IN W MIND

a novel by
JENSEN MOOCK

White Bird Publications
P.O. Box 90145
Austin, Texas 78709
http://www.whitebirdpublications.com

Copyright©2018—Jensen Moock
Cover design: E. Kusch
Flower artwork: Cynthia B. Moock

ISBN: 978-1-63363-358-2
LCCN: 2018964775

To:
Kelly, Alexandra, and Jake,
For saying how proud you are of me.
If you're lying, you're pretty good at it.

Acknowledgments

You spend months and months writing a novel. You stew over it. You grind through it. You revel in it. Along the way, you might give it to a handful of people to review. Just to make sure you're not off your rocker. Unofficial literary critics, if you will.

I had many people who "volunteered" to play that role for me. Know that I am eternally grateful for your honesty and encouragement…both of which were desperately needed. Particularly for a first novel. So, thank you to Kim Sheridan, Rich Ware, Harry Crawford, Christine Sun, and Mom. Also to my wife Kelly, who heard me drone on and on about 'Wisdom' and plotlines for way too many months. Her never-ending patience and subtle critique were beyond valuable.

I also want to thank my father who, after reading the first 100 pages, simply said… "You know, I'm 82. You might want to hurry up and finish it." One year and 200 pages later, he is now in possession of his own signed copy of *In Wisdom's Mind.*

Sometimes all you need is a good swift kick in the pants.

Thank you, one and all.

More to Come

IN WISDOM'S MIND

White Bird
Publications

Chapter One

National Airport

Saturday, December 16th, 1972–11:25 p.m.

As he dropped his jet-lagged body into the cracked vinyl seat of the Red Top cab, it finally caught up to him. His watch said 11:25 p.m., but his body said 5:25 a.m. Time changes were a bitch. Red-eyes were worse. Truth is, he hadn't slept the entire flight. Stress will do that to you. The idiot two seats over smoking incessantly certainly didn't help.

After all these years, it was just a blur. Fly here…work a deal. Fly there…work another deal. It's funny; he thought he'd get used to it. He didn't. So, as he pulled the door tight and the cab began to ease away, David Schneider slowly closed his eyes…if only for a moment. The frantic airport din all now replaced with the low moan of the taxi's Plymouth engine and the muffled silence of a cold winter's night.

His business trip had been productive but brutally long. Managing the takeover of one of the world's largest defense contractors was not an easy task. The military contract ramifications alone would be a quagmire not to mention the reaction on Capitol Hill and the Department of Defense. David and his team had been privately working the deal for almost a year. Of course, it was all very hush-hush. They all are, but if anything leaked on this one the political fallout alone would be enough to shut it down. Shut it down fast.

In the six years since he joined the firm, David had worked over a dozen M & A deals as one of Solomon Brothers top bankers. Each deal had its own sensitivities. Its own peculiarities. But they all had one thing in common. They were all a pain in the ass. This one? Exceptionally tedious. Getting separate groups of powerful men with competing agendas to agree to generalities was one thing, but signatures at the bottom of a 187-page tender offer was quite another. The ongoing Vietnam War certainly didn't lighten the stress. A defense industry merger smack-dab in the middle of a major U.S. military conflict? That was a first for David. For anyone. Seven cities, three countries, ten days. He barely had time to sleep, much less breathe. Calling his wife Sarah was almost pointless. Sure, he slipped in the occasional "Hey, love ya" call but having a real conversation was like trying to tie your shoelaces while running. Simple enough task…if you weren't running. But now, the reality of it all sunk in. It was over. Signatures secured. Chaos subdued and…he was home. Finally.

The initial wave of the season's first storm had passed through earlier that evening, but it had left an opening for David's flight to sneak into National Airport at around 10:30 p.m. A few hours late. Better than being stuck at Heathrow. While waiting to clear customs, David had telephoned ahead to have Moshe, his regular cabbie, meet him curbside. He had come across Moshe years ago on a rainy afternoon after a particularly grueling set of meetings on the Hill. He found the awkwardly attired driver with the thick African accent to be pleasantly efficient…and most importantly, quiet. That was more than good enough for David. So, he kept coming back to Moshe almost like he was his personal chauffeur—albeit, one who operated out of a banged-up multicolored sedan. It was a strange partnership but one that worked just fine for David.

The weatherman had said up to ten inches of snow would hit the District that evening. The first layer started with freezing rain and by the time David had landed, five or six inches of the white stuff had been added to the mix. National Avenue to the George Washington Parkway was the most direct route home, but direct didn't mean smooth. The roads were an absolute mess. No matter how careful Moshe was, the old red and black cab seemed to have a mind of its own—slipping and sliding like a hockey puck. If David was hoping for a nice easy drive, he wasn't getting it.

But as they moved down the GW Parkway, David turned and glanced across the Potomac River. The monuments and government buildings were lit-up and draped with a fresh layer of snow. Their reflections shining off the water's surface. It was pristine. Peaceful...and for David, it was a welcome sight. And so, as Moshe slowly made his way over Key Bridge and onto to 'M' Street, he let out a slow sigh of relief. It didn't completely remove the embedded stress that hung on him like a wet blanket...but it was a start. David Schneider was glad to be back home.

The weather had thinned the typical Saturday night ruckus. The streets, unusually still. The bars, tepid at best. With the snow piling up, Georgetown had more of a burdened feel than anything else...like it was carrying a load it didn't ask for. It looked like David felt. But as they passed the occasional storefront with Christmas lights twinkling above the now almost white landscape, he couldn't help but be suckered in. It was that time of year. David smiled.

And so, with a quick illegal left on Wisconsin, then passing three short blocks of eerily empty bars, followed by a right onto 32nd, David would soon be home. He began to think about what he had accomplished. On Monday morning, his banking team at Solomon would be able to announce the largest corporate takeover in American history. Managing this deal, with all its layers of perfections and imperfections, was going to be a big feather in his cap. He was pleased. Couldn't help it. But when he dug down deep, he realized just how tired he truly was. Christmas vacation couldn't come fast enough.

Sitting slumped in the back of that dingy Red Top cab, one more telling smile came over David's face. Some well-placed government ops were going to be more than pissed. Sneaking one by the very people who thrived in secrecy had its own rewarding irony, and he couldn't help but get a small thrill from that alone. His old man would've been proud.

David lifted his travel bag up on the seat to his right and tucked it next to his briefcase. Inside that worn leather satchel, a most important document lie waiting for the market's opening bell. He reached over and pulled the case tightly to his hip, protecting it as if it were his own flesh and blood.

Now that it was almost over, David felt like he could finally relax. He lifted his hands to his tired face, rubbing his temples and bloodshot eyes, then glanced at his watch. Almost midnight. No need for Sarah to wait up. The wife of an investment banker. Not her first rodeo. A cold beer and then a hot shower would be David's last order of business for the day. He had certainly earned at least one beer…if not three.

Moshe took a careful right onto 32nd. The sound of rolling tires crunching slowly over virgin snow echoed between the cramped row of old Brownstones, their minuscule front yards offering an almost irrelevant buffer. Quietly, the car moved down the vacant and peaceful street. Only the repetition of front porch lights broke the darkness, their glare providing the snow a sporadic and shimmering spotlight.

"Third on de left, sir?"

"Yep."

As he approached his home, David was surprised to see his wife standing on the front porch wrapped tightly in a long puffy jacket, covering her from knee to neck. Wool hat on, cold hands in pockets. She was bundled up like she'd been there for a while. Sarah hadn't waited up for him in years. The kids always wore her out. Maybe she had been sitting in the front living room reading when she saw the cab turn the corner. Maybe she was anxious to hear about the deal...or maybe she just missed him. Probably, the latter.

Moshe steered the cab up near the curb in front of the Schneider home. "Here you go, Mr. David. I help with anything?"

David grabbed his bags and then handed Moshe a twenty over the seat back. "No, Moshe. I'm good. Thanks."

He opened the car door, its creaking sound filling the cab, then stepped out onto the street before briefly glancing back towards his favorite D.C. cabbie. "Hey Moshe, Merry Christmas."

"Yes, yes. Happy Christmas. Goodnight, sir."

David looked up as Sarah started carefully walking down the front steps. The street was silent, his house lights off and with Sarah wearing that ridiculously big coat, scarf and hat this was hardly the welcoming party he'd expected.

As he stepped out of the car, the sharp snap of the bitter winter air caught him off guard...almost as much as seeing his wife standing there. "Sarah?" he said, as he slammed the car door and the Red Top pulled away. "What're you doing out here?"

She said something through her muffler, but David couldn't quite make it out. He guessed. "I missed you, too." David lifted the briefcase out to her. "You mind, hon?"

A nearly indiscernible "Sure" mumbled its way through the thick wool of the scarf and then, as quickly as he leaned forward to give her the satchel, she stretched one hand for the case and in the other was a gun trained right at David's forehead. Before a breath could escape and with as little sound as a snowball hitting the ground, the trigger of the silencer was squeezed, the bullet instantly piercing his brain. David thumped to the ground as one last bit of tortured air shot from his mouth.

With the briefcase still in one hand and the silencer in the other, she calmly jogged across that tiny front yard and down through a narrow path separating the homes. And then, as if nothing of importance happened at all, she silently disappeared into the shadowy and hushed alleyway.

Moshe, the Red Top cabbie, was back on M Street by now. Long gone. Onto the next fare.

And David Schneider, corporate banker, lay dead on a blanket of white, the Georgetown brownstone he called home looming like a dark sentinel. And then, as a steady flow of blood poured from the back of his skull, the second wave of the winter storm the weatherman had predicted began to slowly fall upon the city.

Barely a sound was heard. Nothing was seen, and the capital city still looked remarkably beautiful. A fresh layer of snow draped across the stately monuments, prestigious government buildings...and the tangled, bloody body of one David Schneider.

Chapter Two

Arlington—The Crystal House

Sunday, December 17th–6:22 a.m.

Joey Wisdom felt it even before he heard it…the rumbling of the morning's first plane taking off from National Airport. 6:22 a.m. Each and every damn day. Where Joey lived, one was better off abandoning the thought of even trying to sleep in. Located no more than a mile from the confines of the airport grounds, in a neighborhood you would hope to miss, stood The Crystal House—a 16 story high-rise apartment building best suited for blue-collar workers, divorcees…and Joey.

The non-descript L-shaped tower stood like the deranged overlord to the battered community below, its rundown row houses and dinky cottages serving as suitable understudies. The neighborhood, which sat just across the Potomac from D.C., was Crystal City. But there wasn't anything crystal about it. More tinsel than anything else. The House, as it was fondly called, wasn't any different. It tried to present an air of austerity. Doormen, faux-marble floored lobby, that sort of thing. It even had a pool, but no one used it. Just seemed out of place with the litany of AC units jutting awkwardly out from each apartment window. Must have been hundreds of them.

The House stoically endured this daily and bitter ritual—the roar of the day's maiden flight smashing the silence of the morning—as if it were a badge of honor. The menace was so abrupt, it was in fact, a very convenient substitute for an alarm clock...if 6:22 a.m. served your purpose. This man-made wakeup call was something that the aging D.C. homicide detective had learned to love. Or at least, accept. It was a routine he couldn't shake even if he wanted to.

Joey glanced over at his semi-comatose wife. The still fully clothed bride of two years looked like she literally poured herself into bed last night. Smelled like it, too. All Joey remembered, was that around midnight he left her behind at The Pall Mall, a junky little bar off 'M' Street where the Precinct held its unofficial Christmas party every year. 'Left her behind' was generous. The fly on the wall would tell you that young Ginny spent most of the night proudly wearing as much bourbon as she drank...and she drank a lot. Much to the delight of every cop in the joint, the highlight of the evening was her little pole dancing routine. Every cop but one, that is.

After telling her over and over that it was time to go, Joey finally got the hint. The words never came out of her mouth, but "Beat it, you ole fart" was written all over her face. God only knows when she got home or more importantly...how she got home. Nights like that...and mornings like today made him wonder why the hell she ever agreed to marry him. Maybe the better question was why the hell he ever thought marrying her would do the trick. Maybe that tight little body might have had something to do with it. But now, looking at her lying there like her own version of a prone murder victim, legs and arm unnaturally askew, smoke-soaked hair and clothes permeating the air, that tight little body just didn't seem to carry the same weight any longer.

Joey sat up in his bed, rubbed his meaty palms to his

temples, and then looked back at the jumbled mess of a wife lying next to him. He had spent almost twenty years working this godforsaken beat, his soul slowly peeled away and replaced with callous. When he had fallen for Ginny, he thought…hoped, at least…that she would make him happy. He knew it was a clichéd dream, but it was better than the alternative. With only the slightest bit of contempt, he mumbled to the coma lying next to him…if no one else… "'bout time for a *sit-down*." A barely perceptible smirk crept from the corner of his mouth.

Each year around this time, the Precinct held annual evaluations for the detectives. Discuss the caseload, citizen complaints, arrest records. That sort of thing. The reality of it was that these reviews were just a warped excuse for Sergeant Frankel to bitch you out…like it was an itch he loved to scratch. Hardly the reasoned *discussions* one might expect or, at least, hope for. Joey called them *Sit-Downs* because *Sit Down*! was about all you would remember hearing before the boss spent about thirty minutes reaming you a new one. Frankel, sporting a seemingly constant dew of sweat beneath his generic Vietnam era buzz cut, usually didn't even bother to wait until year-end reviews to dole out his venom. They seemed to happen about as often as a full moon, like he was operating on his own personal and biting lunar cycle.

Frankel wasn't good for much, but he could sure bitch with the best of them. He'd been Joey's *Sarge* for almost a decade, though *Sarge* was a term of endearment the bastard didn't deserve. Weighing Joey down with overbearing caseloads and unrealistic deadlines was par for the course. It wasn't unusual for Joey to be working three murder cases at once. "Solve it…yesterday" was the usual Frankel bark. It was almost as if the berating bastard had one of those graph sheets of paper with a thousand boxes on it and he wouldn't be happy until every damn one was checked off. Joey had learned to tune it all out…dulling the harshness…but it still wore on him. He truly despised the man.

In reality, The District had been an unmanageable mess for years…particularly since the riots of '67. There were more murders than even the most accomplished detective could ever hope to keep track of...much less solve. Joey batted around .600, awesome for baseball and certainly impressive for this city...in this day, but never good enough for Frankel. So, if Joey had to endure his fair share of *Sit-Downs*, deserved or not, surely Ginny had at least one coming her way. After last night's virtuoso performance, she was more than due.

Just then the radio clicked on. Every morning, about five minutes after the first plane left National the radio-alarm clock would come to life, the static sounds of WRC—D.C.'s Country King, filling the room. It served as a snooze alarm of sorts, and even though it was completely unnecessary, Joey craved the extra intrusion. Nothing better than a little Don Williams to take the edge off the growl of a 737. Joey had always loved country music. Couldn't even tell you why. Made no sense, really. An Italian Jew from Jersey working the D.C. murder scene getting hooked on the sounds of Johnny Cash and Willie Nelson. Go figure. Maybe it was because the only thing they ever sang about was booze, bad women, crappy jobs, and the constant hope that things would get better. Eighteen years after moving here, that was pretty much Joey's life.

He reached over, switched off the radio, and, with stiff knees and stiffer ankles, pulled his aching body off the alcohol layered mattress that he called a bed. Slowly, he trudged over to the john for the other daily ritual...a shit, shower, and shave, as he liked to say. He looked out the bathroom window into the bleak dawn and saw what had to be almost a foot of snow covering everything in sight.

Joey flipped on the bathroom light and peered into the mirror, the remnants of last night's bender clearly written in his eyes. No matter how cleverly he snuck up on his reflection, it would look him right square in the eyes—telling him quite clearly, exactly who he was.

He pulled down his boxers, tattered and worn, and eased his tired ass onto the cold toilet seat. "Maybe just 'shit' today."

Little did he know.

Chapter Three

Georgetown—32nd St.

Sunday, December 17th–6:30 a.m.

Sarah Schneider woke to a start. She looked at her clock and then over to her husband's side of the bed. It was 6:30 am, and David still wasn't back home. Sarah groaned. A "dammit" came involuntarily from her mouth. Couldn't help it.

The last she heard from him was when he called from London just before boarding his flight...before it was delayed, that is. She wanted to wait up for him, but as usual, it had been a long day running errands and chasing their two girls around, and now with the snowstorm, Sarah was pretty burned out. He had been on so many business trips lately, rarely coming home on time, that she'd just given up on being the dutiful wife. She figured he was probably still in London...or his flight got diverted. Either way, she wasn't surprised to see his side of the bed empty.

Sarah was thirty-five, but most folks said she didn't look a day over twenty-five...or at least not much different than the day she had gotten married. Petite with short brown hair…kind of a Mia Farrow page-boy look. Even after two kids, she never lost her fighting weight—as David liked to say. Pretty, for certain and she knew she could still catch an eye, but truthfully, she didn't feel like she was bringing all that much to the table, anymore. With David always out of town, raising two little girls was having its natural effect on her. She was truly beat.

The door burst open to the room. "Momma, there is like infinity feet of snow outside. Can we go play? Can we? Can we?" Five-year-old Allie just couldn't contain her enthusiasm. She was, of course quickly followed by her partner in crime, her three-year-old sister, Emma who was equally persuasive when she wanted to be.

"Outside. Play. PEEAASSEE," yelled Emma.

If not grammatically correct, at least it was to the point.

Sarah looked at the clock again and rubbed her eyes. No school today. No help. No husband. Not ideal. She sighed, looked back at her two little girls both jumping up and down like bunnies. She then took another deep breath, this time in resignation. Just how could she say "no"? "Okay, here is the deal. Allie, if you get your own snow boots on and your coat, I'll let you go outside and get the morning paper. You can check out the snow, okay? See how deep it is. Get your ruler from your school box, and you'll be able to tell…but THAT IS IT. Get the paper. Check the snow. Come back in. Got it? After breakfast, you and Emma can go outside and build a snowman. Understand?"

The girls yelled with an unmitigated joy that only a child could possess and ran downstairs to get their boots on. Sarah rubbed her eyes, stepped out of bed, and shuffled over to the painted-shut window that looked over the front courtyard. "Wow, that is like infinity feet of snow." When she had gone to bed last night, there was maybe just a few inches of icy snow on the ground, and it had pretty much stopped. She glanced over to the trunk of the old crape myrtle tree where the snow had built up. "Geez, gotta be a foot down there. No wonder he isn't home."

The street looked so peaceful and still. So quiet. Deep

snow had a way of soaking up the sound. Just then she heard the predictable pitter-patter of footsteps followed the creaking of the front door as it broke the silence of the morning. She wiped the moisture off the window and looked down to see both Allie and Emma in snow boots—no jackets, of course—bursting out the front door before being met by a foot of dense powder. Emma slipped and fell to her side before warily getting back up…PJs now coated with snow. Sarah smiled and then banged on the glass… "Careful," she hollered to the girls. Either they weren't listening, or they couldn't hear. Pointless parenting at this point. The girls steadied themselves and then just plowed over the snowdrift that met the front steps, rolling down the other side like it was an amusement park ride. She could hear them squeal and giggle. Kind of funny to watch but painful at the same time, knowing it was basically the crack of dawn, and she was going to have a tough time getting them back inside…much less cleaning them up.

Allie ambled down the slippery path like a drunk making her way home. Each step was little more than a wobble as she navigated her little feet in and out of the snow. Little Emma, always the careful one, was basically stuck by the bottom of the steps. Good.

She wiped the glass clean again and watched as Allie continued to make her way to the end of the front walk. Sarah couldn't really tell where the newspaper lay…if they even delivered it. With all the snow, it was taking quite an effort for Allie to even make the thirty-foot trek. She was going to be soaked by the time she got back inside. Thank goodness Emma was too nervous to go any further…for now.

What was she thinking letting her little girls out in a foot of snow with only PJs and boots on and at sunrise, no less? She was either the coolest mom on the block, or she was going to be reported to Child Protective Services. Ah, screw it, she thought. Let the kid have some fun. These are the best memories for kids, anyway. Sarah could remember when she was a kid exploring the acres of fields and abandoned barns behind her house in Potomac…no parents…no permission. Complete blast. Allie's little excursion wasn't nearly as daring, but she'll probably remember it for the rest of her life.

As Allie got to the curb, Sarah spotted the paper sitting idly on top of the snow. But instead of grabbing the paper, she saw Allie reach past it and start to dig just shy of the curb's edge. It was a yard full of white, but Sarah noticed what looked like a faint pinkish hue in the snow atop a small mound that looked strangely out of place. Sarah smudged the glass again to get a better look, but all she could see now was the back of Allie as she furiously began brushing away a pile of snow. Suddenly, Allie stopped digging and began to grab something and pull at it. Whatever it was, she initially couldn't move it, but she kept grabbing and pulling on it until she was finally able to lift part of it out of the snow.

Sarah squinted sharply through the moist glare of the window when Allie turned abruptly towards the house, and let out a horrifying scream that broke the silence of the postcard setting below. The scream was unnatural—certainly for a child. The frantic expression on her daughter's face only made it worse. Sarah's heart began to race as she wiped the watered-glass once more, but the renewed clarity did little to make sense of the anguish in Allie's voice. Whatever she was struggling with, it was dark...and heavy. Too heavy for a child. Sarah turned, bolted out the bedroom, and down the stairs while dodging a baby doll, a pile of tinker toys, and Emma, who had wisely retreated inside. She blew through the still wide-open front door and steadied herself just outside on the snowy stoop. Suddenly, with eyes wide, Allie turned back sharply once more, spotted her mother, and let out another withering scream. It was then that Sarah was finally able to make out what her little girl had been struggling with. Mostly, that is. It was the body of man...virtually covered in snow. Dark business suit. Bold red power tie. The only critical detail she couldn't see was the muddied hole the size of a dime right square in the man's forehead. Just wasn't obvious from 30 feet away. Oh, and the fact that the frozen heap of a human lying curbside was also her husband.

As it turns out, David Schneider had indeed made it home last night. Well...almost.

Chapter Four

Crystal City

Sunday, December 17th–7:20 a.m.

A lima bean green Dodge Dart wasn't the typical ride for a D.C. detective, but Joey had inherited it and a lot of debt when his old man passed away a few years back. It turns out, he couldn't part with the car any more than the debt. Apple don't fall too far from the tree. After his Pop died and Joey had paid off the undertaker, bar tab, and banker, he dipped a little into his own world of debt and lovingly had the engine rebuilt and the vinyl seats replaced. Taped to the dashboard was a photo of his dog, Charlie. Maybe a little more offbeat than your typical cop—having a photo of your dog so prominently displayed in your car—but Joey pushed the bit a little further. Charlie, the mutt, had been dead for years.

Joey also ditched the old AM-only radio and upgraded to AM/FM Kenwood tape deck with Jensen speakers. On the floorboard would be a dozen or so country music cassette tapes mixed with a couple depleted cartons of Winston cigarettes.

It was a bit past 7:00 a.m. as Joey made his way out the front of The House and into the intensely crisp air of the winter's first big storm. He took a deep breath and told anyone who was listening just what he thought… "Fuckin' freezing out here." No one was listening.

It *was* literally freezing, and as Joey Wisdom walked carefully towards his car, kicking aside the snow drifts as he went, he realized he was right to skip the shower this morning. Hell, taking a shower for Joey wasn't so much about getting clean as it was about waking up and rubbing the previous evening's booze and the morning's stupor out of his system. But this morning, the sharp whack of the bitter cold was more than enough to get his heart racing.

Joey approached the Dart to see about nine or ten inches of fresh powder hanging on his car. The ol' Dart was in dire need of ten more degrees or a big swipe of his arm across the windows. Instead, Joey opted for the broken-off tree limb that was laying by his car. He opened the car door as a faint but steady smell of discarded cigarette stubs drifted past his face and into the cold. Joey eased his still rigid body into the equally stiff luxury of the brown with white cord vinyl seats and took a deep breath, steam easing from his mouth. With a turn of the key and several punches of the gas, the Dart finally turned over and began first to stutter then hum to life. Hum, that is, as well as a 1968 Dodge Dart Special could possibly hum. Lima Bean Green, mind you. *The ol' Dart and the ol' Fart,* as Ginny liked to say. The two were truly a match for each other.

In the slot, this morning, was the KTEL "Country Fried—Best of The South" tape he ordered for an early Christmas gift. In reality, giving gifts to himself was a hell of a lot more reliable than waiting for Ginny to treat him to something. It was all his money anyway. Might as well save a step.

With the cool sounds of Don Williams, the crackle of his police radio scanner, and the struggling groan of the heater, Joey was on his way. In minutes, he would get a call from

District and find out his first stop of the day wasn't going to be the station. Nope, the dispatch would tell him over the scanner to head to 32nd Street…Georgetown. Turned out some poor schlep took a bullet to his head last night.

It may have been Sunday, but Detective Joey Wisdom learned long ago, murder doesn't wait for church.

Chapter Five

Dupont Circle—Theodore's

Sunday, December 17th–8:15 a.m.

One might mistake the old man with the horribly misguided comb-over and pencil-thin mustache for simply being downright crotchety. But that might be a bit unfair. Just because Alfred Poeltz spoke to virtually no one in the neighborhood didn't mean he wasn't a friendly sort. Just hard to prove, either way. His solitary demeanor, penchant for vagabond cats, Romeo & Juliet cigars, and Perry Mason reruns had actually made him a bit of a community legend. The kind of person all the diplomat children would whisper about as if he was some sort of strange myth.

He lived above an antique store on P Street, just off Dupont Circle. It was a vibrant community of row houses, embassies, bars, and upscale shops that served the capital's blue bloods, politicians, and foreign dignitaries. The store was called Theodore's for some unknown reason, and it might seem to an outsider that he and his son ran the place almost as an afterthought. If you asked Alfred, the best part of Theodore's was that it was conveniently located right down the block from an old beer hall named Sauf Haus, a crusty joint that had been around in one form or another since just after the Second World War.

When Alfred wasn't puttering throughout the store, he could easily be found at either Sauf Haus or on the back patio of Theodore's where an old splash pool had been converted into a koi pond. The little concrete, algae-ridden pond had terribly dark water. Seeing your reflection was next to impossible, but if one were lucky, you might catch a glimpse of an orange speckled Shusi or the black and yellow Kin Ki, lurking just beneath the stagnant surface. Along with a few old iron chaise lounges randomly placed atop the battered brick patio that bordered the pool, were a series of European landscape sculptures that all the D.C. elite clamored for. With Bruno, the cat slinking around the bases of the spitting marble fountains, stone gargoyles, and iron flower pots, Alfred would smoke his little Romeo and Juliet cigars and wait for Sauf Haus to open its door for its famously greasy bar-served breakfast.

Because of its proximity to the Georgetown campus, Sauf Haus had always been popular with the GU coeds and a handful of professors—retired or otherwise. Alfred was one of those professors, but being seventy-two, he was most assuredly retired. For years, Alfred would hold court around the old writing tables in the back room, dispensing his knowledge to the young students while tilting back a beer or two. There was a bar that suggested students could actually come and work on their course papers and thesis. Whether anyone did this with regularity was up for debate, but legend had it that in the early sixties, the back room, which was partially closed off from the rest of the bar by a painted white brick wall and thin, dingy curtain, was the home away from home for the likes of Jackie Kennedy and Robert Bork.

It was now a bit after 8:00 a.m. and, despite the heavy overnight snowfall, Alfred wasn't going to deviate from his morning pre-breakfast pond-side cigar. At his age, Alfred's life had become a series of repetitions. The habits, if that is what you want to call them, didn't bother him. If anything, it provided a sense of comfort. One thing he couldn't tolerate, in himself or his former students, was a lack of reliability. Repetition breeds reliability. And so, he pulled his son's parka over his tattered bathrobe and carefully slid the wood-framed back door open so that the drift of snow wouldn't creep inside. As his slippered feet crunched on the dense remnants of last night's storm, Alfred reached into one pocket of his robe, nimbly grabbed a cigar, and then lifted it to his mouth to bite the tip off. All the while, his other hand, belying its age, gracefully slipped into the other pocket and gathered the little blue Bic lighter that lived inside. This was another ritual in the life of Alfred Poeltz, and he was so practiced at it that the entire scene was almost imperceptible, seeming to happen in one silent movement.

Alfred ran his thumb briskly along the Bic's spark wheel bringing a small flame to life. With an R&J now delicately pursed between his narrow lips, he eased the fire to its stubby tip. His lungs pulled repeatedly, and within seconds the cigar was lit. It was so cold outside that Alfred's own steaming breath blended seamlessly with the cigar smoke coming from his mouth. As his breath and the smoke danced together in the morning air, Alfred gazed across the snow-topped statues, each seemingly frozen in place by some unknown force. Then Alfred saw something that caught his eye…a koi floating near the top of the patio pond. As he looked closer, he saw that the fish was sideways, fighting to stay alive.

Alfred edged over to the pond, carefully bent down, and reached into the frigid water with his free hand while puffing deeply on the cigar with his other. He gently grabbed the pale orange koi and instead of nudging it back to life, lifted it out of the water. It twitched, and with its mouth open wide, the struggling koi fought the air. Alfred pulled it closer and considered its desperate eyes. And then, in the thick Austrian accent that had never left him, Alfred Poeltz grumbled to only himself. "If only you were smarter. Stronger…"

With an annoyance that bordered on anger, he squeezed

firmly until the fish turned almost as pale as the snow—nothing left to give. Its twitching stopped, its eyes as lifeless as a doll's. Alfred reached back and tossed the thing over the back wall...into the littered alley where the dead fish would mix in well with the rest of the trash.

He snubbed out his cigar and as he cautiously walked past the snow-covered creatures to the back door one could hear the muffled voice of the quirky old man muttering with a contempt that only a disappointed father could deploy, "...but you're not."

Chapter Six

Georgetown—32nd Street

Sunday, December 17th–8:15 a.m.

Detective Joey Wisdom carefully aimed the Dart over Key and through the streets of Georgetown taking, unbeknownst to him, the very same route that David Schneider had taken the night before. The crews had been out early clearing the main thoroughfares, steering deep banks of snow to each side. Save for a slippery turn or two, it had been a relatively smooth drive over from Crystal City, and with it being a Sunday morning, the traffic had also been thankfully thin. But as he came upon 32nd Street that peace was about to be broken.

He pulled to a stop on Wisconsin right by 32nd. The street's entrance had been cornered off by the familiar yellow crime scene tape that had become ever-present in his life. He rolled down his window, scanning the scene before him. Six or seven patrol cars were randomly parked amongst a dozen or so cops who seemed to be doing more meandering about than anything else. Isolated groups of concerned and curious neighbors, still in bathrobes, stood huddled on their front porches, intermittently pointing or shaking their heads. If you squinted, the police lights, rolling amongst all that white, almost gave off a festive feel. Until you stopped squinting.

Wisdom waved his arm at the handful of officers milling about, then leaned out his window and hollered out above the grumble of the Dart, "Hey, someone pull the tape aside…can't be stuck out here on Wisconsin."

One of the fresh-faced cops moved over to the driver's side door. "I'm sorry, sir, but this is an official police investigation. Can't let you in."

Wisdom took a deep breath, steam coming from his nose in more ways than one, then blurted "would this help?" He grabbed his badge from the dash and shoved it towards the young officer's face. "Detective Wisdom. Ring a bell?"

"Oh, uh, yes, sir. Very sorry, sir. I'm kind of new to the force."

"You don't say? Couldn't tell." Then with only the slightest bit of sarcasm, "Maybe that's why they keep you as far away from the crime scene as possible."

"No doubt. Yes, sir, let me pull this back."

The rookie undid one end of the tape from the stop sign pole and waved Detective Wisdom in as he slowly steered the car to the curb. He looked down the normally tranquil tree-lined block with disgust. There were literally hundreds of footprints in the snow and now dozens of tire tracks streaming up and down the street.

Wisdom rolled up his window while putting the clunker in park. As he stepped out of the car, he turned towards the young officer who was now re-tying the crime-scene tape, then took another deep breath, and for several moments, watched it linger in that heavy and frozen air and then said, "You guys did a nice job of securing the scene."

Unsure of Wisdom's sincerity, the rookie stalled… "Uh, what, sir?"

"Let's see if I can be just a little bit clearer," his original sarcasm now clearly obvious. "You guys did a shitty job of securing the scene. Okay?"

"Yes, sir. They just told me to man the perimeter. Very sorry, sir."

Wisdom turned back towards what was once a pristine crime scene with tell-tale footprints and tire tracks now contaminated with the remnants of standard issue shoes and police pool vehicles and then shook his head in disgust, "Who's in charge here?"

"Uh, Sargent Frankel, I believe, sir."

And then almost to himself, "Stunner."

"What, sir?"

He thought about asking the kid if anyone bothered to tag and photograph the prints before the cops overran the place or, god forbid, the snow melted. Thought about it, then thought better. The poor rookie was in over his head. Probably got this gig after twelve months of arresting Potomac teenagers drinking beer behind the Bullis football bleachers. He was surely out of his league.

With no reason to be careful, Wisdom strode straight towards the third brownstone on the left. The scene, with its towering trees, quaint front gardens, brick facades, and colonial entryways had a Currier and Ives feel to it. That is if you could ignore all the police chaos. That, and of course, the telltale sign of a small pinkish pile of snow nestled curbside along a landscape of trampled white and the rigid body of David Schneider.

Hard to ignore that.

"Merry Christmas, man." Detective Wisdom muttered to himself. "Merry fuckin' Christmas."

Chapter Seven

Georgetown—32nd St.

Sunday, December 17th–8:25 a.m.

Sargent Frankel met Detective Wisdom by the front curb of 117 32nd street and proceeded to get Joey up to snuff. As it turned out, the initial officer who arrived around 7:00 that morning actually did do a fine job of preserving the scene. According to Frankel, when Patrolman Jenner answered the call, he had come upon a pristine view. With the heavy weather and it being a Sunday morning, the street was a desolate landscape of white and white-tipped trees. Save for the deceased and his wife, who was bundled up in a coat frantically pacing back and forth on the narrow front stoop like a broken toy robot, there was no one else in sight on 32nd Street when Jenner arrived.

According to Frankel, Jenner approached what he presumed was Mrs. Schneider while being mindful of what appeared to be a few sets of traveling footsteps that moved up and down the front walkway. He purposefully stepped away from the other prints despite knowing that his police-issue shoes wouldn't be easily confused with what appeared to be either children's footprints or smaller adult footprints—most likely those of a woman. Later, upon closer look, the only oddity was a set of somewhat trampled prints that approached the body of Mr. Schneider but then abruptly turned hard left down the sidewalk and then back through a small side passageway between two neighboring brownstones. If Jenner wasn't mistaken, the prints he saw that seemingly moved away from the body had much larger spacing. Possibly the kind of spacing one might expect if that person was running. Specifically, running away from something.

The Sargent said that Jenner briefly approached and consoled the obviously distraught Mrs. Schneider then proceeded to guide her inside the home where he asked her to sit in the living room just off the front center hallway. At this point, Officer Jenner was unaware of the possibility of children as the house was awkwardly quiet and there appeared to be no one else around. He asked her to tell him what she knew, so the distraught Mrs. Schneider stuttered the basics between sobs and tears: that she woke up this morning to find the dead body of her husband lying in the snow by the curb and most importantly that she couldn't think of anyone who would want to harm her husband. All the while, Officer Jenner made some mental notes —namely, that she felt like this must have happened late last night when she was asleep and that she did seem genuinely upset. Meaning she seemed normal...for a woman who just stumbled upon her dead bloody husband with a hole in his forehead. She also stammered that she did not suspect there was anyone in her house to be concerned with. But according to what Jenner told Frankel, just saying this out loud seemed to make her realize something she never considered –that is to say, that the perpetrator could be in her home. She said that the possibility made no sense to her, but according to Jenner, the idea alone just made her more unstable and, for the first time, truly fearful.

Jenner told the Sargent that after checking both inside the

house as well as its perimeter, he assessed there was no imminent danger and quickly stepped outside to make a call on his 2-way requesting forensics and backup...not in that order. He then retrieved from his patrol car's trunk a set of evidence flags and crime scene tape and began to establish what he presumed to be the outer boundary of the scene. This was to Jenner, as you faced the Schneider's, essentially the properties and physical structures of the two homes that bordered to the left all the way to Wisconsin, the three to the right and the five properties directly across the street from the murder...and everything in between. Jenner made notes about the conditions of the area such as the weather, time of day, people present (none), and then took the time to place markers by the series of footprints that lead up and down the front walk as well as those that peeled off away from the scene.

"So, since it took you so long to get here, the guys went ahead and questioned the neighbors who said they heard nothing. Bupkis." He turned to look toward the pool of patrolmen surrounding the scene. "Figures. That's basically where we stand, Wisdom. Got it?" Frankel glanced toward the curbside pile. "Dead husband. A few footprints. Distraught and apparently very clueless wife. Anything else will have to come from you," said Sargent Frankel. "Don't take long on this one. Okay?"

Wisdom hated when Frankel did that...offering up only the very basics of an investigation and then telling him to figure the rest out...and fast. Standard protocol for Frankel, no doubt. This was done with such regularity that he came across as either intentionally perverse or simply inept...or maybe both. Probably both. Wisdom had always wondered how the hell he got to be the head of the homicide division. 'Photos,' he'd mumble. "He must have photos."

Wisdom looked past the Sargent, towards the home, then back to the damp and frozen body of David Schneider. "Par for the course, Sarge. Fine advance work." He had spent years disguising his biting sarcasm around Frankel. Some days it worked better than others. Today may not have been one of those days. He took a deep breath, steam—both natural and unnatural—coming from his mouth, then offered a "Thanks for all the help." It was intentionally pliable.

Joey brushed by Frankel and then carefully worked his way along the front path past a police photographer, who was carefully stepping amongst the snow prints to take evidence photos. Approaching the stoop, he turned around to look at the scene behind him and, very much to himself, recites what he sees… "Husband comes home late on a snowy Saturday night…gets dropped off, possibly a cab or maybe a friend and then never makes it past his front sidewalk. Everything about this looks very intentional. Feels like a hit. Damn, who is this guy?"

He turned back towards the entrance and glanced through a set of front bay windows to the right of the door. Even through heavy condensate, he could make out what he presumed was Mrs. Schneider sitting tensely with an officer by her side. Stepping inside the front door, which was completely ajar despite the thirty-degree temperature, Joey leaned his head around the right towards the room where Mrs. Schneider sat. He wanted a virgin look at her, undisturbed by his questioning, if not her dead husband. He had developed a sense about people in his line of work. He felt that he could always tell if someone was hiding something based almost entirely on the way the event affected their emotions. Specifically, when no one was looking. Much the same way you would approach a stray dog…careful, observant and your focus directly on the eyes…the eyes will tell you almost everything. Almost.

Mrs. Schneider was seated in a high-back, well-appointed Queen Anne chair. The fabric was garish but in step with what appeared to be a professional decorator's touch, a touch that also emanated from the rest of the room. Elegant and overt. Which, of course, is why you pay big bucks for a decorator, no? Got to make a statement. These people were definitely, out of Wisdom's league. Then again, who wasn't?

Mrs. Schneider sat in direct contrast to her surroundings. Certainly, not elegant on any level. Seated, slumped and dressed in a heavy, plain grey bathrobe that she tightly cinched up towards her neck—as if she was protecting herself. A police officer stood beside her asking questions that Joey couldn't make out. Mrs. Schneider's dust grey eyes stared directly but vacantly at the Oriental rug that concealed the humble and flawed thick wooden floor planks that were common in these 18th-century row homes.

She may have been staring at the floor, but Joey could tell her eyes were unfocused and lifeless. Her body was there, but her mind was somewhere else. Joey suspected she was in some sort of state of shock—decidedly not the expression one would have if they had just killed someone...or had someone killed, for that matter. Joey had learned that a killer's eyes were hard and had the tendency to dart about randomly as if looking for a way out. Mrs. Schneider didn't need a way out, she was already gone. Most assuredly not the eyes of a killer.

Wisdom abruptly stepped into the sitting room, stood before Mrs. Schneider and, interrupting the officer next to her, introduced himself:

"Excuse me, ma'am. Detective Wisdom, D.C. Homicide. May I have a few moments with you?"

With her head still trained towards the ground, Mrs. Schneider slowly pulled her eyes up as if it were a struggle. She looked at Wisdom but said nothing.

"Ma'am, I can see you're dealing with a lot right now. Just a few questions. Is that going to work for you?"

Mrs. Schneider nodded reluctantly.

"Look, I know this is probably hard to wrap your arms around. I get it. But I just need to know one thing?" Joey paused just long enough to make sure he had some kind of audience.

"Why did you have your husband killed?"

Mrs. Schneider abruptly lifted her head and dropped her hands from her robe as a stunned "What?" spurted from her lips.

Now Mrs. Schneider was back with the living. Joey had

found pointed and at times inappropriate questions were perfect for getting people's attention. He knew she was not guilty of anything more than being a wife without a husband, but he also knew he needed her to focus. He needed details and details don't come easily from distracted people.

"Mrs. Schneider, what I meant to say was 'Why would someone have your husband killed?'"

"What? Nobody would want to kill my husband. Nobody."

"Well...he is dead so... I'm...ah...guessing you're wrong."

"Detective, uh...whatever your name is. Leave me alone. I have already told the other officer everything I know. Get it from him. I need to be with my kids."

"Kids?" Joey knew there were kids but played it a bit dumb. As insensitive as it was, he wanted to ruffle her feathers. He'd get more out of her if he did. "I didn't know you had any kids."

"As far as I can tell, you don't know much."

Finally. Just what he was looking for. A two-way conversation.

"No. True. True. I don't know much...but what I do know—that you don't know by the way—is that your husband was killed quite intentionally. It was not random on any level. So, when you say nobody would want your husband dead, I would simply say that given the facts, someone went out of their way to specifically do just that. Kill your husband. So, I ask again, who would want your husband dead?"

"Facts? What facts? You mean you see a dead body on a street in a nice neighborhood and you immediately assume that he has enemies. How the hell do you make that leap?"

"Well, I would say that given the fact that he came home in a veritable blizzard well after bedtime and that no ordinary person would be out that late in that kind of weather...and that nothing appears to be stolen...and I have been told that your house, and most importantly you, were untouched. Also, there were no other tire tracks besides the car that dropped him off and the only other footprints besides yours and those of your children were most likely those of the shooter. And, I'm told that you've informed Officer Jennings that you didn't hear anything. Neither, I'm afraid, did any of your neighbors."

"So, I didn't hear anything. Is that so interesting?"

"Well, if it was random, there would have been some racket. And since it was apparently quiet as kittens last night - if you don't mind - then, that tells me it wasn't random. And, if no one in their right mind would be out last night in that weather, then they were here intentionally. And, since nothing was stolen from you, your home or it seems your husband, then...well, I hate to be blunt but..."

"Hasn't stopped you yet."

"The shooter very much wanted your husband. And, since there is only one set of prints that could be tied to a suspect and assassins always work alone."

"Assassins?"

"Hitman. Assassin. Whatever you want to call him but...what I am trying to get across, Mrs. Schneider, is I think it is more than safe to say that the facts, as I have just laid out, tell me quite clearly that someone was waiting late into the night...in a shit-storm no less, to intentionally murder your husband...and no one else."

"So, I ask you again...for the third time...who would want to have your husband killed?"

Chapter Eight

Dupont Circle—Theodore's

Sunday, December 17th–8:45 a.m.

Alfred Poeltz pulled the wood-framed glass patio door tight, sealing out the damp chill. His morning routine intact, he moved across the wooden floor covered with old dusty oriental throw rugs. Each rug had a small circular paper tag pinned to its corner with a price—a price far exceeding what it had cost his son. The rugs muffled the sound of the creaking planks, but each step still brought another rickety groan as Alfred moved past the crowded floor filled with colonial-era bureaus and tables and then down a dark and narrow hallway where early century sconces were hung amongst a series of Scottish red stag antlers. It was an ominous passageway, but at the end of the hall lay the kitchen. A small metal rectangular sign hung from the front of the restaurant-style swinging door. "Private" was all it said and it had, over the years, mostly served its purpose. Most customers did not come into the kitchen. Most. Living in an antique store had its many inconveniences—namely that when you were on the first floor, save for the kitchen, you had no real privacy. The only real sanctuaries were your bedroom and a small sitting room —but those were upstairs and hardly convenient for a seventy-two-year-old. Plus, Alfred loved his morning coffee almost as much as his morning smoke and so the kitchen was his destination of choice. Coffee, another cigar or two and the local morning newscast. Every morning without fail.

Alfred pushed open the swinging door, and the well-lit room seemed to enliven him. The kitchen stood in stark contrast to the rest of the building. Unlike the store, which was dark and cluttered, the kitchen was bright and sparse. Nothing like the muddled mess behind him. To the left, a small garden window hung above the sink, letting the morning light in. The floor was tiled mostly in white linoleum squares with the occasional black piece mixed in. The cabinets were painted off-white with harvest gold Formica counters and matching gold appliances. A rust-colored metal-topped sitting table was placed to the right, and a small TV sat on the counter nearest the table. Next to the TV, was the Mr. Coffee®. A gift from his son, a more ingenious invention Alfred had never seen, and its yellow and white gingham decal seemed to match the kitchen perfectly.

Alfred Poeltz poured himself a cup of coffee and then drew it to his crinkled lips. He left it there for what seemed like minutes as he lightly blew into the cup while pulling in the aroma. It was a pleasure he did not like to go without.

Chapter Nine

Georgetown—32ⁿᵈ St.

Sunday, December 17ᵗʰ–9:00 a.m.

Detective Wisdom finished up with Mrs. Schneider and stepped out to the front stoop. He left the newly minted widow in a shamble. An emotionally flustered mess in a bland bathrobe sitting in her cushy ornamental chair within a stuffy high-dollar home. Ironic, to say the least. Most importantly, she had provided nothing concrete to work with…except the fact that her husband flew in from overseas last night. Was working on some corporate merger. Frankel would get the Business Crime guys to sniff around on that angle, but otherwise, she provided very little to work with. An empty pool…like most women. Or at least of the women Joey knew. The still fresh image of his own passed-out wife slipped through his mind. Just couldn't help himself. Here he was, in the middle of a bloody murder scene and thoughts of Ginny still rolled in and out of his mind. Why the hell was that?

Maybe because she left him wanting…just like the Schneider lady. He needed depth or at least some semblance of it. From the widow, for certain. Good god, he knew he needed it from Ginny.

Maybe his own choice in women had clouded his judgment over time. Outside of his wife being a fox, he wasn't sure she brought much else to the table…besides angst and that gnawing pit in his stomach that made him question his own intelligence. What was it about some well-appointed cleavage, perfumed inner-thigh, and a short skirt that took him off his game? "Geez, I wonder." Not that he even had much of a *game*, anyway. At forty-two, maybe he simply needed something more than T & A.

Wisdom shook his head lightly and then gingerly stepped down from the stoop, the soles of his well-worn desert boots crunching beneath his feet. He looked around at the police presence still milling around the property. Dozens of them. "Overkill, as usual," he mumbled. Scanning the men in their dress-blues, he spotted Officer Jenner and thought sarcastically, "Amongst all these well-trained crime-fighters…apparently, he is the only one who appears to know what the hell he is doing."

"Jennings."

"Ah, sir. It's Jenner, sir. Yes, sir. Do you need me?"

"Jenner. Jennings. Whatever, man. Yeah, I need you. Why else would I call your frickin' name?" Wisdom almost added "you dip-shit" at the end but figured he already alpha-dogged him enough by butchering his name.

"Yes, I need you. Let's cut to the chase…got two leads."

"We do?"

"Don't get excited kid. They aren't that good. Hey, are you still on duty?" It would be Wisdom's luck this morning to find out the only marginally competent officer at his disposal wouldn't actually be at his disposal at all if his shift was over.

"Uh, sir. Yes, sir…for another hour. If you need me for longer, I could request it."

"No need to brown-nose. I can't get you a pay raise, and yes, I do need you. Where was I...ah, fuckin A. Uh...yeah, two leads. At least two. I need someone to go check out the cab companies. Little miss inside told me her husband had come home from National last night and always took a cab if it was late. Safe to say...it was late. So, I need you to check out the main cab companies...you know like ah, Diamond, Red Top, Yellow...the bigger ones...until you find the schmutz who took our deceased friend home last night."

"Got it. Do I pay them a visit or just call?"

"Yeah, why don't you go door to door on this...that'll be quick. Fabulous use of your time." Wisdom was beginning to question his own judgment on Jennings...uh, Jenner...whatever.

"Yes, sir. Sorry. I'll call them."

"Just tell them you are investigating a crime and that we believe one of their cabbies may have been witness to it. Just give them the address and a general time...say midnight or 1 a.m. It couldn't of been much later than that...flights typically won't land after 11 p.m. or so."

"Okay, I'll get back to the station and get right on it."

"Don't go to the damn station...just call from inside. She'll be happy." He paused as he caught a glimpse of Mrs. Schneider, her drained expression clearly visible even through the glaze of the front window. "Well, not *happy*. But, uh...at least it'll look like you're doing something." Then turning towards the milling officers on the scene. "Better than the show these yahoos are putting on. It'll take ten minutes. Listen...if the dispatch guy doesn't play ball, don't be surprised. They like to watch out for their own. If he doesn't give you what you want, just tell him we'll be down there in a half hour, and we'll get it that way."

"That'll work?"

"Hell, yeah. He won't want us there. Half their drivers are criminals anyway. Once you have what we want...the driver...his address or phone number...his next work slot...give me a shout."

"Yes, sir." Jenner paused. "Detective Wisdom?"

"What?"

"You said, two leads."

"Uh, yeah, Jenner. I did." Wisdom had to look at the kid's nameplate to get it right. "At least two. Now, get on it."

"Yes, sir."

Officer Jenner quickly bolted up the pathway to the Schneider's front door. "Two leads. Ha", Wisdom muttered to himself. "Wouldn't call them leads. More like chores." The first one was easy enough. Too easy for even a rookie to screw-up. The second? He certainly wasn't going to trust some bleary-eyed over-caffeinated twenty-five-year-old to handle that one. Nope. Not a chance.

That one was all Wisdom.

Chapter Ten

Dupont Circle—Theodore's

Sunday, December 17th–9:00 a.m.

Standing in that tiny refuge called a kitchen, Alfred anxiously awaited the morning news. What had become of him? Decades ago, he was a well-regarded German psychologist who had been forced to flee his homeland in disgrace after the Second World War only to land on his feet as a professor at venerable Georgetown University—eventually becoming head of the Sociology and Psychology Department in the later sixties. He was well-liked by the students for his quirky demeanor if not by the rest of the professorial staff. Some found his habit of staring down questioners for long periods of silence before answering, completely disturbing. He held long after-class study sessions off campus for select students—usually coeds. The students loved his mentoring and his selfless service, but the staff felt that his interest in offering his personal time to students to be out of character for a department head and self-serving—though no one could figure out in what manner he was being served. His practice of walking around campus with his cat at his heels was downright delightful to students but strange to staff. "Since when does anyone ever *walk* with a cat, especially one named Bruno?" Eventually, age and his unusual deportment caught up with him. In 1969, he was not offered tenure, and it was suggested that he retire or take a lesser role in the department. Instead of taking an insulting and reduced role at an institution he called home for almost twenty years, Professor Poeltz simply hung it up.

This was not the first time he was run off, and he had always landed on his feet. When it came right down to it, he just couldn't leave the students or his role as mentor, so he kept holding his off-campus sessions and ran a small but marginally profitable tutoring practice. While the tutoring and mentoring did provide a little extra cash and some sense of purpose for a man in his seventies, it certainly did not fill up his day…and so he was left to helping with menial tasks at the store and of course…he was left with the morning news.

On top of the harvest gold countertop and tucked into a corner, sat the small RCA Victor color TV. It lay virtually untouched unless the TV9 news was on or *Perry Mason*…or *Gunsmoke*. That was it for Alfred; the news, *Perry Mason* and, if he was really bored, maybe a little *Gunsmoke.* He never found much pleasure in sitting the hours away watching television. If you asked him, the only reason he liked to watch *Perry Mason* was because he loved to solve the crime before the star…which was something he did with quite a bit of regularity.

Alfred checked his watch—a Swiss made Croton with rose gold numbers and a moon-phase and calendar set within its pearl dial—then picked up his coffee from the metal topped kitchen table. It was just a tad before 9 a.m. as Alfred took another sip of his coffee and walked over to the counter. He turned the power knob of the RCA to the right with a click, stopping just after to keep the volume low. Then he rotated the channel dial from 4 to 9 as it clunked its way past several stations of static snow until he saw the familiar TV9 News

Desk—its big red 9 logo adorned to the front of the Desk. Sitting behind the desk was Bob Althage, the balding and be-speckled morning news veteran who had presided over Alfred's *breakfast* of coffee and cigars for about 300 days a year. Bob Althage was a seasoned news anchor, but a couple of years back, he was moved from the evening desk to AMs…a slight that reminded Alfred of his own track. Bob was done in, as was always the case in TV, by his looks. Or rather, by his aged looks. Glasses, wrinkles, and thinning hair were hardly the profile of a major news anchor in a major news town. But unlike Alfred, Bob took his demotion gracefully. He was happy to have a job at his age and probably a well-paying one at that. So, every morning at 7 a.m. on weekdays and 9 a.m. on weekends, Bob Althage would throw his journalistic heart and soul into the news—giving the good people of the D.C. metro area everything the day had to offer.

Alfred appreciated Bob's will…and his news-casting talent. You see, Bob may have been too old-looking for evenings, but he could give you the news as good as Harry Reasoner and with significantly less gruff. And there had been no shortage of gritty news in D.C. lately. With the Spiro Agnew situation and that Watergate robbery scandal, there was hardly a day that went by when the newscast wasn't heavy. That kind of serious news required a deft hand and Bob Althage, thinning hair and all, was a pro. After two years on the morning desk at TV9, he and Alfred had become close…or at least Alfred became close to Bob. Every morning as the news jingle came on and Bob Althage would stare prominently into the camera, Alfred would stare right back at his *friend*, smile and wait for the intro:

"Good Morning, Washington. I'm Bob Althage with the latest news…for you…and your day."

Alfred would promptly answer back as if Bob was speaking only to him. "And a good morning to you, Bob."

Alfred was grateful for this *friendship*, one-way though it was. Hell, he's spent so many days with Bob Althage that they might as well be drinking buddies. And today was no different. Bob Althage gave him a connection to someone real...not a student but a peer of sorts and Alfred cherished the simplicity of that relationship. He always looked forward to his time with Bob and the news.

Today was no different. Yes, there would be the ancillary Watergate trial story, an update on the big snowstorm overnight. Heck, with the Redskins on a roll, maybe even a Billy Kilmer interview. But today, Alfred wanted more than that. He wanted to see how it had all played out...and he wanted to see his *friend*, Bob Althage, tell everyone about it.

Chapter Eleven

Georgetown—32ⁿᵈ St.

Sunday, December 17ᵗʰ–9:10 a.m.

The snow was a godsend. In all the years of trying to track down criminals, Joey Wisdom had never had such a prominent trail of evidence gifted to him. Footprints of the killer, no doubt, that began right next to the rigidly frozen & bloody body of one David Schneider. Poor dead Mr. Schneider, his lifeless body didn't even have to wait for rigor mortis…it froze up stiff as a pile of bagged bricks all on its own. And now, you could probably just place a big *GO* sign and arrow right next to him just like that Monopoly game. A starting point to solve the crime and all he had to do was follow the footsteps.

Wisdom walked back to his car and opened the passenger door with a loud screech. If all the ruckus of twenty or so police officers and the comings and goings of all the black and white cherry tops didn't wake the slumbering neighborhood…the sound of the Dart's creaky door certainly did.

Leaning into the car, Wisdom grabbed his walkie-talkie and radioed the dispatch. Pressing the talk button, he bellowed to no one, in particular. "It's Wisdom. Frankel around?" Followed by a few seconds of static.

A click…then soft buzzing air before the dispatch finally answered. "Good morning to you too, asshole. Hell, I don't know where Frankel is. Last I saw him, he left for the scene in Georgetown."

"I am at the damn scene right now, and he's sure as hell not here, Okay? Left about an hour ago. Check his log, man. He ain't that slow."

"Look Wisdom, he isn't here. I'll leave a message for him. And yes, he is that slow."

Click. Static.

"Fuck him," muttered Joey.

Wisdom walked carefully back to where the body lay. He looked down at remnants of Schneider and now, clearly angry, yelled out to a bunched group of patrolmen, whispering amongst themselves. "Hey. Surely someone's called in an ambulance, right? Do I need to do every fuckin' thing myself? Stiff's been parked here like a car for god knows how long." Now pointing at the grieving widow staring through those misty front windows, "Look at her. That lady is having to sit there watching all you a-holes walk around her dead husband all morning…like you know what the hell you are doing. Fucking A, man." Wisdom stared back down the contorted heap beneath him then back up. "He's dead, okay? And I'm pretty sure he's been murdered. No damn mystery. Get 'em out of here."

Of the four or five officers milling around, no one responded. They stood there slack-jawed until someone from beyond the cluster of cops hurried a weak, "Ah, uh, yes, Detective. Gotcha. Ambulance is coming. Already been called."

Joey glanced down at the frozen and bloody mess that *was* David Schneider. "What could this ole boy have done to deserve a bullet to the frickin' brain…point blank…right in front of his home...during Christmas time, for god's sake?" Joey hadn't considered much of anything when he arrived on scene. Just too damn tired. Hell, it was just another day in D.C., anyway. Another day, another murder. No big deal. Probably wouldn't even make the news. But something was off about this one. Wealthy man, yet nothing was stolen. Wealthy neighborhood, yet nothing disturbed. This was quick and quiet. Very quiet. Too quiet for a jealous lover killing...unless that person was just naturally cold-blooded. Doubtful. He was only half serious when he suggested to Mrs. Schneider that her husband was assassinated—just wanted to get her attention—but this was incredibly intentional. No doubt. Someone wanted him dead, and that person planned it out. He took a deep breath and stared back down at Schneider. "Nope. This is not just another murder. This one's gonna be a big deal."

Just then, The Channel 9 news van pulled up to the police barricade off Wisconsin. The grimy and dinged up white van with the big red 9 on its side panel stood motionless for a moment.

"Ah fuckin' A. That's all we need."

From a few houses down, Joey squinted and tried to peer into the front cab of the van. The morning sun's glare off the frozen and snow packed street made the windshield shine, obscuring the view. The door screeched open, and from the passenger-side an overly made-up bottle blonde with way too much hairspray, stepped out. She stood there prominently and expectantly as if someone was supposed to sprint over and let her in.

Joey turned his head back towards David Schneider. "What have you gotten yourself into, son?" He wasn't sure if he was asking the dead man on the ground the question...or the live one standing in a pair of well-worn desert boots.

Another deep breath...the steam filling the crisp morning air. "Well, Mr. Schneider, at least you didn't die in a boring way. Heaven forbid. Hell, Schneider, you might even make the morning news."

Chapter Twelve

Erinnerungen an Berlin, Germany

1941

S. Rauscher Journalprotokoll VII:

My blood name was Sigmund Rauscher. Christened after my grandfather. Also, a doctor. But by the time the war effort was at its pinnacle, we had adopted sobriquets. For security purposes, I suppose. All the major contributors participated. Nothing cryptic. Quite the opposite. Josef Mengala was known as Dr. Death for reasons, I think are obvious. Dr. Fredric Werner was called Dr. White for his experimental work in low-temperature tolerance...and me? Well, I was commonly referred to as Doktor der Sinn. Or as you would say in English—Dr. Mind. I was known for helping pioneer what your government called the German Mind Control movement. Studies that would eventually be replicated in the U.S. and secretly known as MKUltra.

Heinrich Himmler was fascinated by the human brain

and had a cranky obsession with what he believed was its shocking lack of efficiency. Himmler was aware of published studies by Harvard psychologists in the late 1890's that concluded, unless put under pressure to perform, the average human brain only met a fraction of its full mental potential. This charge was further pushed to the forefront in the 1930's by U.S. military scientists who in studies comparing child prodigies with their more generally normal peer group, concluded that most humans only use about ten percent of their brain's power. This theory both absorbed and infuriated Himmler, who felt that any inefficiency—be it mental, emotional, or physical was tantamount to failure.

Himmler's own astonishing capacity for work and his naturally efficient, meticulous, and calculating tendencies made his rise to the head of both The Schutzstaffel and The Gestapo hardly surprising. It was from this position that Himmler developed and approved all sorts of studies on the body's and brain's abilities and inabilities in an effort to push the boundaries of their perceived limits.

As Medical Chief for the SS, I was charged not only with maintaining the health and wellbeing of those men under the Schutzstaffel but, with Himmler's urging, I was also given reign to explore ways of not only maintaining but enhancing the men under our burden. It was in this capacity that I developed and ran experiments to test and push the body's and mind's ability to handle high altitudes, extreme heat and cold, as well as the body's ability to heal from wounds. It was during this study that I discovered certain natural compounds could reduce the bleeding from gunshot wounds. Using prisoners from Dachau, subjects were given a polygala tablet made of extract from beet and apple pectin who were then shot through the neck or chest. Comparing these subjects to others who were given a placebo tablet and subjected to the same wounds, I could substantiate a notable improvement in blood-clotting using the natural Polygala. This proactive treatment then became part of the daily ritual for all SS officers, much as one might drink milk daily for bone strength.

This natural solution to an unnatural condition led me to

consider ways for certain earth-borne resources to help improve and develop a human's efficiency. It was under Himmler's encouragement and tutelage that I too developed a grand interest in if one can manipulate the mind to be, not only more effective, but also controlled. Previous efforts by my constituents at mind-control using a sodium fluoride-laced water supply proved way too time-consuming and mostly inconclusive. However, pirating published data from Soviet studies, I developed an alternative theory that suggested that by combining hypnosis with a consumption of mescaline, a peyote cactus powder, one could expand the brain's ability to not only focus and solve problems more effectively but also become more susceptible to suggestion and direction.

On May 15th, 1941, I sent a communique to Himmler requesting permission to use Dachau inmates for mind control experiments. The response was enthusiastic. I was ordered to begin experiments immediately and to directly provide detailed analytics to him on a weekly basis. He concluded in his response…

> *"All of us, who are members of the Germanic peoples, can be happy and thankful that once in a thousand of years, fate has given us such a genius, a leader, in Adolf Hitler, and you should be happy to be allowed to work with us. Go forth and bring to your Fuehrer what is needed so that the world will never have to wait 1000 years again."*

I spent weeks developing the proper mescaline balance. Ingesting it in an undiluted state proved problematic as patient after patient developed such severe psychosis that they were rendered uncontrollable, the opposite of the desired effect. Several subjects died from cardiac arrest due to pharmaceutical over-concentration.

Finally, on August 28th, 1941 I ran a series of tests on three subjects who were put under hypnosis and then were told to ingest a 5-95 Mescaline/Water dose. Each patient was held in separate isolated chambers and was, while still under the effects of the hypnosis and mescaline, subjected to a series of mental challenges that previously proved difficult to accomplish. Each could perform the tasks with ease, allowing us to give way to the next challenge— namely, can they perform physically and emotionally difficult challenges based purely on suggestion. At this point, a male Dachau child prisoner was brought into the chamber. Prior to the youth's entry, our subject was told to strangle to death the next person who entered the room. On each occasion, the test results were one hundred percent effective. The net result of the combined challenges provided a subject with an unusually high intellect for problem-solving combined with the ability to have their actions under complete control.

The data was sent to Himmler who requested a plan for how it could be incorporated into both the military branch and the espionage branch. This task proved daunting.

Chapter Thirteen

Georgetown—32nd St.

Sunday, December 17th–9:10 a.m.

Wisdom had had just about enough. The last thing he needed was the clichéd blood-thirsty bleached blonde morning street reporter from Channel 9 banging around his crime scene, hoping for someone to give her a gritty eyewitness account…or, even better, a meaty chunk of footage.

As her cameraman scanned the scene seeking a good shot of the bloody body, distraught wife, or maybe a shocked neighbor, Clichéd Reporter Lady hollered out to Wisdom,

"Officer, Sir, Officer…can we have a word with you?

Wisdom looked her way…realized she was speaking to him. He knew he had a badge on but calling him "Officer" was not going to work this morning. Joey turned away and began to walk back to the scene, Mr. Cameraman catching his every move.

"Please, Sir. Can we just get an update please?"

Wisdom looked back…noticed her trying to use her

bimbo looks to her advantage…and stopped.

"Okay—what the hell," he mumbled to himself. "She's going to keep hounding me…or someone else who knows even less…until she gets *something* she can get on air. Better me than some duffus traffic cop."

"Were you talking at me?" Joey yells back above the din of cop activity with just a tinge of sarcasm.

"Yes, officer. Yes, sir. What's the story here? Looks horrible"

"First off, it's Detective…not officer. I haven't been an officer in years. The officers are the ones in uniforms, ma'am. They give you tickets for parking violations. You're welcome to talk to any of them, but, trust me, they don't know shit."

"Very sorry, sir… uh, Detective. I guess I can, uh… assume you *do* know shit. How 'bout some color here? What's happened?"

After years of working around these scum, Wisdom knew that sometimes—when you feed them the right info—the news media can help a case. But as of right now…he just couldn't see the advantage. He barely knew anything. He certainly was not going to give her the leash to create her own narrative. Clichéd Reporter Lady was going to get just north of diddly. He walked toward the eager floozy, microphone firmly in her hand, cameraman at her side and over the next couple minutes proceeds to give her as little information as possible. The basics. Only. Confirmation of a shooting death. Estimated time of the crime. Nothing else.

Professional anchorman Bob Althage had spent almost his entire adult life giving the D.C. metro community the bad news of the day. It was rare when a morning newscast would start off with something pleasant, rewarding, or even some dribble that might make you smile. In reality, that would be considered a very slow news day if that were the case. No, the producers always saved the happy stuff—if there was any at all—for the last thirty seconds of the broadcast, much preferring to start off the show with as much ugliness as possible. The overnight desk scoured the police scanners for killings, fires, accidents, while candidly hoping these events occurred in the *better parts of town*. People didn't care about murders south of the Capitol. Those things were supposed to happen there. However, even the smallest amount of blood on the streets of Alexandria, Potomac, or Georgetown was definitely news. As crass as it was, this newsroom strategy had for years meant better ratings, and better ratings meant better advertising dollars. Without question, Channel 9 was the best at breaking down the barrier of decency when it came to the news. They were the *New York Post* of the D.C. television news market…big gritty storylines always equal big ratings.

Today was no different, and Bob was, as usual, up for the task. And so, near the end of the newscast, he leaned ever so slightly towards the camera and with his virtually imperceptible trademark tilt of the head… "Overnight the Georgetown community was rocked with what appears to be a grisly murder. Let's send it to Barbara Bell who is on the scene…. Barbara, what can you tell us?"

Alfred Poeltz's heart began to race. Setting his coffee down, he pulled his ever-present R&J towards his mouth, took a large drag, and edged forward in this chair. He felt nervous. Actually, nauseous…like someone awaiting potentially daunting news from a doctor.

"Good morning Bob, I am on the scene here in idyllic Georgetown just a few doors down from the hustle of 'M' Street. Bob, this normally peaceful neighborhood is now the scene of what appears to be a violent overnight murder." The camera panned over Barbara Bell's shoulder to show the teeming bustle of a typical murder scene: "On a day when most children would be playing outside in the first big snowfall of the year while counting the days until Christmas, the children of this community woke to a much different and unimaginable horror. Moments ago, I spoke with the lead Detective on the scene."

Channel 9 coverage cut to a recorded interview with a

representative of the D.C. police force. The camera zooms in on the grizzled and barely compliant face of one Joey Wisdom:

"Detective Wisdom, can you offer some details on this morning's shocking events?"

Alfred Poeltz lifted his creaking body up from the chair and while keeping an eye and ear keenly focused on the newscast, walked to the kitchen counter to retrieve a pencil from a cabinet drawer. He sat back down and scribbled the name *Wisdom* on the upper corner of The Post while the detective reluctantly recited the basic facts of the case:

"Uh, sure. At about 6:30 in the a.m., we received a call from this address indicating they had discovered a homicide outside their residence. As of now, we are not in a position to confirm the victim's identity."

Barbara Bell pressed on: "You said homicide, can you tell us how the victim was murdered, and do you have any leads?"

The camera panned past the detective's shoulder and zoomed in for a close-up of the now tarp-covered body...small amounts of blood seeping through the cover could be seen. The camera pulled back for a better view of the stately brownstone before settling back on Detective Wisdom as he continued, "I can only confirm the crime appears to have been committed sometime after midnight and, as of now, we do not have any leads to discuss with you. Thank You."

The camera followed Detective Wisdom and then pans back to Barbara Bell. "Bob, according to neighbors on the scene, it appears the victim is one David Schneider. He is a husband and the father of two small girls—one of which appears to have...tragically enough...been the one to have found her father's body curbside early this morning. Ironically, she had come out to play in the very snow in which her father lay dead."

Alfred Poeltz was beside himself. He intensely ground out his cigar, then grabbed another from his bathrobe pocket before quickly lighting it up. Channel 9 coverage cut back to Anchor Althage who asked: "Barbara, were there any witnesses?"

Back to the Barbara Bell: "No Bob. No witnesses and though the police have not revealed the exact cause of death, unconfirmed reports on the scene are suggesting Mr. Schneider was killed by a single bullet to the skull…execution style." Barbara Bell paused, then went to her hard close: "Bob, a violent start to an otherwise quiet and beautifully winter Sunday morning in The District. From 32nd Street in Georgetown, this is Barbara Bell reporting."

Once again back to the anchor desk where Bob Althage shook his head slightly then offered back: "Thank you, Barbara. That's a tough one to take. Great reporting." Brief pause, then: "In other news, The White House announced a press conference scheduled for this evening at 6 p.m. to address the impending resignation of Spiro Agnew…"

Alfred tuned out his friend Bob, grabbed his pencil, and jotted down *32nd St —GT* on the paper just below the words *Detective Wisdom*. He stood, arched his back, took a sip of coffee, and with a sense of relief let out a low, deep breath, and then, to no one in particular, a simple, "Well, well, well."

He walked over to the TV, clicking off the set. For today at least, Alfred Poeltz had heard all the news he needed to hear.

Chapter Fourteen

Georgetown

Sunday, December 17th–9:30 a.m.

After his dealings with Clichéd Reporter Lady, Joey felt rushed. He'd been there an hour and had yet to attack the one reasonably decent lead he had. Sending Jenner off to track down the cabbie was like a homework assignment—necessary but probably not entirely rewarding. The footprints were a different story.

The snow provided the canvas for a painting that could lead him—if the temperature remained near freezing *and* if he got his ass moving—to a quick resolution to this whole mess. The way Wisdom looked at it, these tracks…if they did not disappear…might point straight to the killer or more likely right to the killer's car. If they led to a car, he could look to put a trace on the tires. A challenge and not the easiest lead but better than nothing. More importantly, he might be able to secure an eyewitness. Someone who saw this *person* leave in the car. Long shot, but with the snow and light Sunday morning traffic, maybe the car may have left its own trail straight to the killer.

Wisdom considered the scene. Every set of footprints that came after sunrise was clear, crisp and deep—the obvious remnants of stepping on the last snowfall of the day. There was only one set of footprints that looked different. That was the set that very likely belonged to our killer. These prints began right at the foot of David Schneider's body, and they were shallow and much less specific than the others. They had been made prior to all the snow that fell after midnight. Weather reports suggested that about six inches fell on Washington-proper prior to midnight with another four or so inches arriving afterward, before sunrise. These were unique prints that left a vague impression in the snow. But, they sent a very specific message to Joey. These were, undoubtedly, the killer's prints.

Wisdom's plan was to simply follow the steps to where they led…hoping that they remained somewhat intact along the way. With the Schneider home located just a few houses off busy Wisconsin, there was the risk that the steps might lead straight there and get mixed up among the leftovers of the late-night bar traffic around Martin's Tavern or Third Edition. The good news was, with half of Georgetown University students likely gone for break and the other half probably lying low due to the weather, that hopefully there wasn't a lot of bar traffic last night. Bar traffic meant foot traffic. Sure, Wisdom was at the Pall Mall last night, but he's a veteran and even he was home before midnight. His wife, on the other hand, was apparently not home before midnight. She was an outlier.

Leaving the scene, Wisdom walked carefully beside the tracks leading away from the victim. They led down the sidewalk and then snuck down a narrow passageway between the two brownstones. Not every step was clear, but it appeared that the steps were far enough apart to suggest that the killer was running.

They led to the edge of an alley that was behind the row of brownstones. At this point, the pace of the footprints began to narrow as if the killer was now walking. Taking his time. Since 32nd runs perpendicular to Wisconsin and is literally no more than seventy-five yards away, the killer had two choices...: Head right back down the alley behind the brownstones of 32nd and then work himself deeper into the city...or cut left. If he went left, within seconds the killer could have likely cut through the Quikee-Mart parking lot that sat at the other end of the alley of 32nd and the corner of Q Street and Wisconsin.

Going right, back up the alley might set off some of those new-fangled motion sensor security lights that some homes had pointed towards their backyards. Going left could lead him into eyewitnesses that might still be meandering around Wisconsin. Wisdom looked at the steps, imagining the killer pausing here in the darkness of the alley, considering his quandary. Both getaway routes provided risk...but both provided cover of some kind. He figured a seasoned killer would prefer the possible crowds of Wisconsin—assuming there were any. The more people around, the easier to get lost in the shuffle. Plus, if he went right and anyone saw him lurking in a dark alley in a snowstorm late at night, it's pretty likely that alone would trigger a call to the cops.

Wisdom and the killer agreed. The steps, now at a walker's pace, led left and he followed them straight to the small parking lot to the side of the convenience store. He expected the trail to end somewhere near here...most likely beside the tracks of a previously parked car. One that had waited patiently for its owner to return from his hit.

Wrong. They continued through the lot beside the store and now off on Q where they headed straight to the corner light at Q and Wisconsin. This guy was smarter than Wisdom hoped him to be. Parking in that lot would have been a bad idea...very likely the store had some kind of video surveillance that may have caught his image or maybe even his car. If he parked there, this case was going to be over in a day. Frankel would be pleased...or at least as pleased as any overbearing, run-of-the-mill asshole could possibly be.

However, the muted but still visible prints continued

their trek towards the corner and the hustle of Wisconsin. His hope for an open and shut case was very likely over. Wisdom had only been trailing these tracks for two minutes, and he already had a real dilemma. It was a quiet morning on the streets of Georgetown, but any small amount of traffic on Wisconsin was going to ruin any possible trail of footprints.

If he had pulled the trigger, Wisdom would want to separate himself as best as he could from the murder. Crossing Wisconsin would accomplish that better than scooting up or down the sidewalks that fronted the road. Unfortunately, it was here where the steps kind of blended in with the foot traffic around the store and there was little if any regularity to any of the footprints before him. The steam coming from the gutters and sewer tops of Wisconsin seemed otherworldly but very much in step with a murder...a strange sort of cover. Would the killer cross here and get lost on the other side? He guessed and cautiously stepped out onto the slick slush of Wisconsin, hoping that once he hit the other side, he'd find the trail again.

After dodging a beat-up Vega coming one way and a family-filled station wagon on the way to church coming the other, Joey finally made his way across Wisconsin. Luckily, the steps continued with some regularity up Q Street and into the quaint row house neighborhood where beyond, several blocks away, stood the University. As he walked up Q, he stopped and looked behind him. Something clicked with Joey here that he hadn't noticed before. The footprints he had been following were noticeably smaller than the ones he himself was leaving behind. Sure, the extra snow that hit after the shooting partially obscured the size of the prints that the killer left behind...but this was different.

"We either got some kind of midget for a killer...or this guy's got really small feet."

Chapter Fifteen

Georgetown—32nd St.

Sunday, December 17th–9:45 a.m.

Jenner had returned to the Schneider home hoping to find the commotion inside more contained. Almost three hours after he first arrived on scene, the normally quaint side street of 32nd was still in a perpetual state of turmoil, bubbling over with even more heated activity. Crime scene investigators manned the operation now, but the place was still littered with police officers. Add in the local news teams and the huddled groups of curious neighbors bundled in heavy parkas, and the place had an overbearing feel…and no one seemed to want to leave.

Inside the home, the place felt drained—empty of the activity that had so rudely invaded this place earlier. Mrs. Schneider still sat in her overpriced Queen Anne, dingy robe and all. Almost no energy came from her body as she seemed to have slipped further down the seat cushion until it looked as if her body would just slide right off. The children had been taken over to a neighbor's home, several blocks away. All that was left in the house were two crime scene investigators dusting for prints and taking photographs, one detective, and the victim's wife.

Mrs. Schneider was accompanied by a female officer from the Sex Crimes unit. Normally, Homicide would have someone working with Mrs. Schneider but the holidays…and weather had left the department a bit short staffed. Reinforcements were called in, but truthfully Homicide was never very good at comforting anyone. The officer, sitting in a chair next to Mrs. Schneider, specialized in helping women deal with the trauma of a very personal crime. This wasn't a rape case, but Detective Sally Maroney had an expertise and temperament that were well suited for the situation.

Jenner stepped into the foyer and breathed in the stale air of confused calm and strode over to Maroney.

"Excuse me, Detective… Mrs. Schneider…?" Jenner asked as evenly as he could. "May I ask a favor?"

Mrs. Schneider looked up, glazed and unaffected by the pending request. A bit frustrated by the intrusion, Maroney stood up in front of Mrs. Schneider offering a barrier along with some much-needed psychological protection. "What is it, officer?"

"Detective Wisdom requested I contact some of the local cab companies. There might be a cabbie lead. Just wanted to save some time and see if I can use your…" Jenner switched his sympathetic stare towards the widow Schneider "…telephone to make a few calls. Save us from having to head back to the division."

Maroney stepped back and looked at Mrs. Schneider, "Would that be okay, Sarah?"

An almost imperceptible "yes," softly slipped from her lips while she turned her head slowly to the right and nodded lightly towards what Jenner assumed was the kitchen and a waiting telephone.

"Thank you, ma'am." Jenner bowed ever so slightly. "I'll be quick."

Jenner quickly made his way to the kitchen…an equal blend of dark wood counters and cabinets balanced by cream linoleum flooring. On the wall, a new-fangled matching cream push-button phone hung. It had one of those ridiculously long handset telephone cords that allowed you to walk far away from the unit. Jenner looked around quickly but was unable to find the Yellow or White pages. Not wanting to disturb Mrs. Schneider again, Jenner made a series of information calls for the local cab companies' phone numbers. Yes, this might cost her twenty-five cents for each call but something told Jenner that this wouldn't be the first information fee this house ever got…and frankly, that would be the least of her concerns.

Yellow, Red Top and Diamond Cab were the big boys, and Jenner proceeded to contact the shift manager on duty for each. Taxi companies were required by law for safety reasons to make note of each ride. Both the pick-up and drop-off. This process also helped to protect the company from the cabbie taking a fare on the side and skimming the cash. Even though it was a simple handwritten accounting in someone's random spiral notebook and that no one ever bothered to make sure there was compliance, the shift bosses usually had it pretty handy. After all, it wasn't the first time the police came calling.

Both Diamond and Yellow were no help at all. Plenty of fares from National last night, but nothing going to Georgetown. Red Top, on the other hand, came up aces. After some prodding and digging, it turns out that they did indeed have a single passenger fare around 11:30 p.m. from National to Georgetown. The street wasn't referenced, but this narrowed down the possibilities quite a bit.

Jenner pressed for the cabbie's name, but the taxi companies loathed to give out that information. Most of their drivers had either done time or were illegal…or both. So, Jenner took Wisdom's advice to threaten the shift manager with a personal visit from the lead detective if he wouldn't provide the needed information. The manager took the bait, and without delay, a name came flying from his mouth faster than a snap—the name of one, Moshe Azizi. According to the shift manager, when Schneider would call in, he would always ask for Azizi.

Chapter Sixteen

Georgetown University

Sunday, December 17th–9:40 a.m.

Across Wisconsin, Joey worked his way up the slight incline of Q Street, following closely the muddled footprints of the killer. At Q and 32nd, where Volta Park lay, the prints headed south, crossing diagonally through the now hushed and white covering of what is normally a vibrant springtime greenspace for dogs and neighborhood little league games.

At the corner edge of the park, the steps continued down Volta Place and peculiarly enough, now led straight towards the campus of Georgetown University. Snowprints were an unlikely ally for Joey, but for them to lead to a college campus seemed far-fetched...and unexpected. What kind of gripe would a college kid have with a high-profile investment banker? Was he having some kind of fling with some little blonde coed? Possibly. Did he piss off some frat kid in the process? Maybe. Joey knew that most murders had sex...or money...behind them. Could Mr. Perfect-Husband with perfect-life and wife have been getting his rocks off on the side with some naïve college hottie? After all, according to Schneider's wife, he was traveling a lot. On the other hand, maybe he had some beef with a professor—like maybe some Economics or Government Studies guru he had hired as a consultant for his practice.

Ah, that just doesn't seem right. The chick story is a much better fit. God knows he's had plenty of his own run-ins with the opposite sex that could've turned ugly.

He continued up Volta and straight onto Copley Lawn…a large tree-lined common area on the campus where students would toss frisbees or footballs around on sunnier and warmer days. But not today. Not this morning. The scene this morning was pristine and very still. The great thing about a wintery Sunday morning on a college campus was that there was no one about. Literally, no one appears to have made even the slightest move outside…and why would they? They were either hungover or gone for the winter break. It was an unspoiled scene, and it gave Joey the clearest series of prints he's had since the alleyway behind the brownstone on 32nd.

He followed the steps left and straight south through the snow-covered space until Copley blended into Healy Lawn, the equally picturesque and normally vibrant meeting place in front of iconic Healy Hall. The gothic façade of Healy, with its famed clock tower, seemed to loom over that campus like an overlord. Joey had heard about the tradition of students stealing the hands of the Healy Clock Tower and mailing them to unsuspecting dignitaries. A slap in the face of the austerity of the institution itself, but what student could put up with such a gloomy presence day in and day out without retribution? An amusing prank no doubt and a much more benign crime than the one four blocks over.

Joey stopped and looked up to the tower. Today the hands were there—properly adorning the black face of the clock and quite clearly showing the current time of 9:55.

"All right, buddy. Any idea what was goin' on here." Wisdom glanced down at his marginally trusty Timex. "Oh, I don't know…say, about nine hours ago?"

If only that eerie clock tower had eyes. If it did, it wouldn't be giving up any secrets. Not on this cold and silent Sunday morning.

Chapter Seventeen

Georgetown—32nd St.

Sunday, December 17th–9:55 a.m.

"I drive Mr. Schneider all the time," Moshe proudly offered.

The shift manager had suggested the same, but Jenner was looking for a little more. "What do you mean, 'all the time?'"

"Mr. Schneider likes me. I drove cab for him one time sometime before. He liked me. I leave him alone. Just drive him home. Good tips. He calls and asks for me. No one else," Moshe said smugly.

"Hmm. Always from the airport? Does he ever go anywhere else with you?"

"Airport always."

"Tell me what you know about last night? Was anyone with him? Did you stop anywhere along the way?" Jenner immediately regretted his anxiousness—jamming three questions at once at the English-challenge Paki cab driver was pushing it.

Moshe was unaffected. "No. He was alone. Always alone. Took him home. Lots of snow. Took longer, but home."

Moshe then asked…his curiosity more than peaked, "Why? Mr. Schneider okay?"

Jenner knew better than to offer the cabbie anything of detail. Telling him they were looking for a killer would scare off the currently cooperative Moshe. If he witnessed anything—that'll come out on its own. Hell, for all Jenner knew… Moshe might even be involved. Highly doubtful but no use gambling.

"Sir, there was a crime reported near Mr. Schneider's home around midnight last night. Your cab was there at about that time. Simply wanted to see if you saw anything unusual."

"No. No. All good." Moshe said a bit too quickly.

That wasn't going to cut it for Jenner. Certainly, wouldn't fly with Wisdom. Suspecting that Moshe's immigration status was sketchy at best Jenner took a more direct tact. "Look, sir. We can come down and take you to the police station for a formal interview if you like." Putting extra emphasis on the word *police*. "I'd prefer to save you from that if you understand."

"No. All good…just drop off. Zawja, waiting for him outside. All good…no problems."

"Zawja?"

"Yes. Wife. Wife watching for him."

Jenner froze. Raised his eyebrows… "His wife was waiting for him…outside?" …his heart now racing.

"Yes, yes…Zawja outside."

Despite saying very little and using very choppy English, Moshe had given Officer Jenner some real gold. This was going to have to alter Wisdom's original premise…namely, that sweet Mrs. Schneider had nothing to do with the murder. Using the full length of the long phone cord, Jenner walked towards the kitchen entrance and peered out the kitchen corner towards the teary Sarah Schneider. Mother, wife, widow. Murderer? Was this all just a clever act?

Jenner was ticking with the youthful energy and

adrenalin that probably comes naturally to a rookie on a murder case. But now, with this new info, he was in overdrive. This seemingly innocent tidbit from Moshe was going to put a wrench in Wisdom's theory. With forensics suggesting he was murdered about the same time Moshe dropped off his fare and now having an eyewitness who can say the wife of the victim was standing outside at about the same time. Well, let's just say they weren't done interviewing Mrs. Schneider.

Chapter Eighteen

Georgetown University

Sunday, December 17th–10:00 a.m.

The still of the Georgetown campus was in direct contrast to the bloody scene over on 32nd…and certainly dissimilar to what was going on inside Wisdom's mind. It was scrambled with possibilities of jilted lovers, angry boyfriends or irate…better yet…devious professors. Hell, an even more random alternative also crossed his mind: Could the killer, having no connection to the University at all, have simply used the campus as a thoroughfare for his escape? Maybe parking his car in some half-empty school garage or even better, leaving it curbside on one of the many small isolated residential streets in exclusive Foxhall, just west of the University.

Sure, but as Wisdom looked at the trail of prints lying in front of him, he noticed no deviation…no meandering. They went straight across Healy Lawn and right to the front steps of The New South Hall. The trail had ended, and it ended right at the foot of a building that housed a couple hundred students…the jilted lover theory was taking even greater hold.

New South, which opened about fifteen years earlier, was one of two student dormitories on campus…the other one being called, fittingly enough, Old South Hall. Old South, which had changed its name to Ryan Hall, was designed in step with the theme of campus' gothic centerpiece. New South, however, was in notable contrast to the campus's sister buildings. Having been constructed with money from the Federal government, it required a no-frills design. Its monolithic appearance was just a shorter version of those ugly, bland and repetitive low-income housing towers you'd see in the inner cities. With its plain orange brick exterior, it diverged significantly from the ornate style of the rest of the campus…but, it was now looking quite likely that behind its tasteless disguise, a coldblooded killer hid.

Wisdom followed the isolated footprints across the lawn and up the steps of New South to the front door. Pulling open the door, he noticed three things right away. One, that despite some slushy steps on the inner entrance mat, the trail most assuredly ended right there. Secondly, that a young student— probably the Resident Advisor—was manning a counter just beyond the entrance. And thirdly, Homicide Detective Wisdom probably stood out like a sore thumb to anyone in sight.

Looking up from her Econ-Theory textbook, the RA offered up a curious "May I help you?"

Wisdom stepped inside and rubbed his hands together. "Chilly."

The RA looked suspiciously at the clearly out-of-place visitor and offered a drawn out and very cynical, "Yeah."

He walked toward the RA as she cautiously sat up straighter. She looked like a brainiac—no makeup, plain with glasses, and wearing the traditional collegiate ensemble of an oversized Georgetown sweat outfit. This was comforting to Wisdom. Maybe she'll have her act together. Maybe an overly ambitious brainiac who worked overtime as an RA was just the reliable female…err, source…he was looking for.

"Yes. Good morning, miss. Yes. I am looking for someone. How long have you been at this desk?

"May I ask why?"

"Uh, yeah, sure." Walking right up to the RA's desk, Wisdom reached into his jacket's inner front pocket and pulled out his badge. "Maybe I should've introduced myself a little better. Detective Wisdom, D.C. Police."

"Holy shit. What's wrong?"

"Well, we are not sure exactly. We are trying to figure that out. Have you been here long?"

Worriedly, she answered, "Uh, this is my second year. I'm a sophomore."

Wisdom let a little smile creep from the corner of this mouth—the only amusement of the day. "No. No, miss. How long have you been at this desk?"

"Oh, sorry...sorry," she stammered. "Didn't mean that. I'm here from midnight 'til six.

"Midnight 'til six? It's after nine. Why are you still here?

"Oh, yeah. Well, my replacement didn't show...so I just stuck around. Extra pay. Always happens."

"Overnights. When do you sleep?"

"Oh, well I only do this like once a month. No big thing."

"Hmm. Okay. So, you've been here since midnight? Did you see anyone come in around midnight or a bit later?"

"Well, uh...yeah, there were two girls that came in around 12:30 or so. Can't really remember, but they were pretty fueled up. One girl looked like she was going to get sick. Kind of made a scene." She paused, "Are they in trouble?"

"Not from me. Anything else?"

"Uh, let me think. I dozed off a bit later...but...uh actually, yeah. A girl tried to sneak a boy in with her around 2 am, but that's not allowed."

"Okay, you sent him away?"

"Yeah, but they both left anyway. Probably tried to go to his dorm...but that's it. No one else. It's been real boring. Most kids already left for break."

Wisdom looked around the lobby area. Two narrow and

lightly lit hallways going in separate directions. One elevator to the right. Behind the RA desk was a small, dark and empty cafeteria—apparently closed. "Girls only dorm, right?" The RA nodded.

The fact that only girls lived here surprised him. He hadn't honestly considered a teenaged girl to be a likely suspect. Didn't make sense. Joey stalled for time—hoping for a better opening. "This elevator. I assume it leads to the upper floors."

The RA drew out a slow, confused, "Uh, yeah. Of course. Why?" Then quickly stopped and spluttered "Oh, yeah, yeah. There was one other that came in. Forgot. It happened around midnight...right when I took my shift. She was quiet. Not drunk...or at least I don't think she was. Didn't say a word. Just went straight to the elevator. Pretty sure she took it up to 3... Do I need to call the campus cops or something?"

"No, no. Not yet. Can you take me to her room?"

Emboldened by the excitement, the RA blurted out "I should call security. They should be here."

"Okay, Miss. Fine, have it your way. But as far as this is concerned, I *am* the cops and we are *not* waiting for anyone...and I *will* need you to take me to her room." Wisdom firmly replied while throwing in the always helpful, "She may be in danger."

32nd St.

After hanging up with Moshe, Officer Jenner had briefly toyed with the idea of putting Mrs. Schneider under another round of questioning. Jenner was raw but not so raw to not know that such a move would have sent Wisdom parabolic. He stepped back through the kitchen into the hallway that opened to the living room. There sat Maroney still consoling Mrs. Schneider as if no time had elapsed at all. Jenner walked tentatively down the front hall and snuck out the front door. He did not want to engage Maroney *or* Schneider, for that matter. Best to leave that to Wisdom. Jenner quickly stepped around two evidence team members on the stoop and then down along the front path skirting through a group of loitering policemen and then towards his patrol car. Most of the officers surely had somewhere better to be by now, but they hung on...just like the neighbors. Gawkers to a highway traffic crash. *I swear these bastards are just burning clock.*

Being the first on the scene, his car was parked virtually on top of the body. Like Mrs. Schneider, who *said* she hadn't seen the snow-covered mess of a dead husband until looking more closely, Jenner had literally almost run over the body when he arrived at first light. After support arrived, he had asked Sargent Frankel if he should move his car. He was ignored and then thought better of the move...damage done. Moving the car would only serve to contaminate the crime scene further.

Jenner opened the passenger door, set his now tired body into the seat, and reached for the 2-way mike while switching on the power. A low hiss filtered out of the dash mounted Motorola system. With a click on the mike, Jenner called out to dispatch.

"Officer Jenner, here."

A hiss and click and then the Dispatch Officer offered an impatient "Yeah, what do you want Jenner?"

"Uh, Yes, sir. Yes, sir. Uh, I am here at the 32nd street scene. Need to reach Detective Wisdom."

Hiss-Click

"Yeah, well, he's on a call," the anonymous and irritable voice offered back.

"How can I reach him?"

Hiss-Click

"Try 14..."

...Hiss...

"What an asshole," mumbled Jenner to himself. "Try 14? Yeah, I'll try 14, you mother," like it was some kind of threat.

Jenner flicked the channel knob up the dial until he reached 14. A click and a hiss... "Calling, Detective Wisdom. You there?"

Georgetown University

They moved toward the lobby elevator in tandem—an odd pair. In front, the rumpled and slightly pudgy forty-something Wisdom trailed by the eager and geeky young coed.

Wisdom's walkie-talkie went from stale silence to a low murmuring hiss. Static came online, and with a tick he heard a voice he did not recognize:

"Calling Detective Wisdom, are you there?"

His immediate response was to ignore it. Click it off. If he doesn't know the voice, he was not interested.

But then an anxious and energetic, "Detective Wisdom? Officer Jenner here. Are you online?"

He had the primary suspect just two floors up. Having to let a persnickety RA, with her campus cops in-route, escort him around the dorm had already set him on edge. Now, he the rookie patrolman was abruptly edging in, as well.

Pausing at the elevator door, Wisdom pulled the Motorola from his waist-belt and brought it up to speak. He hesitated a moment, debating whether he should even bother with Jenner but then pressed the talk button.

"This is Wisdom. What is it?"

Hiss-Click

"Uh sir, uh, yeah, uh, just spoke to a cabbie that drove the deceased home last night and uh…"

Hiss-Click

"Yeah. Yeah. I don't got all day. Spit it out."

Hiss-Click

"Well, uh, sir, he said um, that he saw the deceased's..."

Hiss-Click

The RA gave a shocked glance up to Wisdom who abruptly turned his back to her.

"Geez kid, just call him by his name."

Hiss-Click

"Yeah well…you see the thing is he saw the deceased's …I mean…Mr. Schneider's wife standing on the front porch when he dropped him off."

Hiss-Click

"Huh?"

Hiss-Click

"Yes, Sir. He says his wife was right there."

Hiss-Click

Wisdom was stumped. The wife was there for the murder, and yet he has a trail of footprints leaving the scene that could have only been left by the killer...or an accomplice...or...

With hushed intensity Wisdom blurted, "Fuckin A. Okay. Okay, look, kid, I don't have time to fuck around right now. I've got a suspect 60 seconds from me...and it ain't the sweet grieving Mrs. Schneider..."

...Hiss...

A long pause came over the line as if Jenner had fallen deaf. He couldn't believe what he was hearing.

Click

"Holy crap, Uh, yes, sir...should I come to you...err, call in backup?"

Hiss-Click

"No. Just meet me at Booeymonger's in an hour. If I am not there by 11...come over to the New South dorm at Georgetown."

Hiss-Click

"Dorm?"

Hiss-Click

"Yes. The dorm... Out"

...Hiss...

Georgetown University

As he stepped off the elevator onto the 3rd floor, an inappropriate draft greeted the two. It smelled of chemicals...or maybe it was just really bad mold. Hard to tell.

"They painted the hallways yesterday."

Wisdom nodded and then turned left down out of the floor's lobby area and immediately picked up the faint sound of music coming from further down the hallway.

Wisdom moved his badge from his waistband and clipped it to the front of his jacket. He then placed his right hand on the butt of his holstered revolver while he slowly eased down the hall.

He stopped short of the music room, whose door appeared to be slightly ajar. He listened for a moment. Save for the music, it was quiet. He paused and turned back towards the RA and whispered, "Which room?"

Pointing towards the partially cracked door. "Pretty sure it's that one."

Barely above a whisper, "Look, I want you to go down to the lobby. Wait for the Campus Security."

Without a word, the RA scurried off as if welcoming the exit. Seconds later, Wisdom heard the faint ding of the elevator as its door opened offering an escape route of sorts for the young RA. On cue, another door creaked open further down the hall and out stepped a groggy looking girl in PJs. Joey took a firmer hold of the gun's grip.

Startled by seeing a man on her floor, the girl dragged herself back inside her room then leaned her head out. "Who the hell are you?"

Wisdom raised a finger to his lips and breathed a virtually silent, "Shhh." Then pointed to his badge. "D.C. Police."

"Good, will you get her to turn off that god-forsaken song—been going on all night."

He nodded and flipped the back of his left hand toward her in a signal to go away…which she promptly did. More irritated than concerned, she turned, quickly closing the door behind her.

Wisdom cautiously moved towards the opening of the cracked door…the song now clearly heard as it drifted out of the room. He slowly opened the door to find an empty and made-up bed to his left—the song now fading to a close. On the floor of the room were a heavy coat and winter gloves, a sweatshirt of some kind, some other clothes—all piled in a clump. A sharp clack from the back of the room startled the already edgy Wisdom.

The record player arm moved up and then slid back towards its rest…briefly paused and then shifted back to the still spinning 45 on the turntable. Pausing again before slowly dropping down and resting its needle on the album. Wisdom thought of the girl across the hall. No wonder she was pissed. The record was starting over again…again.

The song was haunting. A hypnotic Pink Floyd piano solo that blended with the wailing angst of a female's voice. There were no lyrics, save for a few repetitive melancholy mumblings barely perceptible beneath the melody:

"I'm not afraid of dying. Any time will do. Why should I be frightened of dying?"

And despite the never-ending music, the room had a muted sense to it…as if it had been abruptly left empty.

With his hand still firmly on the grip of his revolver, Wisdom offered a tentative, "Miss, are you okay?"…hoping that the concern in his voice would be more welcomed then his typical abrupt entry.

Nothing.

And with that, Wisdom carefully eased the door open to reveal the other half of the room and the answer to the question. Upon the second bed, lay something that he would later recall was startlingly familiar to him.

Chapter Nineteen

Erinnerungen an Dachua, Germany

1943

S. Rauscher Journalprotokoll XII:

Who is the greatest hypnotist of all time? I think without question, it is Adolf Hitler.

Though we both eventually and equally became enamored with the possibilities of mind control, Hitler's curiosity came long before I arrived. I had heard through my collaboration with Himmler that The Fureher's initial interests came from his absorption of a book written in 1908 by famed French psychologist—Dr. Gustave LeBon. The book, "Psychologie des Foules"—or as one says in the English, "Psychology of the Masses"—clearly describes the psychology of crowds and the techniques used to control them. He identified that group behavior could be manipulated by hypnotic suggestion and that only a few individuals in a crowd possess sufficient personality to resist.

The book suggested that one of the primary ways to command and direct people was through the use of film...something that was becoming more prevalent by the age of Hitler's rise to power. While Hitler's use of prepared films to press his message of uprising and ascension of the Aryan race became commonplace at that time, there were still few outlets that could produce competing imagery at the pace that Hitler's Third Reich could. This modern technological deployment of propaganda—as one might call it—was paramount to reaching the masses.

However, as important as film was to Hitler's manipulative power grab, he knew that Le Bon's theories on crowd control didn't end there. When speaking to large crowds, LeBon theorized that a positive and confident approach was the essential backbone to command an audience. Further, repetition of keywords or phrases had a way of seeping in the subconscious...such as Jew, Jew, Jew or Blame, Blame, Blame. This was something Hitler did in an unrelenting manner. Hitler also grabbed hold of the LeBon's third leg of the manipulation tool...the idea that when telling a story, a Big Lie was far more powerful than a Small Truth. Additional techniques such as pacing, hand gestures, verbal confusion can also lull an audience into submission, and Hitler used all of these stylings to a great degree.

But that was not enough for Adolf Hitler. He felt, like both I and Himmler, that the brain was an easy target for not only manipulation but also improvement. His quest for a single powerful race would be furthered if he were able to not only manipulate the masses but also expand the will and mental strength of the very people he relied on to reach his goals. That being, the military.

After the first series of our successful mind manipulation trials using Mescaline and hypnosis, Himmler had directed me to carry out tests using captured Russian soldiers. The quest was to run the same tests on these subjects as before and then release the unsuspecting dupes near the Front where they could be rescued by their own forces. Under the influence of both the peyote-based mescaline and hypnosis, they would be directed to assassinate any military member with a rank above Colonel. There was, unfortunately, an immediate problem with this plan as we learned quite clearly that the apparent effects of the mental manipulation did not last long enough for the soldiers to fulfill their task. Reportedly, each subject appeared clear-headed well before they were released and at that point very likely to have lost the medically induced longing to carry out such a treasonous task.

Under intense pressure from Himmler, I took a new direction. Using the same techniques but in smaller doses spread out over several days, we believed we could contaminate the mind deep enough that it would last longer. Again, we released our subjects at various points along the Front only to discover our Russian counterparts found these returning comrades suspicious. While they could communicate fine and they would surely carry out our suggestive orders, we knew from our own tests that they appeared unemotional and almost trance-like, even days after treatment. Reports from our own spies told us that upon their rescue each soldier was almost unilaterally sent to a military mental hospital where they were cared for until the 'shell-shock' went away. Had these victims been allowed to immediately return to their unit we felt assuredly that they would accomplish our goals. Sadly, despite over fifty efforts of treasonous infiltration, we received not one report of success. Yes, through proper mind control techniques, we could get the unsuspecting to carry out whatever orders we desired. But, for how long would they cooperate and more importantly...would their demeanor give them away?

Chapter Twenty

Georgetown University

Sunday, December 17th–10:30 a.m.

She rested there peacefully enough—her bed still properly made, flowered comforter neatly aligned atop the thin dorm style mattress. Matching small decorative pillows placed at the head of the bed and on top of all those pretty fabric flowers lay, perfectly centered, a lifeless girl—naked to the waist.

What set Wisdom back was the girl's head. It was cartoonish. Bloated and almost cherry red from the tip of her concerned brow down her face to her shoulder-line. Bright red save for a blueish tint to her lips—slightly parted as if calmly preparing to take one last breath.

Wisdom had seen all kinds of death in his job from all walks of life. Nauseating bullet holes left in all kinds of body parts. Indescribably ragged knife wounds in spots you would've never considered for murder. Ballooned bodies pulled from the Potomac. Headless dupes and needle riddled dope heads. Children murdered by their own parent—limbs removed. There was even a string of killings in the sixties where all the victims were found in some dark littered back alley with their sex organs mutilated. They were all thought to be prostitutes.

Yes, Wisdom had seen all kinds of death, and even though the net result was always the same, each seemed to have its own special twist. Its own unique story. But what set this young girl's death apart was not its originality. No. It was the similarity of it all that threw Joey. He *had* seen this before. At least once...and what troubled him *were* the similarities. The last time he saw a body like this was four years back. That body's head was also puffed up and inflamed. It was also naked and female, and most importantly, the deceased was also a Georgetown University student.

Chapter Twenty-One

Dupont Circle—Sauf Haus

Sunday, December 17th–10:55 a.m.

The snow had more then stopped, and the sun had begun making an effort to push through the thick air as Alfred Poeltz carefully stepped onto P—an ash-laden cigar in one hand and a worn burgundy leather notebook tucked snugly under his other arm. Married to the notebook was today's *Washington Post*. Bruno, Mr. Poeltz' ever-present cat, trailed close by his side.

Sauf Haus was only a minute's walk down P, but he would still choke back that cigar well before getting there. As he shuffled his stiff legs through the slush, his mind wondered. He was both elated and nervous. Had he finally figured it all out? But those thoughts of success were quickly replaced by the specter of paranoia. Would anyone make the connection?

As he got closer to Sauf Haus, that familiar smell eased him back to center. There was nothing quite like the welcoming but strange blend of aromas that came from the joint each morning…particularly on a cold, wet morning like this one. It was the stray scent of fresh bacon and eggs on the skillet blended with the funky aroma of stale beer that had been spilled on the bar's contorted hardwoods the night before. It all seemed to drift with purpose out the seams of the front door, blending flawlessly with the morning's dank air and carrying with it a barely tangible scent of refuse. A pungent aroma that was courtesy of the steaming gutters and patient trash cans that waited pointlessly each day for the city's garbage man. It was Sunday…so they'll wait longer.

This strangely pleasant blend was only viable because his favorite watering hole also doubled as a greasy spoon each morning. Truth is, without the smell of bacon on the griddle the whole olfactory sensation would probably lean more towards nausea than anything else. The aroma of old beer, wet air, trash, and eggs would hardly seem inviting to anyone. It was the welcomed scented drift of bacon that put it over the top. Without it, it'd be like a cake recipe without the sugar…in its place, salt. A repulsive treat, no doubt.

As he walked up to the entry of Sauf Haus, its rickety door slightly ajar, Poeltz pulled the last drag out of his smoke and blatantly tossed it aside. It rolled into the gutter—no doubt adding to this morning's potpourri.

Chapter Twenty-Two

Georgetown—Booeymonger's

Sunday, December 17ᵗʰ–11:00 a.m.

Booeymonger's is a dumpy little place on the corner of Prospect and Potomac—half a mile east from New South. It used to be called Randy's, and then Bull Dogs, but a few years back new owners changed the name to try and make it cool with the hippie crowd. It may have changed names over the years, but it has always been a coffee and bagel place...all kinds of bagels, all kinds of toppings. If you were real daring, you might try the Booey Box Car Bagel—which was really just a couple of eggs and bacon dumped on a smear-topped garlic bagel. The Booey hallmark? Each and every breakfast was served with a ridiculously large amount of bacon ...whether you asked for it or not. Probably, too much bacon...if that's even possible

This morning, all Joey Wisdom needed was a giant cup of coffee. The bacon wasn't necessary. He headed down Prospect to meet up with Jenner at Booey's. Halfway there, he passed a ruckus by the steep and isolated narrow stair steps that descended to Canal Road towards Key Bridge. The scene was blocked off by a couple cop cars and a large RV trailer.

After Schneider and the Georgetown girl, Wisdom had had about enough. At least for today. *If I have another frickn' murder on my hands this morning, I'm gonna crap my pants.*

Wisdom looked for a familiar face wearing blue but saw no one he recognized. He walked over to the least offensive hippie in the crowd of people peering over the patrol cars. Half expecting to see the discouraging answer to his question before he even asked it. Joey still managed to muster a defeated, "Who died?"

"Shh—no one died, man. They're filming a movie."

Wisdom looked again towards the scene temporarily appreciating the distraction. "Huh, what's it about?"

"I don't know, man. Some weird murder story."

"Wouldn't be the first."

"What?"

Wisdom didn't answer. Just kept moving. It was a bit after 11:00 by the time he got to Booey's. Hoping the place was close to empty and hoping to see Jenner, Joey pulled open the door to find the place virtually vacant, only a young post-church couple and a mildly disheveled and peach-fuzzed patrolman sitting anxiously at a rickety table near the ordering counter. Jenner, nursing his second cup of joe, looked up sharply at Wisdom as the entrance door slammed shut.

"I almost left, sir."

Too beaten down to offer a witty reply or any reply for that matter, Wisdom made his way towards the kid's table and sat down. The folding chair's metal legs screeched against the concrete floor, briefly turning the heads of the couple three tables over. Joey turned toward the lady behind the counter...

"Large coffee," was all he said.

For several moments, the place was silent. Well, except for the whispered voices of the couple sitting three tables over and the dull hum of the fluorescent lights hanging above. Finally, Jenner's impatience got the best of him. "What the hell happened over there? I heard on the scanner...there was a body found on campus. That you?"

Joey said nothing as he waited for the only nutrients his body and mind craved right now. Martha—or at least that was what her named tag said—brought over a tall Styrofoam cup brimming and steaming with what Wisdom always called *black gold*.

"Sugars on the table. Cream?" she offered.

Joey shook his head sideways, waited for "Martha" to leave and then looked up to Jenner. "We got some seriously strange shit going on this morning."

Chapter Twenty-Three

Erinnerungen an Nuremberg, Germany

1947

S. Rauscher Journalprotokoll XXI:

I was given two choices: I could either be taken to the United States and work for the military complex at large, or I could go to prison and possibly spend the rest of my undoubtedly short life in continuous Siberian winters and torturous pain.

Several of my medical colleagues were not so fortunate. Brack, Gebhart, and the Brandt brothers were all subjected to death by hanging. As was pronounced by judges at The Doctors Trial of Nuremberg, their involvement in mass murder under the guise of euthanasia, doomed their longevity. Most of the others received a kind of prison camp sentence. I never saw any of them again.

My saving grace? Expertise in mind control...and a fierce aspiration by the United States to make sure the Soviets didn't see my expertise as a way to further advance their progress in that field. It didn't hurt that I could speak English fluently. My official judgment was "Twenty Years Hard

Labor," but shortly after sentencing, I was approached by a Dr. Sidney Gottlieb—a clubfooted American Jew.

Gottlieb told me he understood that my work in the field of mind control might benefit the US's own advancement in that endeavor. He was very young...maybe late thirties...and he was uppity, like most of the successful German Jews I knew before the war. Pompous, self-righteous, officious...and a stutterer—an odd contrast to the way he otherwise carried himself. I did not like him in the least, but I played coy. He said he worked for a new Intelligence division of the American government and that under an executive order called Operation Paperclip he was authorized to provide special employment to select German scientists, engineers, and medical experts. Gottlieb told me in no uncertain terms that allowing me the option of a Russian prison sentence was a non-starter for him. Undoubtedly, the Soviets would eventually have me marked as a trophy and that he suspected I would be forced into service for their cause if I didn't take his offer.

His offer? I would be relocated to Washington D.C., supplied with housing, earn a salary, and work under a false biography and employment. My official occupation would be as a medical researcher at Walter Reed Army Medical Center. Once bleached (as Gottlieb called it) of all official Nazi affiliations, I would begin collaborative examination within a project called MKUltra—America's effort in deploying mind-controlling drugs and techniques for use against the Soviets and Chinese.

The alternative was very likely a Siberian reality or a slave-like existence working for the MGB—the Soviet's notoriously vicious spy division. They were known for torturing their captured scientists into compliance. The Americans were thought to be much more prosaic than that, and I actually hated the Soviets more than I hated the Jew...or at least as much.

Gottlieb slapped a pen and a document on the table between us then he said something that sticks with me to this day. "Look, I'm a Jew, and I know working for a Jew is probably not preferable. You'll get over it. You can either gamble on Siberia and the Soviets or come to America and get paid to work."

I sat silently for several moments and stoically stared down Gottlieb until it was completely uncomfortable...hopefully, at least for him.

With the words, "You'll get over it" still piercing my ears, I grabbed Gottlieb's pen. I chose America. I chose the money. The job. I chose the Jew.

Chapter Twenty-Four

Georgetown—Booeymonger's

Sunday, December 17ᵗʰ–11:15 a.m.

Wisdom and Jenner proceeded to fill each other in on what they had uncovered. What started off as a wild goose chase following ghost-prints through the snow and interrogating every witless taxi cab dispatcher in town ended surprisingly with two prime suspects: *The Wife*—if you asked Jenner…and *The College Girl*—if you asked Wisdom.

"So, here's my problem…you got a cabbie that'll swear he saw the wife on the stoops…allegedly moments before he was shot, right?

"Yes, sir."

"So, how does this cabbie guy know it was Schneider's wife, and why would she be waiting *outside* in the snow and cold at midnight…assuming she was waiting *at all* at that time of night? These are real problems if that is the angle you're going with. Too many holes. She'd have to be stupid or sleepwalking to shoot her own husband on her front stoop and then walk back inside only to send her darling daughters out the next morning to find their bloodied mess of a daddy piled up on the curb."

"Ok, I admit I never liked it in the first place. She doesn't fit the bill. Very distraught. Too distraught to not be real."

"I hear ya, man, but don't let seemingly 'distraught' fool you. I've seen better performers turn out to be guilty of all sorts of shady shit. Look, we won't ignore her, but she seems pretty weak. Our real problem is the College Girl."

"So, how do you think she killed herself?

Wisdom grunted, "Hell if I know. I left forensics over there to do their deal…couldn't stand hanging out with those numb-nuts twice in the same day."

Joey paused, took a deep breath and rubbed his hand over his eyes. "Jenner, I don't know for sure how she killed herself. Hell, I don't even know for sure if she *did* kill herself, but I can tell you I am almost one hundred percent certain she was standing right next to that Schneider guy before he hit the ground. There is just no way those tracks accidentally led to a dead girl and it not be related.

"Here's the deal, kid. A few years back there was another GU girl found dead in her dorm. It looked like some kind of overdose. LSD or something. The deal is, no one—the coroner, the forensics guys—I mean, no one had ever seen a body react like hers did to an overdose. It seemed like an OD, but it didn't act like one on almost any level. Despite how off it all seemed at the time, they declared her death accidental due to complication from recreational drug usage. And the thing is, that girl never did drugs."

Wisdom took a sip of his coffee, let out a deep sigh and then looked squarely into Jenner's eyes. "The problem…" Wisdom paused. "The problem is…this girl. The one lying over in New South right now… Her body looked just like this other one. And I mean, exactly the same."

Jenner leaned forward and widened his eyes. "Shit, sir."

"Yeah, shit is right." Joey leaned back in his chair, stretching his arms back. If Joey was wiped out…and he was… God knows Jenner was pushing the limits. Working the overnight and then rolling right into a murder and suicide investigation was a bit much. For anyone. But especially for a rook like Jenner.

"Go home kid—get some sleep. Meet me back at the station in the morning. Nine. Hopefully, the crime scene guys will have something more for us."

Chapter Twenty-Five

Dupont Circle—Sauf Haus

Sunday, December 17th–11:00 a.m.

Poeltz had drifted past the grungy bar top with little more than a knowing nod to Timothy, the morning barkeep who knew exactly what the old man wanted: two fried eggs over easy, rasher of bacon, and coffee…black.

With Bruno in tow, he ambled beyond the thin curtain that separated the main bar from the back room and proceeded to take up his regular spot at an old writing table. Before sitting, he placed The Post on the table and slid it to the side then pulled off his scarf and removed the old heavy tweed smoke-scented jacket he wore with too much regularity. Today's paper would be filled with news of newly re-elected Richard Nixon and his fumbling minions. Spiro Agnew's tax evasion drama would undoubtedly make the cut. Poeltz always liked Agnew—thought he would make a good German. The Redskins were 11-2…one game left that afternoon to lock down the NFC East title. So, that would also get some front-page press. But nothing about 32nd Street…too late to make the print deadline. Tomorrow's paper would fill in the gaps that Bob Althage and his crew had missed.

Poeltz lifted an R&J from his dinged-up silver cigar case. Bit the tip, lit the end, pulled in a deep drag and proceeded to open the leather journal he had brought along. The journal had become a diary of sorts. When pertinent, Poeltz would document the day's dealings. At times, the journal would serve as an autobiography recounting, as best as his memory could handle, events from days gone by.

He began writing in the journal shortly after arriving in the States and taking up service for Gottlieb and his team. The journal served Poeltz's way to keep track of his progress. He may have been forced to come to the U.S., but he wasn't going to leave it without making a mark.

He flipped towards the end of the journal until he came to a page with the notation "Case #3—Jennifer B." He flipped past several notations and remarks before coming to the end, an empty page beneath his last comments. Drawing another drag from his smoke, Poeltz leaned forward and began to review his previous entry:

S. Rauscher Journalprotokoll LXVI:

Update—Case #3, Saturday, December 10th: Jennifer B."
arrived for her weekly session. Psych finals were scheduled
for that coming week. She has seen notable improvement in
her test scores since she began hypnotic tutoring in the Fall.
Her anxiety levels had recessed. Additionally, the hypnosis
training for Operation Rache' was on schedule. I deployed
ABS Steps for hypnosis. Patient was more accustomed to the
process and quickly fell under the suggestive condition.

Beyond the prerequisite exam training, I submitted three
additional instructions while under the state:

When contacted by phone and hearing my voice, she was
to immediately ingest a specified dose of the previously

prescribed mixture.

She was to obtain the prearranged tools and proceed by foot to the selected location at the specified time.

She was then to implement the designated plan and return by foot to her residence."

Poeltz took a tentative sip of the steaming coffee that Timothy had just delivered and then pulled a pen from his front pocket. Pausing for a moment to compile his thoughts, Poeltz leaned forward and entered the following simple transcript:

S. Rauscher Journalprotokoll LXVII:

Update—Case #3, Sunday, December 17th: By all initial accounts, Operation Rache'—A success."

Chapter Twenty-Six

Arlington—The Crystal House

Sunday, December 17ᵗʰ–2:00 p.m.

The intensity of investigating two deaths in one morning after a late and foggy night at the bar had left Joey a bit drained. He needed a break, and a simple cup of coffee wasn't going to do the trick. After he sent Jenner home from Booeymonger's, he stayed behind firing up several smokes to go with Martha's endless cup of coffee. Just needed to get a handle on it.

Murder? Yes. At least one.

Suicide? Maybe.

OD? Suspicious, but likely.

Theory: Jilted college girl kills her secret lover after he breaks off the relationship. Goes back to her dorm distraught. Proceeds to ingest something to ease the pain or eliminate it altogether. Dies.

Wisdom had seen enough over the years to know that it usually isn't all that complicated. Probably as simple as it seemed. However, something about the death of the girl and the way her body presented itself had him questioning the simplicity of the knee-jerk analysis. He was actually kind of hoping the crime scene guys would come up with some drug use evidence that would put his logical theory to bed. Yes, he'd have to prove the girl did the shooting. However, with the new gun powder residue kits that the department was test-driving for the FBI, this would seem a pretty simple step. Yes, poor Mrs. Schneider would be devastated—her husband is dead…and he was cheating with a college girl. Hard to take, no doubt. This would all suck, but from Wisdom's perspective, he could wrap up two deaths in one morning in about 24 hours. He just needed some crime scene goodies to make it all go away.

So, before he headed back to Crystal House, he stopped by the station to get the initial crime scene reports from the New South death. He had wanted to take a quick look at the file but decided to wait until he got back to The House, so he could settle in. Damn sure wasn't going to hang out at District reviewing it while waiting for Frankel to bust his chops or worse…send him out on another investigation. No, he could do all of this just fine from his couch. Hell, maybe Ginny would be up by now and make him a late lunch. Maybe.

After parking the Dart in the same spot he left from seven hours earlier, Joey entered the Crystal House lobby and moved past Frank, the ever-present and aged doorman, as if he didn't actually exist. Some days he'd take the stairs up the fourteen floors to his apartment. Ginny said he needed to lose some weight. Not today. Too damn tired. Today he'd take the elevator.

Opening the apartment door, Joey found the place quiet. Too quiet. Surely, she was up by now. Surely, she hadn't gone to church. Ha. That'll be the day. Joey called out "Ginny?" as he moved from the den past the kitchen towards the still very dark bedroom. Bedsheets tossed aside and no Ginny. Gone.

"No lunch for me, I guess," Joey mumbled as he wandered back to the den, took off his jacket, holster and gun, and then plopped down on the couch. It was a beat-up piece of furniture that he dragged from apartment to apartment ever since his rookie days. Just couldn't live without it. It wasn't even that comfortable anymore. But for Joey, the thing was still soft enough for his tired ass. Never that picky, anyway.

Joey grabbed the police file that he had set on the coffee table and opened it up. Awfully thin. Two pages. Nothing else. The summary section was as long as the detail section. Never a good sign. Certainly, not if you were hoping for something to work with. Hell, he could have read this at District in about sixty seconds.

It took a few years, but long ago he learned to expect very little from the crime scene guys. It wasn't that they didn't do their job. They just didn't do it very well. Half-ass might be a good description. He skimmed the report hoping his past experience and initial reaction were at least marginally misguided. That maybe there was a useful nugget tucked in the simplicity of it all. But no. There was little depth and fewer answers.

It read:

Criminal Investigation Division #12

ASP -3A
Incident Date: December 16th or 17th, 1974
Dictated By: Inv. Stan Witt
Documented: December 17th, 1974
Copies To: David Frankel, Joseph Wisdom

Crime Scene Search Summary

The crime scene search was conducted on December 10th at 9:55 a.m. at the New South Dormitory at Georgetown University. Room # 312 (Photo 1)

The conducted search consisted of visual observation and photographs of the deceased body of Jennifer Bard and the surrounding room.

The body of Ms. Bard was lying face up on a dorm-style bed common to every room at New South. The body was naked from the waist up. (Photo 2)

Visual observation of Ms. Bard's body showed a red sunburn-like coloring to her upper shoulder area and face. The head was bloated in an unnatural condition, not common to natural death. There was not any visible bruising or marks on the body. Eyes were open. Hands and arms were at rest by the torso. (Photo 3)—Autopsy reports TBD

Visual observation of the room indicated a well-kept environment. The other bed (presumably the roommate's bed) was fully made and untouched. The ceiling light was illuminated. Music was coming from a record player that was placed on a desk near the center of the south wall...opposite of the door entrance. (Photo 4)

Page 1

Additional Crime Scene Details

-No roommate present

-No indications of drug use or paraphernalia –Toxicology reports TBD

-Winter style coat on the floor (Photo 5)—
evidence analysis TBD

-Women's style blouse on floor (Photo
5)—evidence analysis TBD

-Book Satchel on desk...2 notebooks and
2 textbooks inside...3 pens, 1 pencil
(Photo 4)—evidence analysis TBD

-Calendar: Opened to December with
notations entered on multiple dates—
evidence analysis TBD
 (Photo 6)—evidence analysis TBD

-Interviews with dorm-mates, roommates
and Resident Advisor ongoing.

<u>Summation:</u>
Cause of Death: TBD
Crime: TBD   FILE   #:
01-674-96...12-10-74

Page 2

"Shit." Not much to work with. Frankly, Joey had a hard time
believing the lack of drug evidence meant anything. Sure, she
could have died from some medical malady, but this one felt
drug-related. Definitely.

Joey set the file down thinking how much easier this
would all be with a witness. Where had she been? Who had
seen her comings and goings? What do her friends know
about her love life? Did she have any friends? Unfortunately,
being winter break there was next to no one on
campus...much less in her dorm. Outside of the one girl down
the hall that Joey had encountered, he only found three other

rooms with a current occupant and they were worthless. Didn't hear or see anything and didn't know the deceased. Joey thought for a moment and then glanced back to the report and scanned down to the Detail section…:

"Calendar: Opened to December with notations entered on multiple dates."

"Okay, then…maybe we do have something to work with."

Joey was speaking to only himself. Certainly, wasn't speaking to Ginny. Nope. She was gone…literally, and if Joey had looked a little closer, he would have known this. Because, sitting on the coffee table right next to his service issue .38 revolver, sat a nice little folded over note…with "Joey" written on the front.

Joey kicked his feet up onto the coffee table…folded his arms and closed his eyes. Just a rest…fifteen minutes was all he needed.

Two hours later, Joey was startled awake by the sound of a plane taking off from National…the other forty takeoffs hadn't done the trick. Rubbing his eyes, Joey stood up and arched his back, then looked down to the coffee table. For the first time, he finally noticed a small card addressed to him sitting on the table. Well, isn't that sweet, Ginny left him a nice little love note. She never did that.

He reached down and opened it up. Inside it read: *I have gone to my sisters. I might not come back. Don't call me.* She didn't even sign it.

"Bitch."

Chapter Twenty-Seven

District of Columbia—Station House

Monday, December 18ᵗʰ–7:30 a.m.

Joey spent the rest of his Sunday watching the Skins while slouched in his Eames lounge chair, the only relevant and reputable piece of furniture in his dumpy little apartment. Ironically, a birthday gift from Ginny.

He chained half a dozen Winston's to blend perfectly with a six pack of Schmidty. Not that he was trying to kick the habit or anything, but he always figured he'd allow himself no more than one smoke for every drink…that way maybe he'd manage to keep the lid on both compulsions. Drinking Schmidty came with a curse and a blessing. It *was* the cheapest beer on the shelf, but it was also the smallest…only a ten-ounce bottle. The funny thing was it took Joey about a year before he noticed it wasn't even a twelve-ounce bottle. So pleased with the price, he never bothered to even look at the label. By the time he figured it out it had become his cost-effective beer of choice. Never mind that he could be drinking twelve-ounce Schaeffer at almost the same price. Twenty percent more beer for an extra dime. Math was never Joey's forte.

By the time the Redskins had finished off the Rams 42-0, Joey had finished off the beer. The initial buzz had helped him forget about Ginny…and Schneider…and the college girl. At least for a while. Once he got through three or four beers though, he just got plain drowsy, slipping further into the lounger and fading into a deep snore-laden sleep that lasted through the night.

Joey found that daytime drinking had its benefits. Most important was that he usually passed out way earlier than if he spent the *night* boozing it up. So, while on the surface there is nothing good about waking up in a lounge chair at the crack of dawn still in your workday best, at least he'd get a long night's sleep, and the likelihood of a cheap beer hangover usually faded sometime around 2 a.m.

So, on Monday morning, Detective Wisdom arrived at the 2nd District Station house both refreshed *and* early…just after 7:30. Located on Idaho past the National Cathedral and just off Wisconsin, the District HQ was tucked in a neighborhood of tenement apartments about a ten-minute drive up from M Street. This part of the District was in stark contrast to the tony neighborhoods of Georgetown and Foxhall. Littered with street dwellers, liquor stores, and strip clubs like Archibald's, the area around the station usually kept Detective Wisdom more than busy. Certainly, busier than any drama that typically came from the high-priced brownstone community down the road.

Breezing past the bleary-eyed desk manager who undoubtedly had been there all night, Wisdom made his way to the Evidence Room. To his surprise, Jenner was already there. Under the watchful eye of the Evidence Room Director, Jenner had laid the contents of the Jennifer Bard case box neatly around the evidence table.

"I thought I told you 9. It's like 7:30."

Startled, Jenner jumped up from his chair stammering out a quick "Yes, sir."

Wisdom almost laughed out loud. Giggled, for sure. Mostly to himself. Mostly. Looking at Jenner all polished up in his blues emphasized the difference in the two of them. Hell, he could still smell the Barbasol on the kid. He was so eager and nowhere nearly as jaded as Wisdom…yet.

The kid reminded Wisdom of himself…twenty-years ago. Unfortunately, the differences didn't stop at enthusiasm. twenty-years on the 'beat'…hell, twenty-years doing anything…will put a bit of wear and tear on the body and the mind. Jenner's posture was ramrod straight…Wisdom's slumped. Jenner was fit like any recent Police Academy grad should be. Wisdom was paunchy like someone with a couple decades of Schmidt's under the belt…literally. Jenner's attire…spit-polished. Wisdom was wearing the frumpy exterior of someone who just didn't care (maybe that's why Ginny left him). Save for a pimple that he thought he saw, Jenner's complexion was baby-faced. Wisdom's? Weathered and wrinkled. He was sure the smokes didn't help his cause.

"Relax, kid. Tell me what you got."

"Honestly, Detective…"

"Just call me Joey, Okay, kid?"

"Yes, sir…You can call me Richard,"

"Yeah. Okay, kid, what do ya got?"

"Yes, sir." Jenner paused, looked down at the articles he had spread out on the table. Some textbooks, study folders, a few pieces of clothing, some makeup and toiletries, a prescription bottle. "Honestly, I don't think there's much here. I'll let you be the judge."

"What's the story on the prescription?"

"Best I can tell it was for stress or something. They didn't test it yet, but the label says Diazepam. Valium."

"Hmm. I'm not narco but I'm pretty sure valium doesn't do what *I* saw to a body. What else?"

"Not much. The tox report won't be completed for a couple days. Forensics left a note on the GPR test: *TBD…eta = late Mon.* Most of the stuff in the evidence box is pretty drab. Study folders all had school stuff in them. No drug paraphernalia. Nothing interesting. Well, nothing interesting for us. No diary, either. Which is odd. Kinda thought all girls had a diary. She does…did…have a calendar. Got some notes on it."

"Well, okay…maybe we've got something to work with. Show me."

Jenner pulled out the calendar—a theme calendar. This one had a cat theme. Each month had its own mascot…an artist's rendering of a different cat for each month. You know, Siamese for September. That sort of thing. Jenner flipped it to December and handed it to Wisdom. The mischievous grin of a grey-toned Cheshire cat stared back at Joey. Poetic.

Most of the notations seemed innocuous. Reminders of tests. A lunch date with a girlfriend. That sort of thing. Boring stuff. Not that you could tell from her bloated body, but from photos in her dorm room, Jennifer Bard seemed like a pretty girl. Unfortunately, that didn't translate into much of a social life…at least not one that showed up in her calendar. If she was having a fling with the good banker over on 32nd she certainly didn't make a note of it. At least not in her cat calendar.

"Okay, well, not much to work with. A couple notations of meetings with teachers. We'll need to check with them. Also, track down this girl she had lunch with last week…see if she is up on anything."

Wisdom flipped back to November and October then back to December. Everything seemed very basic. He dragged his glance through every day and stopped abruptly at December 10th. Marked clearly were the words "Prof Poeltz, 7 p.m." …followed below with the cryptic reference of "tut…1812 p". Flipping to November, he noticed the same scheduled meeting on every Sunday during the month of November. October, too.

Pointing to the notation on the 10th. "What do you make of this, Jenner? I got what looks like a meeting with a professor every Sunday. Tut *could* mean tutor, I guess. She *is* a student, after all. But what the hell is 1812 p?"

"Well, I'd say it's not a time…they met at 7 p.m. Maybe it's a location…maybe it's a campus code or an abbreviation for one of the buildings."

"Nah, pretty sure Georgetown doesn't have a code system. Not like that at least Certainly, not one a student would know. Might be an abbreviation. Can't think of any buildings on campus starting with P, though."

Jenner stared at the notation hoping something brilliant would come to him then blurted out, "P Street?"

"Huh...well. Maybe. Hmm. P Street, huh? The 1800 area *is* over there by Dupont. Address makes sense...kind of. But why the hell is a student going over there to see a professor? Why not on campus?"

Wisdom paused for a moment, wondering if he could answer his own question. "Okay—normally the campus is pretty dead with winter break, *but* I'm pretty sure the school's Admin is fully staffed today. It's going to be busy handling the Bard situation. So, check in with Admin and see if you can get the contact info for her roommate and that girl she had lunch with.

"What about this Professor?"

"I got that. Want to see what his story is. Why the hell would a cute little college coed visit her professor off campus...every week?"

"Are we going to pay him a visit?"

"Damn straight."

Chapter Twenty-Eight

Erinnerungen an Bethesda, Maryland–Walter Reed

1949

S. Rauscher Journalprotokoll XLI:

I had arrived home from Walter Reed to find two of Gottlieb's go-fers in my apartment. A large frumpy woman stood off to the side with a child supported in her arms. Her name was Charlotte. His name was Jonathan. There were two luggage bags and a cradle on the floor next to her. She was moving in. The two men stood side by side. They were well dressed, each sporting a felt trimmed Bailey hat to match their grey suits. They were focused. There was no doubt these gentlemen were straight from National Intelligence.

"It has been decided that you need a family...for appearance sake. You'll be happier," said one of the minions.

In actuality, I understood this to be a security precaution of the highest level—a threat more than anything else. Gottlieb wasn't about to let me run free without oversight, especially since I had been making significant progress for MKUltra. This woman...this Charlotte...was most assuredly full-blooded NIA. Definitely a spook of some kind but one of a more subtle order. Where the child came from was anyone's guess.

According to Gottlieb's man, as a cover, the plan was to move the three of us into an apartment over an old antique store over by Dupont Circle. A store that Charlotte would theoretically operate. As for our relationship—she would be my wife in name only, and I was not to initiate any physical interaction with Charlotte. Anything on that level would be at her discretion. (This would not be an issue...for either of us). She was apparently a wonderful cook, and she would tend to the boy...our child. I was also told, in a very offhanded manner, that she was fluent in German, very observant, and she could certainly take care of herself.

"Not to worry, Dr. Poeltz. All is well. You need a family. It is better this way. This will make you content. We are sure of it," said the second minion.

Even four years later, I was still having a difficult time accepting my identity—Dr. Poeltz. To bleach me, I had not only needed a new name but a new biography. Rauscher was most assuredly German. So, a suitable alternative was found in Poeltz—more Austrian than anything. And while there was nothing you could do about my accent—which was thickly Germanic—it could, in truth, easily pass as Austrian or possibly from the regions of northern Switzerland. Either, a realistic heritage for me.

So, in Gottlieb's infinite wisdom, I became Dr. Alfred Poeltz, a doctor of science from Paris Lodron University in Salzburg. According to my profile, due to the overwhelming prejudice of the Nazi movement, I fled the border area near Germany in 1943 then hid in Switzerland temporarily until making my way to the United States. Because of my ability to speak English and my expertise in science, I was 'able' to find a medical research position at Walter Reed.

All of this was very convenient.

In their eyes, this metamorphous was for my protection

more than anything else. I was told that a Nazi doctor living in America right after the war was surely a death sentence. They were probably right...and besides, erasing my past was, for them, a simple process of paperwork. For me, it was more like an attempted obliteration of who I truly was. What I truly believed. How I truly felt.

They could change my name. Where I came from. They could even burden me with a wife...and a child. Gottlieb could do all this...contorting my life like I was a warped medical experiment...but he could not change the core. He may have stolen my future, but he could not change my past. He would NOT change me.

Chapter Twenty-Nine

Dupont Circle—1810 P Street

Monday, December 18th–10:58 a.m.

After a few well-placed phone calls to the Georgetown University Admin office, Wisdom was able to get the low-down on the Poeltz character that was so regularly mentioned in the Bard girl's calendar. He was indeed a professor at GU, but he was retired. A bit of a character on campus and a student favorite. He headed up the Psych department for several years, but when he applied for tenure and was denied, he abruptly retired. This was several years back.

After he left, and this is apparently backed mostly by gossip, he started up a fairly robust tutoring service for Georgetown psych students. According to their records, his last known address was indeed on P street in the Dupont Circle neighborhood…but it was 1810 P, not 1812. Since he was not under tenure and he was off the university's payroll they had no real reason to keep tabs on him. This was the best they could do.

"A tutor wasn't very ominous," thought Wisdom but the Bard girl *was* a Psych major, so the tutor deal kind of made sense. Hell, who better to tutor you than the guy who used to run the whole department? The address being off by two digits? Probably just a simple typo. Meeting at his house was perhaps just the way he did it. Since he left GU under less than happy circumstances there is probably not a chance in hell he'd want to be near or, for that matter, on campus for any reason.

They also discovered that the roommate was indeed home for the winter break. California. Flew home on Friday after her last exam. So, a phone call to her parents would wait a bit. Pacific Standard Time. Too early. Wisdom had sent Jenner back to New South...interviewing anyone or anything left in the building. After that, he was to retrace the path the Bard girl took from the Schneider's two nights earlier...making sure to look for anything left along the way.

As of now, there were only two people he was certain were familiar with Bard...her roommate and this tutor. Potentially three, if you want to include the deceased David Schneider. Outside of him...who was worthless to the investigation, she presumably talked to her roommate every day. The tutor? Well, he was probably a limited resource, but at least Wisdom knew she saw him once a week. With Jenner knee deep in discovery, Wisdom thought it best to go on his own wild goose chase venturing over to Dupont and one, Professor Poeltz.

Leaving the 2nd District Station, Wisdom picked up Mass Avenue east. Even though it was a busy route this time of morning—particularly on a workday—it was by far the most direct route to Dupont. Taking the 4th right on the roundabout onto P, Wisdom pulled up curbside to an elegant three-story brick home right at the corner of P and the Circle. There was no street parking out front, so Wisdom made sure his portable cherry top was placed front and center on his dash. Not interested in getting the Dart taken away by some overzealous tow company, he then pulled partially up on the curb and flipped on the red flashing light.

The main entrance to the house was beneath a covered porch right between a decorative bay window and a small bricked arched portico. The number of the house was 1810, but it didn't seem like a home. On the large wood-framed glass door was a gold stenciled sign that read "Theodore's." Wisdom walked up to the big glass doors and peered inside. Inside it was dark except for a bleeding light that came from beneath a closed door near the back and a rumor of light that came from the upstairs landing.

In the main room off the entrance was a cluttered assembly of chairs, tables, bureaus, and grandfather clocks. On the walls, an abundance of dusty bleached mirrors and wall mounted candelabras were hung seemingly everywhere. Down the hallway to that closed-off room was an assortment of mounted antlers. *If* he actually lived here, Poeltz sure had a pretty strange decorating style.

Wisdom stepped away from the front stoop noticing for the first time a black pole planted near the gated entry…a non-descript iron sign hung heavily from a small extended arm. It said simply, "Antiques."

So, good ol' Professor Poeltz was an antique dealer….*and* a tutor. Wisdom glanced up at the façade taking in the entirety of the structure. It was impressive by any judgment. By the look of this home, he must have been a very profitable dealer. This place was undoubtedly on the pricier side.

As he scanned the place for any sign of life, Wisdom saw what appeared to be the slightest movement of a closed pale cream curtain faintly settling back into its place…as if someone had been watching him. An upstairs light promptly went out.

Wisdom looked back at the awkwardness of the parked Dart and rolling police light flashing from the inside. "Well, guess I got someone's attention. Let's see what the old professor has to offer."

Chapter Thirty

Dupont Circle—1810 P Street

Monday, December 18th–10:48 a.m.

Alfred Poeltz heard the visitor way before he set eyes on him. He was seated in the 3rd-floor parlor room reading The Post when the distinct sound of a car jumping the curb shattered the calm. Poeltz abruptly turned his head toward the front window. The sound of a creaking lima bean green Dodge Dart settling on his sidewalk followed by the opening and slamming shut of a car door had made a bit of an impression on him. This part of Dupont wasn't used to that kind of racket.

Poeltz promptly crushed out the last bit of his teetering R&J, carefully set the perpetually sleeping Bruno on the floor, and walked over to the window. He peered through an open sliver between the thin drapes that otherwise would've provided little more than a hazing view to the street below.

A man wearing a fur-collared dark brown Towncraft coat lumbered his way up to the front stoop. Looking confused, he rolled his gaze around the front of the house…down P and back –like he was looking for something that made sense. As the man walked up to the front door, Poeltz completely pulled the curtain back struggling to follow the visitor's movement. It was then that he noticed the flashing red police light centered firmly on the old Dart's dash top.

There must have been a skip in his heart because, as the visitor stole a glance to the upper windows, Poeltz immediately felt faint. He staggered back a bit from the window, the curtain settling back into its traditional dormant position.

"Not possible" was the only thing that escaped his now uncertain mouth.

The sudden chime of the doorbell rang as a startling echo moved throughout the silent structure. Poeltz steadied himself…desperately hoping to recapture the internal confidence that he was now so clearly void of.

Turning off the light and gathering his cat, Alfred made his way down the back stairs that led to a private kitchen off the store's main showroom. He moved slowly enough that another ring sounded throughout the house, followed by three loud rhythmic knocks. He paused on the safe side of the swinging kitchen door, took a deep breath, and walked purposely to the front door that was Theodore's primary entrance…cat still in tow.

He stopped just short of the door, the visitor clearly visible through the other side of the glass. The man appeared uncomplicated but carried a focused air about him. The two stoically looked at each other. Longer than necessary. Certainly, longer than appropriate. Taking each other in. The tired and confused man on the inside…the serious but simple gentlemen on the outside…looking in.

Poeltz took a quick glance at his Croton…10:50. Naively hoping to send the visitor away…for good, Poeltz presented an apologetic "Sorry, sir, but we are not open 'til noon. Please come again."

The visitor looked at his watch. A Timex…11:00. "I'm looking for Professor Poeltz, sir."

Poeltz said nothing…just stared at the visitor through the

wavy clarity of the old wood framed glass door. Finally, "We are not open until noon."

"Yes sir, but I am not a customer. I'm looking for Professor Poeltz."

"What is it about?"

"I'd prefer to not yell through the door. May I come in?"

"Pray-tell...may I ask who you are?"

"Of course, sir... D.C. Police."

And with a silent thud...there it was. As if the rolling red police light hadn't clued him in enough. Alfred Poeltz now felt cornered...if ever so briefly. Police at his doorstep...less than forty-eight hours after. Hardly seemed possible.

With an almost imperceptible slump to his shoulders, Poeltz offered up a plaintive "Please come to the other entrance..." now pointing to the visitor's left "...on the side here."

As Poeltz headed back through the swinging kitchen door, the visitor walked off the front porch and then down the side of the house until he saw a door with the number 1810 stenciled on the threshold. If Poeltz could've seen him, he would have noticed a glint of a narrow smile ease from his otherwise focused expression...and it wouldn't have made any sense to him at all.

From inside the kitchen, Poeltz reached forward to open the door to the side entrance...the visitor waiting. What the visitor found was a man who carried himself a bit differently than the one he witnessed at the front door. Sure, it was the same man, but gone was the cat; and the gentleman now in front of him had an appearance of superiority that now trended towards pompous irritability.

"What can I do for you, sir?" His now noticeably thick European accent dripping off every syllable.

"Like I said, I'd like to speak with Professor Poeltz. Is that you?"

"Your name?"

"Like I said...Detective Wisdom. D.C. police." Pausing then tauntingly adding in... "Homicide."

Poeltz hesitated before answering. The name Wisdom

had hung in the air ever so slightly. Poeltz knew the name...
knew exactly who this visitor was. "Well, uh actually...you
never gave me your name...but yes, my name is Alfred
Poeltz".

"Professor Poeltz?"

"Like you said, "Professor Alfred Poeltz."

"Sir, I'd like to talk to you about a student of yours."

"I am retired...several years now. I don't have
students...anymore."

"Well, I mean someone you tutored. I understand you do
some tutoring."

"A bit."

"Yes, well sir, there has been an incident over at
Georgetown. One of your students. A death."

"Well, I thought you said you were Homicide."

Detective Wisdom felt like he was being poked at, and
he didn't like it. It was the kind of poking that felt intentional
versus habitual. He firmed up... "I am Homicide, sir."

"Well, if that's the case, then it's not merely a
death...wouldn't it more directly be called a murder? No
reason to be subtle with me, officer."

"Detective," Wisdom offered firmly. "It's called being
polite, and no, sir, it *is* a death. In my experience –they are all
deaths. Whether we call it a murder or not will depend on a
lot of things. May I come in?"

"No."

"Sir, I am not trying to be difficult. I just have a few
simple questions. I'd appreciate you giving me a bit of leeway
here."

"I'd appreciate it if *you* wouldn't park on my sidewalk
with your little police light running."

Wisdom decided to take another more apologetic tact.
"Sir, I know this can be a bit confusing to you. Some cop
showing up abruptly at your door. Some student of
yours...dead. Yes, your name came up in our preliminary
investigation, but I can assure you, it's all quite benign." He
paused, then tilted his head slightly, a concerned wanting
clearly visible on his face. "Look, sir, I got a dead eighteen-

year-old several blocks away. It's Christmas, for god's sake. I could use a little help. Was kinda hoping you wouldn't mind pitchin' in some."

"Pitching?" Spoken as if he truly had no clue what the hell that meant and then, "What was her name?"

Wisdom hesitated...thought, "Did I say female? "I'm sorry, how did you know it was a female?"

Poeltz turned and pointed towards the newspaper on his kitchen counter...the header below the fold reading:

"Georgetown Coed Found Dead"

"Last I looked coed meant female...plus all the students I tutor seem to be females...for some reason, I can't explain. What was her name?"

"Jennifer Bard. A freshman. Do you know her?"

Just the sound of her name made the stern façade that Poeltz wore, fade just a bit. It was replaced with a strange giddiness that he could only hope was undetected.

"Do you know her, Professor?"

Poeltz gathered himself... "I did. I, uh, tutored her this fall. How did she die?"

Wisdom paused. This guy was just a longshot witness, but he had such a wall up that Wisdom couldn't help but want to know why. Was he just a grumpy old man who didn't like him parking on his sidewalk or was there something else? He decided to call the old Professors brusque bluff and press the issue. "Well, sir, as of now, I can't say for sure. That's why I am here." And then with a bit of a forged grin on his face. "May I come in?"

Chapter Thirty-One

Erinnerungen an Frederick, Maryland–Camp Detrick

1951

S. Rauscher Journalprotokoll XLIX:

With the Korean War in its operational peak, it was decided that our research was to become a priority for the Army. Walter Reed was lacking in security and operated in too public of a domain for our team to carry out the kind clandestine and controversial study in which we were engaged. So, in '51, we were all moved out to Camp Detrick— an old military base, retrofitted into the government's headquarters for chemical and biological programs.

The 400-acre camp was located by an old abandoned airfield in the middle of Maryland farmland about an hour outside the Beltway. I regularly arrived at the lab every day but Sunday—always arriving by the prompt hour of 7 o'clock a.m. This meant I departed the city by 5:45 each morning. The roads were mostly empty. The drive peaceful. The rolling hills faintly reminiscent of my homeland. It was my only opportunity for private reflection. It was a welcome part of my day.

Amongst other research, I was charged with the responsibility of conducting a study on manipulating psychological battle readiness as well as evaluating various medicines for the improvement of mental effectiveness in battle and after. While my German team made advancements in wound recovery during the war, this exploration was fascinating and different from some of the more baleful work I conducted on behalf of Himmler.

That was until our department received word that the Swiss drug company Sandoz had 100 million doses of the mind effecting hallucinogenic Lysergic Acid Diethylamide (or now more commonly known as LSD) available to purchase.

At this point, much changed...for Gottlieb, for the CIA...especially for myself. You see, it had become known that the Russians had researched possible methods to infect large populations with a chemical that could allow for manipulation of the masses—to become unwitting and involuntary participants to a third party's bidding. There was great fear within our department and the higher levels of the government that with LSD in the hands of the Soviets, entire U.S. cities could be driven mad or made to revolt from a contaminated water supply.

I had informed Gottlieb that we had tried a similar method of mind control during the 1940s using a spiked water supply, but it had proven largely ineffective and inconclusive...particularly so in more developed communities where water treatment facilities had a way of dampening any possible and temporary side effects. It was, in my opinion, just not a concern that he should be worried about. However, Gottlieb secured the authority to purchase the entire supply only to find out it was a mere 40,000 doses—hardly enough to have the impact the U.S. Government had previously worried about but still worth keeping for our own studies.

This began the CIA's fascination with the mind-altering drug LSD. Gottlieb wanted to procure a pharmaceutical potion that was either a predictable and reliable method of mind control or at the very least a truth serum. I discussed my previous failed studies using mescaline—a similarly constructed natural hallucinogenic. According to Gottlieb, these were dismissed as outlier samples. "Not enough study...too weak of a solution." It had become apparent that Gottlieb was more interested in keeping me from the Soviets then using me for himself. I began to withhold what I believed to be helpful information...most notably the possible benefits of other medicines he had yet to consider and the benefits of incorporating hypnosis with mind-benders...or as Gottlieb called them... "m m m m mind b b b benders."

Regardless, the little clubbed-footed, stuttering Jew put me and a colleague (Dr. Edward Obendorfer) in charge of carrying out the LSD research. Most of the MKUltra LSD experiments were conducted under the traditional scientific method using informed, willing test subjects at universities. These test results were favorable. While their behavior was, at times, odd, we reported the net result was reliable measures of truth management and temporary suggestibility.

However, it was determined that using subjects that were knowledgeable participants provided an inappropriate evaluation...namely that the espionage subjects we would seek to manipulate would need to be unwitting on all levels. At this point, the tests fell outside of the bounds of acceptable protocol. Nothing new for Gottlieb. All sorts of unwitting subsectors of the population had been secretly tested using all kinds of pharmaceuticals over the years. But with a large supply of LSD now at his disposal and with Gottlieb desperate for a breakthrough, these nefarious experiments became even more commonplace. One study lured heroin addicts to participate as test subjects by paying them in the very drug they were hooked on. Another studied the effects of LSD on black inmates in prison. Other experiments carried at Gottlieb's behest were less scientific. These tests included surreptitiously administering LSD into the drinks of unsuspecting bar patrons...all under the watchful eye of note-taking MKUltra staffers. Each subject presented an inconsistent reaction. Sometimes it would resemble elation, sometimes tortured anguish. We had no way of knowing in advance. Each person having their own very personal reaction to the acid.

In all studies, at the peak of the LSD effect, the subject was released into the public and presented with suggestibility challenges. The goal was always to seek to program a person's mind to do one's bidding. One common method was to suggest to the unwitting case study that they could perform miracles. The administrator might propose being able to fly or possibly stop a moving subway train with one hand. Several subjects died. In all cases, the police labeled the death as accidental or suicide.

The problem, as I had repeatedly informed Gottlieb, was that much like the behavior in my prisoner-of-war case studies, all the subjects had the appearance of being peculiar. They were either trance-like (mescaline), or they were quite clearly out of their minds (LSD). While you could get a subject to do your bidding, you could not reliably get them to perform these tasks in a way that wasn't suspicious. In other words, their behavior—strange or otherwise—gave them away. The drugs we were using had behavioral side effects that rendered them unreliable—even if, as I learned long ago, those drugs were used in tandem with hypnosis.

If Gottlieb and his team had known about scopolamine— a plant-based drug derived from the Borrachero tree...a tree that grew wild and abundant in much of South America, the story would be quite a bit different. Discovered before the war by my former colleague Alfred Ladenburg, scopolamine was used by German doctors to put mothers in labor into a kind of twilight sleep—an amnesic condition characterized by insensitivity to pain without loss of consciousness.

I, however, had found another use for scopolamine. A use more in step with the name more commonly used in the jungles and villages of South America. Before my indentured service to Gottlieb, I had briefly experimented with the hallucinogenic. Though the sample size was not considered extensive, the results brought alarming success. Inhaling even one small dose of the Borrachero powder would present a completely suggestable, even-tempered, and conscious patient who was impervious to pain...for about three to four hours.

That is why the locals called it "The Devil's Breath."

Chapter Thirty-Two

Dupont Circle—1810 P Street

Monday, December 18th–10:55 a.m.

Wisdom crossed the 1810 threshold to find a surprisingly uncluttered and well-lit kitchen—quite the contrast to the entrance at 1812. It was a simple room—mostly white save the harvest gold countertops. A tiny Norman Rockwell soda fountain print hung slightly askew on the wall next to an old cuckoo clock. A small television set on the counter…rabbit ears pointing to the sky. A window above the sink looked out to the back patio. There lay a mishmash of assorted garden fountains and stone benches set around a shadowy pool…much more in-step with the inside the rest of the home.

Poeltz pointed Wisdom in the direction of the metal-topped table. "Have a seat. Coffee?"

"No, thank you, Professor. Please don't go to the trouble."

"No trouble. It's one of those new-fangled coffee makers. Pretty simple. Already made." Poeltz's thick accent prominently presenting itself.

Wisdom took a seat. "No, thanks. Look, I don't want to take much of your time. Just a few questions and I'll be on my way."

Poeltz looked at Wisdom. He *was* indeed the man from Bob Althage's newscast the other morning. The morning *after*. On television, Wisdom looked like the kind of man who didn't take much guff. That impression didn't change with the cop now sitting in front of him. Quite the contrary. He looked like the kind of man who not only didn't take shit from anyone but also expected to be very much in charge…and Poeltz didn't like that. So, he poured a cup of coffee anyway and set it on the table next to Wisdom. Like it or not, Poeltz was going to be in control.

He sat down opposite Wisdom, crossed his legs tightly, pulled out and lit up an R&J…then offered, "Cigar?"

Wisdom smiled, mostly to himself and offered up an, "I only smoke when I drink."

"But I have served you coffee."

A stifled giggle seeped from Wisdom… "Not that kind of drink." Pausing ever so briefly. "Listen, Professor Poeltz, I appreciate the hospitality, but I rea…"

"So, how did she die, again?"

It was abrupt—almost too abrupt—and it set a tone of *enough of the bullshit. Let's just cut to the chase.*

"Well…like I said before…I can't say."

"You can't or won't?"

Wisdom smiled. "Aren't they the same?

Poeltz took a deep drag off his cigar before slowly letting the smoke fill the air around the Detective. "To me, Mr. Wisdom, *won't* means you are choosing not to tell me."

"Well, I can't say how she died because I don't know for certain. If I did know, why wouldn't I tell you?

"Protocol, I presume."

"Professor, you may be watching too much *Mannix*."

"*Perry Mason*"

Wisdom couldn't help but be bemused by Poeltz. The old man appeared to be having fun with him. Wisdom got to the point. "Labs are not back…but she appears to have overdosed. We are trying to establish if it was intentional or accidental."

"Why would Homicide care in either case?"

"I appreciate your curiosity, but I am simply here to investigate her state of mind."

"But how would I be able to help with that?"

"You saw her every week…spent time with her one on one. From what we know she wasn't much of a social butterfly. You appear to be one of just a small group of people who she regularly interacted with."

"Ah, well I can tell you, Mr. Wisdom, that she wasn't any different from any other student I tutored: Respectful but needy."

"How do you mean…needy?

"Well, they only come to me if they need help…so they are needy. They are respectful because I am fifty years older than them and an expert in the field in which they need help…so …they are respectful. Make sense?"

"So, Ms. Bard was no different from the others?

"Mr. Wisdom…"

"Detective"

"Okay. Yes, she was the same. If you are asking if she told me about her life issues I can assure you, we don't get into that sort of thing. I tutor them in the Science of Psychology…not the science of boyfriends."

"Just to be clear Professor, she never talked about being stressed or depressed?"

"She was stressed…getting a *C* in Psychology will do that to you. Depressed? I wouldn't have a clue."

"She was getting a *C*?

"I believe so…or at least it *was* a *C* when she first came to me in October. Fairly certain she had gotten her grade up to a low *A*.

"Well, that's impressive work."

"Not that it is doing her much good now, but…yes, it is impressive. I hope you don't think it is surprising."

"No…just impressive."

"Mr. Wisdom, I may have retired from GU several years

ago, but I presume you didn't just guess at my pedigree. As Dean, I literally wrote the curriculum. I think I know a thing or two about what is needed to get a strong result on the very coursework that I designed."

Wisdom picked up the cup of coffee, still steaming and took a deliberate sip before setting it back down. "Yeah, we have a good working relationship with GU Admin. They're especially informative when it comes to deaths on campus. So yeah, they filled us in on your work history. Tell me, why did you quit?

"Oh, Mr. Wisdom...it's no great secret... I got passed up for tenure...so I retired. If you want to know why I got passed up...ask them. I assume I moved beyond the point of usefulness. The amusing part is..." Now using his cigar to point towards the space beyond the closed swinging door, "...I probably make more money with this store...and with the tutoring practice then I would've over there."

"If you don't mind me asking...since you knew the curriculum and I expect, for the most part, the exam questions...doesn't it just come down to memorization?"

Poeltz took a deep frustrated breath. "If you want to boil it down to its most basic tenant...then yes, it *is* about memorization. Isn't everything? However, the student will have to apply memorized theory into random case studies. This is where suggestive hypnosis comes into play."

Wisdom leaned forward... "What, now? Hypnosis?"

"Oh, Mr. Wisdom...surely you are not naïve to the basic tenants of hypnotic therapy?"

"You tell me."

"Look, I understand that it's been largely disregarded by mainstream society, but hypnosis is still widely considered a most effective method of psychological training by the scientific community."

"I'm sorry, but wouldn't it be illegal to use hypnosis on a minor?"

"Oh, I don't know. I would assume you would know the laws on that subject far better than I but none of my students are minors, Mr. Wisdom. They're in university, after all. As far as I'm concerned, it's all beyond reproach."

Wisdom paused…took another swallow of coffee, then asked, "How does one become an expert in that kind of specialty? You know, hypnosis. You just don't hear much about it anymore."

"Too old-world for you Mr. Wisdom? I *am* a Professor of Psychology. That should pretty much cover it. But if you bother to dig a little deeper, you'll probably discover that I served for years at the HSA.

Not one for the plethora of acronym-laden government departments, Wisdom asked, "What the hell is the HSA?"

"Health Service Agency. It's a division of the DOD."

"Defense Department?"

Poeltz laughed, enjoying the curveball he threw at Wisdom. "Ah, I see the coffee is kicking in. Yes, *that* DOD. We spent a great deal of time working with soldiers on recovering from the psychological effects of war. We used hypnosis therapy quite openly and, I should also say, quite effectively. Regardless, I have much experience in the arena." Poeltz abruptly stood and looked down at the visitor… "Now, will there be anything else, Mr. Wisdom?"

Wisdom took out his notepad. Wrote down four simple words: Poeltz, Hypnosis, D.O.D, Asshole…and then slipped the pad inside the pocket of his Towncraft jacket. He then took one last sip of his coffee. "Nah, I think that'll do for now."

"You know Mr. Wisdom, earlier I asked you why Homicide would care about an overdose."

"Yeah, so?"

"Well, you didn't answer. Why's that?"

"Oh, I'm sorry, Professor, I just can't get into that sort of thing."

Poeltz turned his back, walked over to the sink, and then looked out the patio window, "You can't or won't?"

Wisdom said nothing but smiled and stood up.

With his back still to the visitor, Poeltz offered a nearly hollow, "Well, anyhow. I certainly hope I was of at least *some* help."

"Well, we'll see, Professor. We'll see."

As Poeltz squinted through the misty glaze of the window, he took another drag of the now ash-heavy R&J, paused, and then asked… "You know, Wisdom is such an interesting name, don't you think?"

Clearly irritated, "How do you mean, Poeltz?"

"Well, what kind of a name is it, old boy? Heritage. What's the heritage?"

Wisdom laughed. Couldn't help it. And then, as succinct as he could offer, the Italian Jew from Jersey simply said, "American."

Poeltz turned around to face Wisdom eye to eye… "Oh, I doubt that, Detective." Finally addressing the visitor with the title that, after twenty years, he had undoubtedly earned.

Wisdom stared at Poeltz for just a moment—long enough to make a point—then made his way towards the exit. Poeltz followed behind before reaching forward to open the door.

"Just one more question. Off topic, I'm afraid."

Slightly annoyed at the clearly intentional repartee, Poeltz answered curtly, "What is it?"

"Well, you have such a distinct accent. Where are y*ou* from?"

Poeltz paused, then smiled. "Austria, Mr. Wisdom."

Just then the German-made Black Forest cuckoo clock announced the arrival of 11:00. Wisdom looked at his Timex. It read 11:10.

"Austria, huh?" and then with his own barely perceptible tinge of sarcasm, "Yeah, right."

Wisdom turned, walked out the door and down the side path as the sound of ten more very telling cuckoo chirps echoed out the door. Much like a countdown.

Chapter Thirty-Three

Georgetown University—Delta Sigma House

Tuesday, December 19ᵗʰ–10:15 a.m.

The music from Rod Stewart's new album blared as Julie
Brenneman unabashedly danced around in her fluffy slippers
and red flannel PJs. *'You Wear It Well'*...and a full-length
mirror provided the inspiration.

With the House essentially empty she was free to blast
the music all the way to 10...and she did. No one was
complaining because no one was there. It wasn't until the song
ended and the only sound coming from those big box
Panasonic speakers was the scratching of the needle against
the spinning LP that she finally heard the phone. Its ringing
had a shrill to it...like it was pissed that she hadn't picked it
up yet.

The phone was hung from the wall by the entry door, and
she skipped over and anxiously grabbed it. It was less about
interest and more about getting it over with. With everyone
gone for winter break, the place was a veritable ghost town.

Anyone calling now was probably a wrong number. She answered just as she turned down the volume on the Kenwood knowing full well that "*I'd Rather Go Blind*' was about ready to crank up.

"Hello," …she barked into the receiver while wondering why she was even yelling. Geez, the music was off for god sakes.

No answer from the other side. She tried again. "Hello?" This time much softer.

"Julie. This is Sigmund." A Germanic inflection dripping from the other end of the line.

She paused, confused. The voice was familiar, the name was not. "Excuse me?"

"Julie. This is Sigmund." He paused, waiting for the recognition to kick in. Her prolonged silence indicating his success. "I need you to take one tablet with a full glass of water. Wait fifteen minutes, and then call the following number…363-3124."

Another pause. "Please confirm."

"I understand," and with that, she softly slipped the receiver back into its cradle and then slowly walked to the Jack and Jill bathroom she shared with her sorority sisters. She opened the mirrored covered vanity door above her sink and reached in to pick up a small antique metal pill box. Inside were four tablets. Julie grabbed one and placed it on her tongue while she gripped her glass, turned on the water, and carefully filled the glass until it was just about to overflow. Closing the vanity door, she briefly considered her stoic reflection in the mirror, then watched herself as she diligently swallowed the pill and the full glass of water in a matter of seconds.

Julie put down the glass and looked at her watch. 10:18 a.m. She sat down on her bed and waited.

She watched the record player continue to spin as the needle continued to scratch. She did this until her watch read 10:33 a.m.

She promptly stood up. Walked over to the phone and dialed the number that she had been given. It rang twice before the same thick accent answered by saying simply, "Julie?"

"Yes"

She listened intently as the voice on the other line spoke for several minutes, occasionally interrupted by a plaintive "yes" from Julie. Finally, the line went quiet on the other end and then settled into a dial tone. Julie set the phone back into the cradle while reaching for her car keys and winter coat that hung by the door.

She opened the door and then for little apparent reason, stared back into her room—a curious look on her face. She stared at the record player—still spinning—and then shook her head lightly as if she was dismissing some random thought. Shrugging her shoulders, she stepped out into the hall closing the door behind her.

In a few moments, she would be out in the cold rain-soaked morning steering her mustard yellow Pinto through the narrow Georgetown streets until she came to 1619 32nd Street. She parked her car several doors down. She would wait there. Wait, until she found what she was looking for.

Chapter Thirty-Four

Georgetown—32nd Street

Tuesday, December 19th–11:15 a.m.

The showers that poured down on the city demolished the virgin-white landscape to reveal its true natural grit and grime. Gone were the tantalizing but all too temporary pillows of powdery snow, replaced rather ominously by the damp and depressing blend of oily exhaust-laden slush. Forty degrees and rain will do that to any idyllic wintery scene. Fast.

Jenner parked his patrol car outside the Schneider home. It had been two days since he first discovered the wasted body of one David Schneider. Thankfully the police chaos that engulfed the normally quiet enclave had dissipated, leaving in its place a stale reverence.

Turning off the engine, the screeching wiper blades came to an appreciated halt. Jenner looked out at the drenching scene thankful that he already wore the rubbery police-issue yellow rain jacket. He clipped the final two buttons on his slicker and stepped out of the car, slipping on his plastic encased officers cap. He paid no attention to the dingy little yellow car that sat idling several houses away…nor should he.

Because the campus was mostly void of students, he had spent most of Monday conducting interviews by telephone with Jennifer Bard's dorm mates. What he discovered was that she was a shy girl—kept very much to herself. Even her roommate, whom he reached at home in California, seemed to barely know her. She stated that the girl studied a lot. Spent most nights in the Launiger Library. No real partying. No boyfriend…or none that was obvious. When Jenner asked if it was possible that Ms. Bard was seeing a boy all those nights instead of studying in the stacks, the response was a stifled but knowing laugh… "No, I don't think so."

"Drug use?"

Again, a sassy "No." Jenner wondered if the girl was secretly happy to be rid of her roommate. Dead weight removed. Place to herself.

The *loner* description was also consistent across the few friends she was known to spend some time with. Even her parents labeled her as a "bit of a wallflower…socializing is…was not her thing," said her father.

"Boyfriend?"

"No. Never had one bef…" Saying this out loud to the faceless cop on the line caused Mrs. Bard to stop abruptly and just start weeping. Who could blame her?

It appeared that Jennifer Bard was certainly not the kind of girl you would expect to be messing around with an older man and drug use seemed to be very much out of character. Based on photographs pinned on her dorm room bulletin board, she *was* pretty but not in a sorority girl way. Nice? Apparently, but in a subtle forgettable manner. Apparently, the only thing she seemed to do was study. It certainly would not have been in step with her profile to be doing recreational drugs, but maybe she was lonely and so wired tight with her studies that she *did* kill herself. Intentionally. Jenner thought the idea was plausible…but killing a man? Not likely.

According to Wisdom, the preliminary lab results were coming back today. The GPR analysis would tell them if she did indeed pull the trigger…or at least pull *a* trigger… and the toxin report would hopefully tell them what caused her head to balloon up turnip-red.

In the meantime, Jenner was to retrace the steps the Bard girl took late Saturday night. Wisdom had provided him a detailed map straight from the passageway beside the Schneider home to the alley and then across Wisconsin, the main quad and then straight to the New South dorm. Look for any clues along the way. Knock on a few doors…see if the convenience store had any security camera footage. Doing this in a driving rain, however, seemed pointless if not downright criminal.

With rain dripping off his officer's cap, he looked up to see Mrs. Schneider staring at him from the front window…still wearing the same slightly tattered bathrobe, she wore the morning before. Jenner gave her an awkward nod and then made his way through the mess towards the narrow pathway between the two brownstones. This looked like it was going to be a pain in the ass. Literally.

Chapter Thirty-Five

The Pentagon

Tuesday, December 19th–1:45 a.m.

Making your way from the city to the Pentagon required the rather dubious challenge of navigating the multi-level Mixing Bowl junction just after crossing the Memorial Bridge. Here, there were three interchanges that crammed cars into one ill-designed funnel hopefully resulting in your vehicle being spit out on just the right transit ramp. They called it the Mixing Bowl for a reason. Making the trek in the driving rain only amplified the drama.

For Wisdom though, this was old hat. His apartment at the Crystal House was no more than two miles south of the Pentagon, so he had made this trek countless times before. In a twisted sort of way, he enjoyed the challenge, and while there were three ways to make it to the Pentagon from the Mixing Bowl, Joey always preferred taking the Mount Vernon Highway, which bordered the Potomac River and normally gave you an outstanding view of the Jefferson

Memorial. He considered this route a reward for the chaos of The Bowl and even though the view today was a wet mess it was better than the alternative...a backed-up Jefferson Davis Highway.

Wisdom parked in the South Lot and stepped out in the rain. With rubbers on and his Towncraft coat cinched up to his neck, he splashed his lumbering way to the Navy entrance. Once inside, he shook off the wet and loosened up the jacket. The rubbers protected his shoes, but all the splashing had made his pant legs as drenched as his hair.

On the wall to his right hung an exceedingly detailed office listing board. Wisdom was looking for "Health Service Agency—Records Division." After several minutes scanning the listings, he finally spotted the location of the rather innocuous department that he was looking for...6-MC112...which, of course, meant Concourse 6—Mezzanine Level, C Ring, Office 112. Of course.

Wisdom always found the Pentagon to be depressing. It was a massive monolith that was poorly lit and had almost no natural lighting. It was so big that if you by any horrible chance needed to get to the other side of the building for a meeting it would take you about fifteen minutes to get there. Not only was 6-MC112 on the other side of the building, but it was also in the basement. Needless to say, HSA-Records didn't warrant A or E Ring status—the only Rings whose offices had actual views to the outside world.

He looked amongst the people buzzing around. *Where are all these people going, anyway?* He noticed a tubby negro manning a coffee cart. Still in his rubbers, Wisdom made his way over to the man, flipped him a quarter in exchange for a teeming cup of coffee and began the squeaky trek around the perimeter.

After making his way to Corridor 6, navigating three security checkpoints, one escalator, and two elevators, Wisdom finally arrived at his destination. Stenciled on the foggy glass inlay of the barely descriptive office door was the black moniker he was looking for—MC112.

Wisdom made a light rap on the door. No response.

Another double tap and once again, no response. He cupped his hands around his eyes and pressed his face up to the glass. The lights were on, but there was no movement. He was about ready to open the door when he heard the muffled but unmistakable sound of a toilet flushing from inside and then finally a… "Just a minute."

He backed off the door and waited as he saw the shadow of a man making his way to the door. The door eased open to reveal a singularly tiny and pale man with clunky glasses and only a whisper of hair atop his head. His aged brown leisure shoes combined with a dingy brown Sears and Roebuck suit gave away his status. This man was a lifer, and it was quite possible he had spent the last twenty years of his working days in this one tiny office.

"Can I help you?" he mumbled.

Feeling the generally defeated nature of the man, Wisdom offered up as much respect and information as he could. "Yes, sir, sorry to disturb you, sir, but I think you might be expecting me. I am Detective Wisdom, D.C. police, and I believe my station contacted you late yesterday to inquire about a former employee. I was told I could come down and check some of the records."

"Yeah, I remember, but I told them already…you can't check anything."

"I'm so sorry, I must have been misinformed. Maybe I have the wrong office. Are you John Sniffen?"

The beaten man nodded his head. "I told them yesterday. You can't check the records. Only I can check the records. This is the Defense Department, buddy. We don't just open our robes for anyone."

"Yes, sir, I misspoke. Yes, I'm ah…looking to see if you can confirm a former employee's work history here at the HSA. Maybe provide some detail."

"We'll see," the bitter man offered back. "What's is about?"

"I am so sorry Mr. Sniffen, but it is an ongoing investigation, and I am not at liberty to say."

"Well then, I am not at liberty to give you what you

want."

"Look, Mr. Sniffen… John… I can get a warrant, but that takes a lot of time…"

"Yeah, that will take a lot of time because you aren't getting a warrant to search DOD files anytime soon."

Wisdom hated to give up the goods on a murder case so quickly, but this guy needed to be nurtured. He paused for a moment. "Possible double murder."

The record keeper's eyes lit up. "Murder? Are you saying a former employee is involved?"

"I said, double murder…and if it were only that simple. Your former employee is likely only an acquaintance to one of the victims and a pretty distant one at that. We're just double checking background on all the parties no matter how loosely connected they are.

Sniffen firmed up his glasses, tightened up his tie. "Well, well, well. This might be a fun day after all" as he walked over and disappeared behind a row of grey filing cabinets jutting out from the wall. "Now let's see what we have…Why don't you have a seat?" He pointed to the small rigid chair in front of his desk. "So, who are we looking for?"

"An Alfred Poeltz. Maybe listed as Doctor Alfred Poeltz…P-O-E-L-T-Z"

Wisdom could hear the career paper pusher thumbing through folder after folder… "Poeltz uh? Doesn't ring a bell. Kind of a big department. Guess that's why I got a job. Poeltz, Poeltz…Hmm…."

The newly inspired clerk peered out from behind the row of file drawers. "Ah, here we go. One Dr. Alfred R. Poeltz…Health Service Agency." Sniffen walked over to the desk and opened the manila file folder and began reading privately to himself.

Wisdom began to lose a bit of patience. "Well, what do ya have?"

Nothing from Sniffen…just more lightly mumbled reading and then a resounding, "Hmm."

"Yes?"

"Well, I am sorry you came all the way down here

Detective, but his file is pretty much classified."

"Classified?"

"Well, it is pretty uncommon for the HSA. That's why I didn't steer your department from coming down here. But his work detail is blocked. *I* can't even see it."

"What do you mean...you have several pages of information there. Got to be something I can work with."

"Actually, no. It's unusually empty. There's some detail on his marital status, birthdate... his inception date...a few references to his work locale, his Division Supervisor. Pretty basic stuff."

Wisdom wasn't looking for anything more than some basic profile confirmation on the curmudgeonly old man. Now he can't even get that. "Well, can you at least give me what you got there?"

"Well, Detective...I'll give you the basics...but anything else isn't coming from me. That information will be like getting water from a stone, if you know what I mean. But uh, I'll at least give you what I have."

Wisdom grabbed a pen from Sniffen's desk and then pulled the pad out from the inside of his still damp Towncraft coat. He opened it to the page where he had previously scribbled those four ominous notes on Poeltz. "Okay, give it to me?"

"Employment start date was 1-1-1947...which meant he wasn't always HSA. HSA wasn't even around back then. No mention of marital status. Got his Supervisor listed as a Doctor Stuart Gottlieb."

Wisdom wrote down the start date...and the name *Gottlieb*...followed by *boss*. "Gottlieb?"

"Yep...I have been around here a long while...almost eighteen years. Can't recall a *Gottlieb* in the HSA...at least not that *I* know of." Sniffen paused a bit, sniffed, and then added, as almost an afterthought. "There was one over at CIG, though."

"These frickin' agencies, man. Too many damn letters. CIG? What's that one?"

"CIG is the Central Intelligence Group...it's the part of

the CIA that works directly with the military...which might explain why Poeltz records are linked to him. HSA's work is a service for the armed forces."

"Do you have Gottlieb's contact."

"Oh, no, sir. No, sir. He's dead...a few years back. Kind of a big deal at the time. Made the news some. Probably the only reason I recognized the name...because he definitely wasn't HSA."

Wisdom racked his brain a bit. The name rang no bells at all which really isn't surprising. Despite living in the potbelly of politics most of his adult life, he pretty much blocked out all thing's government based. It bored the hell out of him and anyway their respective worlds never crossed paths. Usually elected officials didn't commit murder. Fraud? Yes. Murder? Not so much.

"Hmm...Okay then... I know this is going back a ways, but uh, do you have anything on his *former* employment? By his current age, I'm guessing he didn't start working here until he was about mid-thirties. Had to be some kind of employment before that."

"No, sorry...under former employment it's redacted. Blacked out."

Wisdom was a bit taken aback by the unexpected secrecy of the old professor's past and asked, "Really? Well, at least give me his last day of employment?"

"Yeah...that's kinda the weird thing. Based on his birthday...he's about seventy-two years old."

"Yeah...so?"

"Well sir, that's uh...well, it's strange, is all. There's no reference of a retirement."

"What the hell does that mean?"

"Well, based on this, he still works for the HSA."

Chapter Thirty-Six

Erinnerungen an Camp Detrick–Frederick, MD

1959

S. Rauscher Journalprotokoll LVI:

Charlotte was a brute. A wall of a wife who spent her time lording over my every move like a hawk to its prey. After her arrival in '49, they moved our farce of a family into a quirky old home by Dupont Circle. The place doubled as an antique store, and she ran it like a drill sergeant –much like she ran our family. I had long ago decided it was best to just play along with her domineering character knowing full well who she reported to.

She conveyed back to Gottlieb weekly with such inane updates as to when I went to bed, what I read, where I would go on my walks. She even made notes of how I engaged with Jonathan—who I found to be a rather delightful boy. He was now almost twelve, and though I was fairly convinced as to where he actually came from, he never seemed to question his place in our awkward home. A son to a father who obviously was much too old for an adolescent of his age. A child of parents who had a contemptuous relationship at best. It was all very uncomfortable...at least for me.

As such, I chose to spend the last decade hiding from my counterfeit wife by engrossing myself in Gottlieb's bondage. It was tantamount to sadistic punishment—trading one domineering dictator for another, but at least the work I did under Gottlieb's direction was engaging. The overbearing little Jew with a stutter and a club-foot was more of a menacing cartoon character than an admired boss, but as the years wore on, I learned to carve out slivers of time to push on with my own private agenda.

After almost ten years of warped study on LSD, our team had acquired access to no shortage of willing participants for case experiments. The government paid well. Over $100 a day. Cash, of course. The catch was that volunteers were permitted to participate in a maximum of two experiments per year. However, due to word of mouth about the pay, we had no shortage of downtrodden citizens in dire need of a free meal and some much-needed money.

This worked in my favor. I found the research into LSD to be suspect and dangerous, but I carried out the studies at Gottlieb's behest like clockwork. Every day we would have up to five or six candidates to test. We administered dose and setting variations as well as various challenges for each volunteer with the goal of procuring the dosage that provided the most reliable outcome. This evidenced as inadequate.

However, due to the large number of case studies I could surreptitiously run separate studies using scopolamine. I was especially careful to only use volunteers who would otherwise most charitably be characterized as vagrants. These unwitting dupes were literal guinea pigs for my study. If the tests went poorly—caused them any harm—they would have no one viable to report to. If they died during testing—which some most assuredly did—the only person that would miss them would be the homeless junkie who called Foggy Bottom his home. I did learn quite quickly that certain doses of the powder led to a most gruesome and quick death. One such test case became distended and heavily feverish to such a degree that his skin turned an almost bright red...as if his body was preparing to explode. He died of cardiac arrest within minutes of dosage.

Dosage was an issue. But I discovered that when it was accurately delivered, the test case was put into an almost immediate continuously suggestible state. More importantly, the individual was even-tempered, calm, and rational. In other words, normal. Or at least as normal as one can be after their brain's chemical makeup had been altered. Regardless, it served its purpose—unremarkably benign and malleable. This was critical, but the overriding issue was being able to trigger the suggestable behavior at a time and place of my choosing. It did no good to have a case study ingest the scopolamine...become suggestible...and then be stuck in a laboratory. The case-study needed to be in the field, so to speak. Additionally, getting someone to ingest the scopolamine outside of my experiments was not realistically reliable. Why would someone voluntarily take this drug? Even if the dosage was accurate and they could expect no harm would come to them, there was no compelling way to get them to take it on their own accord. Why would they? Even more important was the timing. The case study would have little more than a couple hours to accomplish our mission before the effect of the drug would wear off.

How could I get a case-study to voluntarily take the scopolamine at a time of my choosing and then accomplish whatever task I required in an hour or so...all before the condition eroded?

This is where my studies in hypnosis proved most beneficial.

Chapter Thirty-Seven

Georgetown

Tuesday, December 19th–11:45 a.m.

After checking the trashcans of several houses in the alley behind the Schneider home and coming up empty, Jenner came to the Quikee Mart on Wisconsin. He questioned the manager, and then after getting his permission to search the exterior of the store, Jenner found himself standing in the driving rain staring at the opened lid of a large partially filled dumpster. Its contents, a ram-shackled blend of foul odors and fouler things, was far from inviting. Most dumpsters were appropriately hidden behind their store, but this container jutted out from the side of the Quikee Mart while awkwardly facing Wisconsin for all the world to see. Jenner peered into a jumbled mess and sighed. This was pretty much going to ruin his day...and he knew it. Trash—particularly wet trash—kind of had that effect.

On a normal day, he would be casually handing out parking tickets. Not today. Nope. Today he had yesterday's soda cans and candy wrappers to swim through. In hopes of finding what? Some random personal belonging of the Bard girl or Schneider? It all just seemed like a wet and messy waste of time.

But if you wanted to hide something from someone…a dumpster was a pretty viable option. Who in their right mind would ever go inside one of those…except Jenner…or a vagrant.

Investigators had already discovered Schneider's leather business satchel by the bushes near the side of his home. Like the victim, it was hidden under about ten inches of powder. But in this case, there wasn't a big lump and pool of red that gave away its location. So, it lay there untouched, its secrets or lack thereof concealed from police until the heat of the day and some rain betrayed its hiding place.

Once discovered, the dank leather case proved wanting. Locked by combination and with no apparent attempt to access its contents, the satchel was a dead end. Thorough analysis of its contents provided a treasure trove of tease. Several documents, all seemingly untouched, related to the merger of two defense contractors. This led Frankel to send an investigator from the Corporate Crimes Division over to Schneider's bosses at Solomon Bros. The merger, announced the morning after the body of its lead banker was discovered, was indeed provocative. The news shocked not only Wall Street but also Capitol Hill. Whether it was approved by regulators or not was, at this point, irrelevant. What was important was that the merger was on track…regardless of who died making it come together.

If someone didn't want this deal to happen, murdering a banker was probably not the best way to shut it down. Wall Street stops for no one…particularly dead people. What would grind the wheels to a stutter in New York was the accusation of fraud. The recent case of NYSE listed *U.S. Financial* was testament to that. The real estate banking conglomerate turned out to be little more than a Ponzi scheme, and it sent CEO's and Wall Street executives scurrying for cover in a way murder couldn't emulate. At least not one murder. For now, the Wall Street conspiracy angle was dead…just like David Schneider.

So, Jenner put both hands on the edge of the wet metal container and hoisted himself up and into the mess. With one hand over his nose, he stood there frozen in silence before he began the irritable process of rummaging through whatever the world thought wasn't worth keeping.

The sticky remnants of empty Shasta and Craigmont Root Beer cans were mixed chaotically with vacant Pop Rock bags and Pixie Stick wrappers. There was also no shortage of purged MD 20-20 wine bottles and Schlitz tall boys. This was all merged quite offensively with the true refuge of the day…or week…leftover bits of rotting food. Hot dog pieces, molded cheese, and anything else a street bum might tolerate…and all of it was wet. Very wet. The stench and its contents reminded Jenner of the basement in his old fraternity house…the morning after a massive kegger. The only difference here was that it was all confined to a seven-foot by seven-foot metal container, and he was standing right in the middle of it.

At first, Jenner kept his hands free from the chaos, choosing instead to simply kick his foot around the trash hoping to bump into something. After a few futile minutes of poking around, he decided to make a real commitment. After all, he was marginally protected with his officer gloves and yellow thigh-length rubber raincoat. What could possibly get through that thing? So, as to not oblige himself too much, Jenner slowly knelt into the belly of the beast…hands outstretched seeking to find support in its mushy contents.

As his right knee met the pile beneath it, he abruptly felt hard resistance. Jenner reached down into the mess beneath his knee rummaging to remove the obstruction…a derelict wine bottle, no doubt. His hand searched to find the form of the sturdy object lying irrelevantly beneath layers of all that *stuff* when it finally came to a dead-end. And it didn't take him long to realize this was no empty bottle of booze.

Grabbing the object with this right hand, he carefully pulled it up through the trash. This was the mother lode of clues. In his gloved hands lay a most deadly object—a handgun. And not just any handgun. This one had what appeared to be a silencer attached to its muzzle, *and* this was no traditional Smith & Wesson or Colt. No. This was old …and definitely not American made. The gun's long narrow barrel, elevated toggle, and textured wooden grip were seemingly dead giveaways.

What Jenner had in his grime-soaked hands was most assuredly not a Smith & Wesson. If Jenner's high school history knowledge didn't betray him, what he had was far more interesting than some petty criminal's Saturday night special. What he had was likely a Luger…a German Luger P-04 to be exact, and it was about thirty years out of date.

Jenner eased up from the bottom of the stew of trash, Luger in one of his gloved hands and turned to climb out of the dumpster. Hands on the edge of the metal box, he heaved himself up and swung his legs over, landing with a slight splat on the damp asphalt lot. With rain still working hard to ruin the day, Jenner lifted the gun up for a closer look…beads of water gathering on the barrel. It wasn't your typical murder weapon and no reason for a college coed to be carrying it around. Maybe it had nothing to do with the Schneider killing. He popped out the cartridge…no bullets in the casing, and it even looked a bit rusted inside. Pretty old, too. Probably didn't even work. Some street thug probably tossed it after he realized it was a dud. The silencer was curious, though. Who would put a silencer on a handgun like this? Certainly, not one of the ruffians that worked the dark streets after closing time. But if not an eighteen-year-old girl or a street thug…then who?

Just then, as he was staring at the old steel mystery in his hand, Jenner heard the insistent sound of a car's engine revving. He looked up and saw in the background a grimy yellow car in the parking lot across from him. It was pointed menacingly in his direction, and through the windshield, he saw a lady—more like a teenager—staring at him as if she was sizing up a target. Suddenly, the wheels screeched and spun against the wet ground and in a split second, they caught traction lurching the car forward like it was shot out of a cannon.

Jenner froze, the gun still in his grasp, as he stretched both of his hands out in front. It was a kneejerk and silent defense. One that came automatically in such circumstances. It didn't work, of course, and it instantly led to the prone Jenner frantically screaming "stop" …as if the driver had even the slightest intention of doing any such thing. And she didn't.

The rusted yellow Pinto came to a thundering stop with Jenner's limp body smashed between the car's front grill and that gritty black dumpster. The driver put the car in park and stared at the result of her mayhem: a lifeless Jenner slumped on her hood, blood easing from the corner of his mouth, the rain splattering the back of his police-issue yellow slicker…and an antique pistol clutched defiantly in his right hand.

Jensen Moock

Chapter Thirty-Eight

Alexandria, Virginia—Old Town

Tuesday, December 19th–1:30 p.m.

One good thing about being a detective…versus, say a patrolman…was that if you wanted to hit a bar and get loaded in the middle of the day, there was no one stopping you. That probably explains why most detectives were drunks…or at least made major efforts to imitate a drunk. As long as there was a police callbox somewhere near the bar or you had your walkie-talkie handy then you could buy yourself a little downtime when things were slow.

But today wasn't slow. No, quite the opposite. Joey Wisdom got the news about Jenner over the police scanner just moments after leaving the Pentagon. *Officer Down*, has a way of changing the tone of the day. Yes, today was a bitch, and Joey needed something a little bit stronger than downtime.

As he left the massive Pentagon parking lot, he immediately headed south on the Jeff Davis aiming straight for Gadsby's Tavern in Old Town. Joey loved Gadsby's…there was usually no one there in the afternoon,

148

they had a call box outside…and they served *very* stiff drinks. Perfect recipe for today.

The rain had stopped on his way there—the only blessing of the day so far—so the traffic was a bit eased as he pulled off the Jeff Davis and left onto King Street. King led straight into the center of Old Town Alexandria. Joey always liked this area of town. Tucked right by the Potomac, it once had an old shipyard and slave trading port as its heartbeat. This was George Washington's old stomping grounds. Ancient cobblestone streets. Quaint shops. Inns and taverns from the colonial era. It made quite an impression on Joey. Parking was never allowed on King so if you happened to be here late at on a foggy night when the traffic was down, and the streets were still you might actually feel like you were in some sort of time machine. One where a short stately gentleman in a powdered wig might even ask you for a *fag*.

But today was not that kind of day. Despite the traditionally poignant Christmas decorations adorning the street lamps and door fronts, Old Town had a plainly frenzied feel to it. The Christmas season traffic and bustling tourists gave the whole hurried scene anything but a nostalgic sensation. But for Joey, he didn't care what the hell the place felt like. All he cared about was getting a couple pops in him. A couple, at least.

He parked on Royal Street just off King and headed down to Gadsby's—only half a block down Royal. Every time he walked into the joint the same sensation hit him. The place had been there for 200 years, and it smelled like it. Not that the smell was bad…it was just old. There was dankness to the place, and despite a fire burning in the hearth, it still felt cold. However, as old as the building was it was just as elegant. And in reality, it was more of a dining hall than a straight-up bar, anyway. Fancy white clothed four-tops spread evenly around a large social room. Antique silverware accompanying each place setting. Candlelit table tops, providing a sophisticated and natural glow. It was quite a scene. The kind of place you might take a wife or girlfriend for a fancy dinner…that is if she hadn't just dumped you.

As he stepped inside, the slow screech of the front door and the ringing bell that came with every entry startled no one. It was now almost 2 o'clock, and the place was still. Only one table occupied. Two businessmen on a three-martini lunch, no doubt.

The only waiter on staff gave a knowing nod as Joey maneuvered around the tables to the bar. The bar was freestanding and tucked in the corner by the fireplace, and it was small. Very small. Five stools and they were all vacant. Perfect. Behind the bar stood Ralph—the same balding tubby grey-haired gent that had been swilling drinks for Joey for the better part of a decade. Behind Ralph, sitting on a shelf, was one of those new-fangled color televisions. It was tuned to that soap opera Ginny liked so much... *Days of Our Lives*. Volume down...thank god.

Pushing a stool aside, Joey announced his presence to the indifference of Ralph by slapping both hands on the counter. Ralph barely looked up—this was not his first dance with Wisdom.

Ralph took a deep breath of mock irritation. "I see you. Saw you when you walked in. No need to startle the clientele."

"What clientele? Those stiffs?" Joey pointing to the tipsy gents across the room.

Feigning impatience. "All right, Sarge...what'll it be? The usual?"

"Geez man, you're like a bad cliché... The usual?"

"What then...ice tea?" Ralph grinned at his own feeble attempt of sarcasm.

"Boilermaker."

"Oh, the usual then.... You got it, Sarge."

"Man, why the hell you always call me Sarge? You know damn well I'm not."

"You prefer asshole?"

"Same difference."

Ralph sniffed with amusement as he poured a tall Pabst from the tap sliding it over with a shot glass of Old Crow...no use wasting the good stuff on a shot of bourbon that's going straight into a cheap glass of beer.

Ralph stepped back and leaned against the back of the bar while drying a just-washed glass with a small white towel. "It's only 2, ya know. Rough day?"

"You could say that. Partner got killed today."

The drama of the news barely raising an eyebrow…from either man. "Didn't know you had a partner."

"I don't…didn't. Some rookie was helping me out on a murder case. Was."

"What's the deal, man?"

"I don't know. Crazy fuckin' thing—got run over in a parking lot."

A little snicker leaked from Ralph. "The rookie? What, he got an ex-wife like mine?"

Joey took a deep swig off the beer and then plunked the bourbon into the glass…its contents spilling over the side. "Man, you've been a bartender, too long."

"Yep—you've been a cop too long."

"Detective"

"Yeah-yeah."

"The kid got smashed up against a dumpster. Show some fuckin' respect."

"Sarge, I've never known you to have a soft side. Why now?"

Joey took another big swallow, squinted tightly, let out a tight breath then offered a defeated "I don't know."

"Okay, who did it…some drunk?"

Joey looked over his shoulder to see if the three-piece suits were listening then leaned onto the bar and said softly, "Nope. Some college girl. Witness said it looked intentional."

The smashed-against-a-dumpster news didn't move the needle for Ralph…but this did. "Really?"

Over Ralph's shoulder, a TV9 news alert interrupted the soap that had been silently going through its tasteless paces in the background. Joey's favorite blonde bimbo appeared on the screen with *Live from Georgetown* imprinted on the bottom.

Joey shook his head in disgust and pointed to the TV. "Turn it up."

Chapter Thirty-Nine

Dupont Circle—Theodore's

Tuesday, December 19th–2:10 p.m.

Over the years, Theodore's had become the kind of store where customers were almost always met by appointment only. Its reputation was now firmly entrenched after decades of servicing the political elite and embassy row muckity-mucks that so ruled the Dupont Circle community. Yes, the sign on the front door was engraved with...

"Open 12:00-5:00 Daily—Closed Sunday."

But almost no one just *showed-up* anymore. Sure, a random passerby who didn't know any better might poke his head in, but the exorbitant prices and awkward silence of the store would send them on their way before staff could muster the traditional "Can I help you?" Yes, most days it was a very quiet place, and today was no different.

Dr. Alfred Poeltz took advantage of the solitude to avenge his boredom with some television and an R&J in the kitchen. Sitting in the same spot Detective Wisdom sat in only yesterday gave Alfred a chill which he quickly shook off by replacing the thought with the theatre of *Days of Our Lives*. Even though the overly dramatic comings and goings of the Horton Clan hardly met his idea of entertainment, he was still generally bemused by the whole thing. Most importantly, it kept him distracted…and today was a day in need of distraction.

Today's storyline of Dr. Tommy Horton's secret love affair with Maria the nun was a doozy, but before Alfred could get too settled in, the screen went briefly dark as a *Breaking News* banner appeared. Standing in the middle of the Quikee Mart parking lot in Georgetown, Barbara Bell and her bouffant blonde mane steadied herself in anticipation of the big moment.

In the background were the remnants of the *accident*—a beaten down yellow tinged Pinto with a damaged front grill parked just a few feet from the edge of a large black iron dumpster. Investigators were milling about as the report went live:

"This is Barbara Bell reporting live from the parking lot of a convenience store in pristine Georgetown, where moments ago, a district patrolman was literally run down by the young female driver of this small car.

The camera scanned over Ms. Bell's shoulder to show the muddled chaos of the small parking lot…police cars and officers cluttered together with a smattering of witnesses and other reporters. Then the camera zoomed in on the grill of the Pinto and then scanned over to the dented and damaged dumpster. Bouffant reporter lady continued: "It is apparently here where the driver of this automobile pinned the police officer against the large unmovable dumpster behind me. We have been told that the officer—who has not as yet been named—died almost instantly from blunt force injuries sustained in the incident. No report either on the identity of the driver, but witnesses said the tragic event appeared to be intentional…though, there is no known motive at this point."

The camera panned back to Ms. Bell, who glared intently into the camera. "With the recent murder of a local banker, the apparent suicide of a Georgetown coed and today's violent death of one of our District's finest, it has truly been a very rough and emotional Christmas season. More details this evening on the TV9 Evening News. Reporting live from the...normally peaceful streets of Georgetown, this is Barbara Bell." The TV abruptly cut back to Dr. Horton in the middle of an awkward groping session with young Maria.

Undaunted by the tawdry kissing scene, Alfred mushed out his cigar and walked over to turn off the TV set. He looked at his watch...2:20...then out the kitchen window where the rain had started coming down hard again. Then, speaking to only himself, he asked in little more than a whisper...

"But where's the girl?"

Chapter Forty

Foggy Bottom—George Washington University Hospital

Tuesday, December 18th–3:10 p.m.

Joey slammed back one more boilermaker before bidding his barside benefactor goodbye.

Ralph had rarely seen his *regular* so anxious. Most days, Joey never got too lost in his job. He just had a natural ability to compartmentalize almost any drama…trivial or otherwise. Twenty years of investigating murders will do that to anyone, but to see his friend obviously impacted by the young officer's violent death was a bit of a surprise for Ralph. It wasn't sympathy he detected. Sympathy just wasn't in Wisdom's DNA. Irritation *was*, and the more Ralph thought about it afterward, the more he came to the conclusion that the death of the patrolman had mostly just pissed off Detective Wisdom.

Joey quickly left Gadsby's, got into his Dart, put the cherry top on the dash, and sped his way back into the city...rain coming down hard once again. On the way, the dispatch released more details about the incident—information the TV9 bouffant reporter lady wasn't privy to earlier. Namely, where the authorities had taken driver girl. He assumed that she would be at 2nd District for questioning but apparently on the ride back to HQ, she began to show signs of trauma and became virtually non-responsive. She was quickly taken to the George Washington University Hospital in Foggy Bottom and admitted into the ER until she stabilized.

When he arrived, Wisdom was promptly directed up to the 3rd floor...room 320. The hospital had been there for over forty years, and it had become a bit decrepit. Most floors were overcrowded, had poor lighting and cluttered hallways. Two-to-a-room was the norm, but the 3rd floor was much nicer. If you had decent money or better insurance...or if you were someone special, they found you a room on the 3rd floor.

Driver girl was someone special.

Outside her room sat Patrolman Canter guarding against any unwanted guests or unlikely escapes. As he approached the young officer dutifully guarding the entry, Detective Wisdom couldn't help but think of Jenner. While it probably wasn't necessary, he quickly showed his badge and glided past the sentry. Canter gave Wisdom a nod and went back to reading *The Post*.

When he entered 320, he saw the curious young perpetrator lying prone...hospital gown on...sheets pulled up just past her waist...IV tube attached to her wrist...vital sign lines linked to other various body parts. There were so many wires connected to the young girl that she looked like a Bride of Frankenstein experiment. Compared to her body, her face looked puffy, and she was a bit flush. It caught Wisdom off guard. She looked like a watered-down version of dead dorm girl...but this one wasn't dead. She was awake and as it turns out, shockingly alert.

She heard Wisdom's entry, then turned her head towards the clearly unwelcome intruder. "Who are you?"

Not expecting such vigor from a young lady in such peril, Wisdom quickly adjusted... "Detective Wisdom, D.C. Police.

I'm investigating your...uh, accident". A strange emphasis on the word *accident* hung in the air.

With a curt, "I don't remember anything" she turned away and looked out the window at the rain-soaked rooftops and their ugly wooden water tanks. It must have been a better view than the sight of an equally drenched and frumpy police officer.

"I'm sure you don't remember much...you've had a very traumatic day" with just a touch of sarcasm leaking out.

Wisdom paused, walked over, and picked up the *Patient Summary* clipped to the foot of the bed. Driver girl barely batted an eye...just maintained her gaze towards the dreary window. As if everything he was reading was mostly Greek to him, Wisdom gave up and put the report down. "So, what is actually wrong with you? You got a lot of stuff going on here." He motioned towards the wires and monitors.

"I don't know...said I may have had an allergic reaction."

"Really? It says here they're treating you for edema, low blood pressure, and...high fever. Do you know what may have caused it?"

Driver girl abruptly turned toward Wisdom. "No...like I told them...and you already...I don't remember anything. I blacked out. I have no damn idea what happened."

As she let out that last burst of anger, an energy that bordered on frustration, she began to break. A crack in her voice and a watering in her eyes made her quickly turn her head away and roll over in the bed—the plastic covered mattress squeaking beneath her. She began whimpering like someone clearly in over her head.

Sensing a need to tone things down a bit, Wisdom asked simply, "I see your name is Julie. How do you pronounce your last name...Brene..."

She sniffled out a fragile, "It's Brenneman. Julie Brenneman." ...followed by a pleading, "Do I have to talk to you? I don't want to talk...I just want to be left alone."

Joey turned to yell back to the door...still open. "Officer, has she been read her Miranda Rights?"

"Yes sir, I believe so."

Those damn Miranda Rights were a ball buster. Frickin' government mandate that had been laid down as law a few years back by the Supreme Court. Seems some serial rapist from Arizona felt his confession was coerced under duress without any representation. Oh yeah, the punk *was* guilty as hell, but in hindsight, he just didn't want to admit it. Preferred the police figure it out on their own...without his *coerced* confession. That was his right...according to the government.

So now, every time he was investigating someone for a crime he had to let them know that they didn't have to talk to him...then or ever...and certainly they were not obligated to talk until a lawyer was present. This was such a deal breaker for police. Wisdom had learned long ago that the best answers to a crime *were* almost always derived under duress when the suspect was at his weakest.

Wisdom turned back towards Julie. "No, you do not have to talk to me. But I don't want to know about the incident. Can I ask some other...uh ...easier questions?" No response.

Wisdom tried again. "The police report said you live over at the Delta Sigma house...I am guessing you go to school at Georgetown. What year?"

Julie muttered back, "Junior."

"Great school. What are you studying?"

"I'm working towards a BS in Psychology." And then pointing to her herself and all those tubes and wires. "This isn't going to help."

"Psychology? Is it tough?"

"I don't know...yes, I guess...got a 3.4 though, so I am doing Okay, I guess."

Wisdom decided to shift a bit. "You live in the sorority house...I assume you have roommates."

She turned and squinted her eyes at him as if he were an idiot... "It's called a *Sorority...House...* I got about twenty-five roommates."

"Of course. Any of them around today."

"Place is dormant. Everyone's home for vacation."

"Why aren't you at home, then?"

"I wish I was. Parents are on some sort of company boondoggle trip. Easier to just stay at Delta Sig. Okay?"

"Sure, sure...I'd rather be in Georgetown, too."

"I didn't say *rather*...I said *easier*."

"Do your parents know you are here?"

"Yes. Can you leave now?" The weakness in her voice plainly audible.

It was weird. Watching her demeanor—her expressions and responses. She rotated so quickly between traumatized and angry that talking to her was like being on a ride. She didn't seem stable but neither did she seem like she knew anything...or at least she didn't *think* she knew anything. But sometimes you just got to poke around a bit.

"So, no one saw you leave this morning? No neighbor?"

"Like I said...the place was empty."

"Well, let me ask you this. You *say* you don't remember *anything*...but surely at some point, you remember driving around this morning or maybe getting into the car?"

"I remember nothing. I don't remember leaving the House. I don't remember getting in the car. I don't remember driving." Again, beginning to tear up.

"Okay, Okay. What *is* that last thing you remember?"

"I don't know...I was listening to music in my room...just messing around...bored."

"Anything else?"

"No...no. I was just being silly...dancing to music." She paused, now clearly fragile. "Got a prank call. That's it. You're embarrassing me. I remember nothing after that."

"Prank call?"

"I don't know. I guess. It was nothing. Dammit, leave me alone."

"Okay...okay...I know. This is tough. Honestly, Julie, you are far from someone I would suspect of wanting to run a man down in the street. But I just don't understand. Look, just talk to me like I am a five-year-old. You said you remember nothing...that you blacked out. But if you drove around town all morning can you at least explain what led you to end up in the Quikee Mart parking lot..." and then incredulously, "...in your pajamas and slippers?"

Julie looked at him as if she wanted to kill him…with her bare hands…not a car. Then turned away again saying nothing.

"Okay, so I guess you must black out often? Common occurrence, is it? Some medical condition?"

Julie never adjusted her tear-soaked angry gaze. She just simply and calmly offered up what she should have offered up long before. "No Comment."

"Never mind. Never mind. Let me take this another way. So, the last thing you remember…before the incident, that is…was being in the House? If you don't remember driving around, what is the next thing you *do* remember?"

She turned back toward Wisdom and with a voice reminiscent of a child, Julie sniveled, "I remember seeing a man…with a gun clenched in his hand…lying face down on my hood. Blood coming from his mouth. Pinned against a dumpster. Dead. That good enough for ya?"

"Yes, of course."

And then, almost pleading, "Who *was* he?"

"You didn't know him?"

"No. Who was he?"

"My partner."

Julie looked back at Wisdom, now crying uncontrollably as Officer Cantor, hearing the commotion, came in the room.

"Is everything alright, sir?"

"Yeah, I guess. It's okay. We'll be okay. You can go back to your post."

Wisdom shooed Cantor away and then turned back towards Julie. Staring at her…taking her in. She was not ripe for this mess. He waited until she calmed down. "Julie, sorry to upset you. I really am. I know you are out of your depth here…very sorry. I'm going to leave you to rest. We'll dig into this more later…if we even need to." The pause and addendum clearly meant to provide her some comfort.

Julie wiped the tears from her eyes but said nothing as Wisdom walked toward the door before turning back. "One more thing, you said you were a Psych major."

"So?"

Then the Hail Mary. "I'm curious. Did you ever have a tutor for those classes?"

"Why?"

"Just curious…tough school."

Defiantly, "I'm not stupid you know. Psych is really hard. Yes. I had a tutor. Almost everyone did."

"I understand. I know I would need one."

"I'm sure you would."

Wisdom giggled a bit at the dig. "You're probably right. Probably right," as he headed out the door before stopping at the threshold and turning back around. "Curious. What's the name of the tutor?"

There was nothing for a moment, and then Julie let out a deep breath of frustration followed by the two clearest words Wisdom had heard all day. "Dr. Poeltz."

She pulled the sheets to her neck while curling up in a ball and rolling back over toward the window. The view's drizzly gloom blending seamlessly with the predicament she now found herself in. It gave her a shudder as she closed her eyes…tightly. It was as if she was magically trying to wish the world away.

Chapter Forty-One

Arlington—The Crystal House

Tuesday, December 19th–9:30 p.m.

Joey went home after the hospital interrogation with his head in a bit of a clutter. With a Schmidty in one hand and an ash-topped Winston in the other, he went over the conundrum again and again.

It just made no sense.

One college girl apparently killing a high-profile banker while another coed from the same school kills a police officer just two days later…in broad daylight…and *she says* she doesn't remember *anything.* Oh, and as if the other events weren't crazy enough, don't forget to include the death *or suicide* of the first girl. And the thing is…it appeared none of these people had the faintest clue any of the others even existed. There *had* to be a tie-in, and so far, the only common thread is that each girl went to Georgetown and both saw the same tutor for their studies. Big deal. So did dozens and dozens of other kids, and no one is seeing any of them out killing random florists or mailmen or whomever.

It's strange sometimes how seemingly simple things can bring back a flood of memories. Like the smell of a freshly baked pie makes you think of home…or hearing a song can make you think of a certain girl…or maybe it's just a single word that jars a repressed memory. In this case, for Wisdom, it was the fleeting thought of a *mailman* that flew through his brain, sparking a memory that for the second time in a week had made him pause.

It was early one Saturday morning back in 1969 when witnesses saw a teenage girl hurriedly walk down the dirt path from Wisconsin to the Key Bridge Boat House. She had removed her shirt and rushed right past the attendant onto the dock towards the river. It was the days of hippies and free love so seeing a girl remove her clothes and jump in the wading area around the Boat House wasn't completely out of the question. But it was late October, and the water was cold. Too cold for a casual dip in the river. She appeared sunburnt as well which, given the fact that it was fall and had been cloudy for several days, just didn't make any sense. Witnesses thought maybe she was tripping, but in hindsight, she seemed too calm for that. Without a word or warning, she leapt in and paddled towards the middle of the river, the strong current pulling her downstream. According to a jogger on Key Bridge, once she reached the middle, she simply stopped paddling and lay flat, feet first, head back and just floated.

Eight miles and ninety minutes later the girl came out the other side of the Great Falls and into the view of a retired mailman on a morning hike. All the worse for the wear.

Yep, a retired mailman.

He found her down past the rapids of the Potomac River. He was hiking the Billie Goat Trail when he saw her lifeless and battered body. It was floating placidly through the calm narrows near Purplehorse Beach before he frantically waded in and dragged her ashore. She was hard to recognize. The brutal violence of the Falls' rocky currents had done plenty of damage to the young girl. An expert in a kayak *might* make it cleanly through those rapids. She did not. Her body cut and bleeding. Her hair matted with remnants from a cracked skull.

Her shoeless feet were broken and mangled, as was her right forearm. She wore nothing but shredded blue jeans and a tattered bra. Her torso and face were flush red. Her head and upper body ballooned.

Oftentimes, when you find a drowning victim, they are distended with gas but this is usually after the body had been submerged for days—sometimes hours—and the pressure from being underwater for so long just pops them to the surface. This girl had been on the river no more than sixty minutes, and she essentially floated the rugged surface of the Potomac the whole way. The puffy and red look of her body was strange but...according to the coroner:

Primary Cause of Death: Head Trauma & Internal Bleeding.

Secondary Cause of Death: Drowning.

According to the Police...specifically one, Detective Joey Wisdom: *Probable Cause of Death: Suicide.*

No lab tests were run. No real inquires made. It was an open and shut case. Young troubled college girl, identified as Georgetown sophomore Elizabeth Rubin, was merely in over her head. Took her own life. Not the first time this had happened. Sure, most judicious people intent on killing themselves, would simply leap from the top of Key Bridge, get knocked unconscious by the impact and drown within a minute. This girl took the hard way out. But in Wisdom's opinion, it didn't change his determination. She wanted to be dead even if she chose to do it by going through the meat grinder of Great Falls.

At the time, the condition of her body meant very little to Wisdom. Bloated and inflamed was an afterthought to what actually happened to her in that river. But three years later, the similarity of who she was...*and* what she looked like now made him shudder. There had been a couple of unexplained overdoses on campus back in '68, but that didn't seem out of place with the culture at the time. Two or three ODs could be a convenient coincidence but add in that battered coed from the river and now, the Bard girl? Hell, even the Brenneman situation seemed familiar...in an unfinished sort of way.

Chapter Forty-Two

Erinnerungen an Frederick, Maryland–Camp Dietrick

1962

S. Rauscher Journalprotokoll Entry LX:

I remember the day quite clearly. Late April. A near perfect Spring morning that, strangely enough, both belied and mimicked my pending fate. I arrived at Dietrick early, per usual, and was promptly met by the limping and diminutive Gottlieb along with his two armed and ever-present gofers. They quickly ushered me downstairs into a secure and soundproof conference room. It was a room that doubled as a bomb shelter, but on that morning, that purpose was most assuredly not served. The whole silent and plodding scene played out like I was on a death walk and in a way, I was. That was to be my last day at Dietrick. My last with MKUltra.

In short, I was terminated for using valuable lab resources towards experiments that deviated from the predetermined and approved emphasis. Being one of more than a dozen scientists working on Gottlieb's inane LSD adventures—each of us conducting several experiments a day—I had been able to run my scopolamine trials interspersed with the LSD tests. Each week, I would produce my reports. But only 1 set—the LSD results—were readily made available to Gottlieb. I had long worried of being discovered, so I actively produced two sets of scopolamine results. One showing failed data. The other, accurately showing the truth. I provided neither report to anyone. The real results were concealed at Theodore's beneath a faulty floorboard at the top of an attic staircase. To my knowledge, only I ever ventured the narrow and rickety path...Charlotte's weight and age precluding the effort. The erroneous data, however, was technically in plain sight—tucked away in my lab office files. These tests did show scopolamine data, but I had manipulated the results for failure. I knew that at some point, as a matter of simple protocol, someone would examine all my files. I felt, if discovered, that it would be best to admit to the failed peripheral testing in lieu of claiming outright innocence—an argument I was sure to lose. When he finally sat me down, the words, "we have no use for a rogue scientist in this division," told me all I needed to know. They had discovered my project. At the time, I worried that Leavenworth would be my next destination. But, it was quickly evident that only the falsified data had been discovered. Otherwise, I would have been on a slow train to military prison, or worse.

The naïve thing about Gottlieb is that he always acted like he had been doing me a favor...saving me from assured imprisonment in Siberia. I saw it much differently. I was kidnapped from my homeland...my heritage. No family. No real family, that is. It was a vacant and castrated existence. It hardly seemed like a courtesy. Adding in his overbearing narcissism and the myopically abusive LSD ventures made the arrangement almost intolerable. No matter his opinion, I felt like an indentured servant to Gottlieb. A slave. A military sharecropper procured to the detriment of America's enemies...my own people. The guilt-tinged irony of it all, tormented me.

We did, though, have one item in common. We both had an equal and pressing fascination in expanding the ability of the mind. Gottlieb's methods had been ruthless, and up until that day, horribly misguided. For years, he felt that LSD was a wonder drug—one that he could use to rebuild personalities, transforming the unwitting into trained unadulterated killers. The process of re-patterning—as he has called it—consisted of two stages. In the first stage, amnesia was induced through an extreme form of sleep therapy. During this phase, the subject was heavily sedated and given daily electroshock treatments over a period of several weeks...essentially with the goal of killing the old personality. While in this now muted state, the patient was then subjected to psychic reconstruction by making the individual listen to manipulative tape-loops for as long as 16 hours a day for several weeks while repetitive doses of LSD were administered. This never worked—his damaged volunteers discarded like yesterday's trash. The entire brutal process left me empty. On edge.

Furthermore, the suspected suicide of my friend and fellow scientist, Ted Olsen, seemed more like murder than anything else. Just weeks prior to my removal, Ted leaped to his death from the roof of the Hotel Harrington. Ted had no reason to be at the Harrington—he lived a mere 15-minute drive away. He also had no reason to kill himself as he was soon to be married. He, like myself, did not agree with much of what Gottlieb was exploring, but he was a very promising and ambitious scientist. Hardly one to take his own life.

Was Gottlieb getting rid of any weak links? To the suspicious, my firing and Olsen's death would seem odd timing. No doubt.

Gottlieb told me they had secured me a teaching position at Georgetown University. Psychology. With no access to the lab, Charlotte would no longer be necessary. She would be gone within days. Onto her next mission, I suppose. I couldn't help but pity her next assignment—whoever that would be. I was told to (somehow) maintain the operation of the antique store. The child? Jonathan? He was now almost 14, and he would be staying with me. Why? Because what else were they going to do with him. Gottlieb also made a rather ominous note that I would remain on HSA payroll and that "you will continue...to be monitored". How monitored had I already been? And then, with a bit of a vindictive edge, he also said that all *notes and files not pertaining to the LSD studies would be destroyed. Fortunately, the truth was secure, hidden beneath that rickety board and far from my tormentor's reach.*

The ironic reality was, had he known about the scopolamine studies he would have surely retained my services. He was stubborn but not obtuse. With access to the genuine research, he would have found that his thirst for a reliable method of re-patterning would have been satisfied by the advancements I had made. Among other developments, I had discovered that, while he was correct that two phases were necessary to make the mental transformation, his methods were far too time-consuming and mentally abusive. Mine were much more benign. Most importantly, he was simply using the wrong drug.

So, on that spring morning, I discovered in my own tragic way that I had been reborn. Free for the first time since 1945. Or at least as free as one could be under the lurking and watchful eye of the HSA.

Up to then, my experiments had proven consistently reliable. While the success had been procured under the very controlled and pristine setting of the lab they had nonetheless been proven efficacious. The most superb development was that, prior to my dismissal, I had also surreptitiously secured enough scopolamine to proceed with further testing. At my own pace. On my own terms.

With that, I no longer needed Gottlieb nor his lab. I didn't even need his volunteers. If I was correct, those poor saps would be available almost anywhere.

It was time to take my experiments to the field. Time for the next phase.

Chapter Forty-Three

Georgetown—32nd Street

Wednesday, December 20th–9:50 a.m.

Through the misty glaze of the front bay window, he could
see her…pacing back and forth like the lonely wife of a long-
absent seafarer. Anxious and wanting. Only in this case, it
wasn't an angry ocean she contemplated but rather, the restful
confines of her antiquated neighborhood. The contrast was
not lost on Detective Wisdom.

Before he could even ring the bell, she abruptly jerked
the door open.

"What do you want?" The chill in her voice was
remarkably similar to the morning air. Bitter.

It had been four days since he brazenly accused the
young bride of having her husband murdered. Sure, it was a
tactic meant simply to shake her and possibly help steer the
direction of his discovery, but her dislike for his tactic was
palatable. Still.

Detective Wisdom took a deep breath…a deeper breath

than normal. It was the kind of breath that reeked of frustration and the only way to blunt the feeling was to then let it all out with almost as much vigor as the breath itself…maybe more.

"I am sorry to bother you. My dispatch should have contacted you. Is this a good time?"

"I don't know, Wisdom. Did you find who killed my husband?" The sarcastic scorn seeping through the tone in her voice.

Her question was nearly rhetorical. He ignored it. "Well, there's been some developments Mrs. Schneider. Do you mind if I come inside?"

Without a word, Mrs. Schneider stepped back and widened the door entry. Despite the early time of the day, she had moved beyond the depressed bathrobe attire she wore with regularity those first couple days. Now in jeans and a woolly sweater, she was comfortable but focused. As they moved into the front living room, she pointed to one of the high-back Queen Anne chairs that at one time she had been so charmed by. Its sophistication no longer relevant. Detective Wisdom eased himself into the overstuffed cushion making sure to brush his trousers before sitting down. He left his jacket on. Something about her demeanor made him feel like this was going to be a short visit.

Mrs. Schneider took a seat across from Wisdom in the elegantly appointed French styled settee. Wisdom got the impression that this room was rarely used but rather little more than a showcase of their stature to the world outside that big bay window. People were surely looking inside but not for the reason she hoped for.

She got right to it. "You know the last time you were in this room, you accused me of having killed my husband. Have you changed your mind?" she asked mockingly.

The mournful and shocked wife routine of a couple days ago had been clearly replaced by an angry and bitter doppelganger. Wisdom needed to wrest back control…damn her feelings. "Ma'am. Look, I understand your frustration."

"Do you?"

He paused, rubbed his chin lightly and then came right out with it. "You know, and I probably don't even need to tell this, but over ninety percent of murders at home are committed by a family member. I pretty much eliminated your two children right away...just didn't think they were tall enough."

He shifted, "Where are the kids anyway?"

Clearly pissed, she squinted her eyes at him. If she had a baseball bat handy, she would have used it by now. "They are with my mother-in-law. Cut to the chase, Wisdom." The *Detective* label clearly left intentionally aside.

"Okay. Fine. What can you tell me about Jennifer Bard?"

"I couldn't say. Don't know her."

"You don't know her...or don't know *of* her?"

"Listen, Mr. Wisdom. Let's not play games. I have never heard the name."

"You don't read the papers...watch the news?"

"Honestly, reading the morning paper over a cup of coffee has not been in my routine since...last Saturday."

"Okay—well, we have reason to believe Jennifer Bard may have killed your husband. In fact, we are quite sure of it. There are some tests we need to complete, but all evidence suggests that she is the perpetrator. The uh...shooter."

Sarah leaned forward. Clearly upset and stunned. "Why in the hell has no one told me this?"

"I'm telling you now."

Mrs. Schneider shook her head as if to wake herself... "When did you figure this out...is she in jail?"

"Honestly it has been pretty fluid, but we had a decent idea on Sunday...and no...she's not in jail." Wisdom was delaying with details to gauge her natural reaction—a valuable tool he learned long ago. In his mind, The Widow Schneider was clearly not high on his list of suspects. Just not the kind of person who would hire a college girl to kill her husband...but you never know.

"Sunday. What the hell. Why isn't she in jail?" Her voice rose with each word.

"You really don't read the news, do you?" Without

waiting for a response, he continued. "She's dead."

Wisdom spent the next several minutes discussing the details of the Bard girl careful not to divulge too much information. He questioned her about any work or connection her husband may have had with Georgetown University. *To her knowledge, there was no connection.* This was also previously confirmed by Jenner. And as much as it bothered him, he asked if she felt he could have been having an affair with this girl…or any girl? *No. He worked hard but he was always home at 6 p.m.…every day and outside of travel…which was rare…his weekends were always spent with her and the kids. Hell, he didn't even have guy's nights.*

Mrs. Schneider had been stunned by the Bard situation. She didn't know what she had expected, but surely a teenager killing her husband was never in her wheelhouse. But just the idea that they had found the killer brought the whole sad reality of her life full front. As she listened to and answered Wisdoms questions, her eyes began to glisten. She didn't weep outright, but she had trouble talking without halting. Brief answers to shocking questions were all she could muster until she finally turned away from Wisdom and looked out the window.

"I smell him everywhere. I know that's strange. Honestly, I didn't even realize he had a smell. I see his toothbrush in the bathroom and just stare at it…for a…for a really…long…time." She paused and then as if there was a deep-seated fury rising inside. "Damnit. Even his shoes make me cry. What the hell? His shoes, for god's sake. Honestly, I'm just lost… I don't know how else to explain it."

She was silent for a moment as she stared out the front— her eyes fixated…on nothing but what was in her imagination. "You know, Detective Wisdom, I look out this window, and I can see him there…walking up the path…home for the day. Just like every day. The girls jumping at his legs as he walks inside…always singing the same silly little song. *"Daddy's home. Daddy's home...to stay."*

The room was still for a moment. Wisdom said nothing until she finally burst out, "No. He's not." She paused, the tears now clearly running free down her cheeks before finally whimpering out a sad, almost silent, "No...he is *not* home to stay."

The anger and the anguish now having officially bled together for the very first time.

Chapter Forty-Four

Virginia—Dulles International Airport

Wednesday, December 20th–10:10 a.m.

As the lumbering Pan Am jumbo jet banked left over the Virginia countryside on its approach to Dulles, the passenger in Row 5—Seat C began to stir. For the last few hours, he had been sound asleep. Well, that is, as sound as one can sleep on an airplane. Head periodically bobbing up and down like a chicken. Seatmate doing a gymnastic routine to get over his cramped legs. Stewardess nudging him with the prerequisite drink or peanut offer. Accidental seat bumps from the row behind. It was all very soothing.

He hadn't been an international flyer for long but no matter the length of the flight, he had always managed to use the travel time to sleep. From the very first flight he took to Europe, he realized that being cramped next to someone for seven hours—especially some lady who loved to chat—was a punishment equal to torture. These *Chatty Cathys*—as he liked to call them—would ruin any flight and the best way to eliminate the hardship was simply to sleep...or at least pretend to sleep...right from the start. Nip it in the bud. So, every flight, as soon as he would take his seat, he would cross his arms, tilt his hat down, and close his eyes. It didn't matter whether his row had filled up yet or not. He was going to set the tone...early. And it worked. Maybe it was his determination, or maybe it was the thinner oxygen in the plane, but each flight was met with an almost unchecked nap from take-off to landing. Today's flight was no different.

The flight left Managua, Nicaragua five hours earlier, but he had managed to use a big chunk of it for sleep. As the pilot announced the landing instructions over the intercom, his brain began to come alive. Shaking off whatever muddled and exaggerated dream his shallow slumber had been wallowing in, he defiantly feigned sleep...eyes lightly shut with nothing more than a glint of light seeping through. He stayed that way until the wheels hit the runway.

The short visit to Nicaragua was essential. Additional scopolamine was needed. The many batches that had been hoarded away had either been used in trials, actual implementation, or had simply lost their efficacy over the years. Now, the only way to obtain the substance known locally as *The Devil's Breath*, was directly from the source. The Borrachero tree. Native only to Central America, the *Drunken Binge* tree—as it was also called—was marked by tauntingly beautiful white and yellow blossoms that droop ever so innocuously from the jungle plant's slender branches. The irony of the flowers beauty was lost on no one in this region. For it is widely known that its petals, pollen, and seeds possess a powerful chemical substance that, when inhaled or consumed, can eliminate a person's free will, and turn him into a mindless dupe. One that can be fully controlled without any inhibitions...moral or otherwise. And, as he had learned first-hand, too large of a dose, ended in a contorted and ugly death. Warnings to local children, "to not sleep under the Borrachero, for either demise or slavery await you," were common.

Finding the Borrachero tree in Nicaragua was not

difficult. Locating a native village healer who could procure the final powdery substance proved more difficult. Healers are not known to use the Borrachero powder for anything more than the benign treatment of nausea or dizzy spells. They know the damage the drug can do when it is administered for less than charitable purposes. In ancient times, the drug was given to the unwitting mistresses of dead tribal leaders who were then told to lie alongside their master in his earthen tomb. Buried alive. Onto the next plane without even the slightest sound of anguish. Nowadays, local criminals had learned to use the substance for robbery or coercion. They would literally blow the Borrachero powder into the face of an unsuspecting person. Hours later, the victim would gradually emerge from his stupor penniless or worse.

After a couple days of inquiries in the villages on the outskirts of Managua, he learned of a local criminal named Enrique - *Ricky,* for short - whose specialty was The Devil's Breath. He made his home among the lesser knowns in the bleak, dusty alleyways of a chaotic village outside the city. His reputation was earned with clandestine visits into town where he and his maniacal powder would prey on the fortunes of city folk or better yet, tourists.

Ricky was indeed his best option but also a dangerous one. Knowing that he himself could become a victim, a driver named Claude was hired who would also act as an interpreter—his own fluency in both English and French, useless in Central American. Even Claude was not to be trusted, but it was better than being unaccompanied when venturing into the jungle villages to make a drug deal.

The exchange went simpler than he had imagined. It seemed Ricky was amused by the inquiry. He also was pleased by the fact that the buyer was a gringo - not another criminal - *and* he greatly appreciated the American dollar...quite a bit. In exchange for 100 milligrams, enough for twenty-five to thirty doses, he was offered $5,000. Ricky didn't blink, as 5,000 dollars was significantly more than he could have earned using the powdery compound for robbery. The only buying condition was that he had to witness Ricky

grind down the tree's flowers and seeds into its potent white
residue. He had not come all this way to be taken by some
village hoodlum.

After consummating the deal, he hastily dressed at his
dumpy city hotel and had his driver take him back to the Las
Mercedes airport for the long flight back home. He was not
worried about customs in Managua, but Dulles might be a bit
more of a challenge. Having opened to international flights in
1970, Dulles had witnessed several hundred ner-do-wells
trying to smuggle drugs into the country from Mexico and
Central America. Most of the confiscated material was
marijuana—a pungent odor, to say the least—easily detected
by the dogs. Scopolamine was an odorless and tasteless
compound, and the small quantity that he was secreting into
the country was easily hidden. Regardless, there was no
reason to take any chances. So, the substance was packed in
an empty talcum powder bottle—a suitable cover for any
customs agent.

After landing and taxiing down the runway, the hulking
white jet came to an abrupt stop at an isolated structure about
500 feet short of the main terminal. This building housed each
of the separate airliner's gates as well as the customs center.
The passenger in Row 5, Seat C had intentionally packed
light. A small carry-on suitcase with a few changes of clothing
were all (or almost all) that accompanied him. Deplaning was
quick. He was near the beginning of the line as they were all
ushered through a dimly lit hallway and into a large customs
review hall. Rows of ceiling-hung florescent lights provided
a depressingly blueish hue. In front of him lay several small
gateways, each with a customs agent sitting stoically at the
helm.

He eyed each agent with as little angst as he could muster
trying to decide which provided the least barrier of resistance.
They were all wearing the same stern and distrustful
expression along with their customary but intimidating
sidearm, silver shield, and dress blues. Reaching the front of
the line, a bellowed, "Next" came dismissively from one of
the stations.

With measured paces, he cautiously stepped towards the origin of the voice. It was here when he realized that it didn't matter which station he went to. None of these agents seemed like a great option. He had contemplated hiring a mule to bring the scopolamine back to the States. He even thought about mailing the package separately, but both options had their own risks.

He had simply concluded that he was going to lull these guys to sleep with his benign but appropriately nice appearance. Dressed nicely, but not too nice. Hair trimmed and beard well groomed, Jonathan intended to give the impression of reliability—a hard sell to someone traveling from Central America. Right about now, his strategy didn't feel like such a great tactic.

He walked through the nylon roped partitions towards the booming agent's voice. The gentleman was sitting behind a military grey metal desk—passenger log and booklet before him. The aging man with thick silver hair and a thicker belly waved him forward. He stopped just before the desk where a bright red sign told him to do so.

"Passport."

He handed it over wondering if that was a bead of sweat that just rolled down his cheek or just his imagination…or paranoia.

The agent peered through the passport's pages and looked suspiciously up at the traveler for the first time.

"Place your suitcase on the table, sir."

Lifting the case onto the table. "Should I open it?"

Ignoring the inquiry, the agent took a quick glance at the small suitcase now sitting impatiently on the cold metal review table. "I see you've been to Germany…and France quite a few times." Flipping back to the front. "I see you're just…uh…let's see here, uh...twenty-four-years-old. That's a hell-of-a-lot of big-time travel for such a young guy."

"Yes, sir, my family runs an antique business in the city, and I travel to acquire furniture and other articles for resale." *Damn—way too much information…and he didn't even ask me a question. Idiot!*

"Uh, huh. Can you explain Managua?"

He paused, remembering his simple but planned response for such an inquiry. "Uh...the same thing, sir. We sell furniture from South and Central America, too." He redeemed himself with the simplicity of the response.

"Well then, I assume you have something to declare."

"Uh, no sir.... I am not bringing anything back."

"You went all the way to Central America, and you're not coming back with anything?"

"That's correct, sir. Much of what we see down there is kind of junky and we only buy high- end. If it's nice, its usually with the wealthier families, and they don't sell easily. Don't need to."

"Hmm. Sounds like a waste of a trip."

"Yes, sir." The agent flipped through the passport again until he got back to the picture and name. He peered back up...staring at him for an uncomfortably long time he then looked back down and made a brief notation in his log book. Taking out his customs stamp, he soaked up fresh ink from the pad and slammed it down onto one of the few empty passport pages. He flipped it shut and handed it back in an almost singular and practiced motion.

"Welcome back to the United States, Mr. Poeltz. Thank you."

Almost startled at the finality of it all, he quickly grabbed his bag and headed towards the door leading to the Passenger Transport Vehicle—which would take him to the main terminal and then to the privacy and security of a D.C. cab.

He looked over his shoulder for one last glimpse...as a cautious but arrogant smile now leaked from his face. Jonathan Poeltz—barely twenty-four years old, recent graduate from Georgetown University and rising antique dealer...was also, a drug smuggler.

Chapter Forty-Five

Georgetown—32nd Street

Wednesday, December 20th–10:20 a.m.

"When's the funeral?" Subtlety was not Wisdom's forte.

She had hidden her tearing eyes in her hands to compose herself, but the brusqueness of the question hastened the job. She quickly pulled them away and wiped her eyes with her sweatshirt covered arm.

"Saturday," she said between sniffles. "Why?"

"Well, we'll probably have a plainclothes officer in attendance."

"What the hell for?"

"For that matter, we intend to post an officer outside your home for the next several days." He paused and then leaned forward for emphasis, "Mrs. Schneider, someone wanted to kill *your husband*. Not someone else. They specifically wanted your husband dead…and even if our prime suspect is a *sweet* little college girl…someone had a grudge. A big enough grudge to kill him…in cold blood…in front of his house. I can assure you this was not random, and at this point, we don't know who else, if anyone, is involved. Look, it's not just for your protection, okay? It's also for our surveillance."

She thought about objecting…saying that it was crazy she would need protection. *Who would want to kill me?* " The fact that someone actually wanted to kill her husband still seemed so foreign to her. Sometimes, reality can be a bucket of ice water in the face.

Defeated, she blurted out "I get it. I get it." and then slammed her fist against the cushiony and flowery fabric-covered arm of the settee and began to tear up again.

"Mrs. Schneider, I do have some other developments for you."

She took a deep but weary sigh then looked back up at Wisdom and said nothing.

Chapter Forty-Six

Dupont Circle—Theodore's

Wednesday, December 20th–10:35 a.m.

Jonathan arrived home almost as excited as he was anxious. He had grabbed a copy of The Post at the airport and although the paper was always peppered with several ancillary crimes…one in particular, caught his eye. On page four of the Metro section, there was a fascinating development. The death…or more specifically…murder, of a certain Georgetown banker. Though the cab ride from Dulles could have given him the opportunity to wind down; this news clearly had the opposite effect.

Entering through 1810's narrow side entrance, he stepped into the kitchen. The smell of a cheap cigar hung heavy in the air, the origin of which teetered precariously on the edge of a heavy glass ashtray which lay isolated on that tin-topped kitchen table. A string of undisturbed smoke rose effortlessly from its origin. The room was well lit, as the ceiling lamp hanging over that small table beamed with a warm glow that blended naturally with the low winter sun peering through the kitchen sink window. The little RCA was also on...the voices of Marshall Dillon and Doc Adams floating over the empty room. It was *Perry Mason* in the evenings...*Gunsmoke* in the afternoons. Always. Father was definitely home.

Jonathan had grown used to his father's daily fascination with the theater of American television. He seemed to identify with Perry Mason and his shyster way of getting his clients off. *Gunsmoke's* Doc Adams was another story. A grumpy and somewhat dark character, Doc had a varied and some would say unethical past, but over the years he had aged into a warm-hearted fellow of respect...something he felt his father secretly longed for himself.

The slight tinkle of the bell on Bruno's collar signaled his father's arrival. The two were lockstep as usual as they breezed through the swinging kitchen door.

"Jonathan, mein sohn. Sie sind zu hause." His German, a natural default when greeting the boy.

Jonathan's dialect was not nearly as polished, but he covered the basics well enough. "Ja, Vater...Ich kam ...uh... uh..." finally giving up on the challenge. "I just arrived, Father."

Taking his son in a tight hug, the two embraced deeply betraying the aches of the old man's lanky and aging body. Finally, the elder Poeltz pulled back to look into his son's eyes. He stared at him for seconds before asking the simple knowing question, "Well?"

"Father, it went very well. I believe I have acquired more than enough."

"Wunderbare."

Jonathan set the small leathered baggage on the table and unclipped the latch before rooting inside to find his dop-kit. He unzipped the case and there, beneath the toothpaste and shampoo, lay the small green metal container of Pinaud Clubman Talc—the one emblazoned with the image of a stately gentleman sporting top hat and cane. A less suitable spokesman for scopolamine would be difficult to find.

He grabbed the small bottle, made sure the top was twisted and sealed tightly and then extended it towards his father's ear, shaking it lightly. "Father, we have enough for over twenty doses…maybe more."

"Brillante, mein Junge. Brillante. His father was beaming, seemingly beside himself as he took the small bottle from his son's hand. He stared at it for a moment…a slight grin escaping his mouth, then shook it himself as if further confirmation was needed. The thumping sounds of the dense and diabolical powder lightly thudding against the inside of the little metal container was all that he needed to hear.

Jonathan grinned at his father's obvious pleasure. For many years, before his mother left him as a child, he had considered his father a stranger. He was rarely home, and when he was, he kept to himself—alone in his second-floor office late into the night. At times, he could hear the old man mumbling lightly to himself behind those perpetually closed doors. His father had intimidated him…but not for any nefarious reason. Just the fact that his presence was downright vacant left Jonathan feeling insignificant. He had known that he was a scientist or something…but that was all. If he dared to interact with his father, he would get a thick and grumbled, "Talk to your mother," in return. It all had the desired effect. Jonathan kept his distance. But the day his mother left, it was like someone opened a window and let a soothing spring breeze flow through the house. His mother *had* been domineering—constantly hounding his father and for Jonathan, she was more like a taskmaster then loving mother. But at least she interacted with the boy. More than he could say for that stranger on the second floor.

Before she left, Jonathan's childhood was stilted…at best. Any friend he would happen to make at school was intentionally kept at arm's length. Mother would not let any children in their home on P. She always argued that there was no room for children to run about amongst the antiques—"You'll break something."—or that it wasn't safe on the patio with all those lurking statues bordering the small shadowy pool—"You'll fall in.".

To make matters worse, Jonathan was rarely allowed to spend time at other boys' homes. Requests for sleepovers were sullied. The possibility of a girlfriend was a non-starter. Even his phone calls were monitored as his mother would lurk in the hallway outside the kitchen whenever a call, rare though it was, would come in for the lad. It felt more like a prison than a home…and shortly after his mother left, and the sun finally shone on his childhood, he found out why.

Almost a decade ago, on one early Saturday morning in late February, two men in dark, almost matching suits arrived seemingly unannounced. With his father breakfasting at his usual haunt, only his mother stood as sentry to their home. They entered through the storefront. Jonathan heard the heavy wooden framed glass door creak open and then shut with the relevant thud of wood banging against wood. When he heard the racket, Jonathan—then almost fourteen-years of age—was in the kitchen eating cereal. Frosted Bran Flakes. His favorite. It was early…too early for customers and so, the boy's curiosity got the better of him. He set his spoon down and tiptoed towards the swinging kitchen door, easing it open just enough so that he could get a look at the visitor…or in this case, visitors.

His mother had first heard them coming far before the clamor of the front door officially announced their arrival. It was a quiet neighborhood—Saturdays especially—so, the sudden noise of two car doors shutting had startled her. She peered out the large bay window of the second-floor solarium. There, two very familiar men walked with purpose, up to the front stoop. When Jonathan had looked out from the kitchen, he did not recognize them…but his mother sure did. She knew them quite well and had learned over the years that these fellows rarely called in advance, and even if they did it still usually meant something abrupt was in the wings.

She had scurried down the squeaky wooden staircase as best as her sixty-year-old joints could muster. There was an urgency in her manner like she was hoping to catch the unannounced visitors before they could formally doff their hats in greeting…as if that would stop what was coming.

They welcomed each other, but there was a stiff formality to the discussion. Jonathan could hear next to nothing...*mumbled instructions, maybe.* His mother seemed to be breathing deeply...her back rising back and forth. *Maybe out of breath...maybe scared. Hard to tell.* One man pointed behind him towards the front entrance. *Policemen? Was she in trouble? Maybe.* Jonathan was lost. Confused. Whatever it was, the whole scene had an air of importance that was not lost on the young boy.

This mostly one-sided discussion lasted no more than a minute or two before his mother nodded and then ambled up those rickety and foreboding stairs. As she banged around upstairs, Jonathan caught a bit of daring and eased that heavy swinging door all the way open, his presence now naked to the intruders.

One gentleman in black horned rimmed glasses—which was really the only way to tell them apart—turned towards the silent swing of the door, its motion catching his eye. He said nothing but stared at the lad intently for a moment before he leaned toward his partner and whispered something non-descript. Both Glasses Man and his partner then looked directly at the boy...their stares judgmental. While it only lasted for a second or two, for Jonathan, it felt much longer than the tick of the clock suggested. Kind of like the stare you get when the 7-11 cashier man thinks you might be about to steal some Wacky Packs, or something. It was uncomfortable, and he did not fully understand it, but thankfully their gaze was stolen away by the sound of his mother descending those creaking front stairs. A light winter coat hung off her body as if by accident and a knit cap was haphazardly pulled down upon her natty gray hair. She was tousled and rushed.

With a small luggage bag in her right hand, she waved off the two gentlemen with her other hand as if shooing them away. On cue, the two men made their way towards the front door, and his mother used this opening to approach the confused and still pajama laden lad. She leaned forward, almost to eye level of the boy and in her traditionally stern tone, simply said... "I am sorry, but I have to leave. Your father, I am sure, will explain everything."

"Mom?" His simple response, inquisitively plaintive.

She frowned and shook her head lightly as if to suggest he should just stop. She stood, turned, and made her way toward that looming storefront entrance...which, for his mother, was now an exit. For as Jonathan would soon find out, this would be the last time he would ever see her.

He stood there in his PJs with his slight body holding back the swinging door...a drip of milk on his chin and a bowl of half-eaten cereal on the table behind him. His mother gone...his vacant father nowhere to be found. With an empty look on his face, he stepped backward and turned to go back into the kitchen, the swinging door following him like a loyal puppy. From behind the door, a light scoot could be heard as the boy pulled his chair up to the table to finish his breakfast.

The house was now silent, save for the childish sound of slurping and the occasionally spoon clanking on a cereal bowl.

Before she had left, Jonathan had offered one more hopeful, "Mom?" in her direction, but it had had no impact. It was strange, even calling her *Mom* had always seemed awkward to Jonathan. Her firmness and the uncomfortable way she related to the boy were far from motherly.

He would soon find out why.

Chapter Forty-Seven

Georgetown—32nd Street

Wednesday, December 20th–10:50 a.m.

"I am going to guess the name Julie Brenneman means nothing to you."

Mrs. Schneider had privately hung on Detective Wisdom's previous comment of more dramatic news to come. She didn't want to give him the satisfaction and by now, she knew better than to be baited by a carrot from a man who had thus far been more a tormentor than anything else. However, given the circumstances, any developments were of great interest, and she just could not resist the intrigue when he said flatly, "I have other developments for you."

So, she had leaned forward and waited for the punchline like a dog waiting for a biscuit...or at least that's how she saw herself. A dog anxiously waiting for a treat...or in this case...more like a trick.

"No, I don't know a Julie Brenman...or whomever. What? Do you think she was having sex with my husband, too?

"It's Bren-ne-man, and no, I don't think that's the case." He leaned in to meet her as she stared at him with a mix of wanting and dissatisfaction, "I don't think she was having an affair with your husband...but she did kill my partner yesterday."

Mrs. Schneider's hand went straight to her mouth as she blurted out his partner's name. "Jenner? What the hell is going on." She paused, shook her head lightly and then offered her own preemptive, and plaintive addendum to the young officer's eventually obit, "Jenner? Good lord. He was...he was...just so nice."

"Yep, he was nice...and young. Had a wife. Couple kids. Just like you...and we're probably going to bury him the same day you will be burying your husband. Shitty week, all around."

Defeated, Mrs. Schneider collapsed back into her couch while begging again, "What is going on?

"You know, uh..." He paused. Temporarily defeated. "We really don't know." With the District being an over-murdered place and Frankel keeping his department intentionally and perversely under-staffed, the *We* that Wisdom subtlety referenced was actually the *Royal We*. Wisdom was now...and, as usual...the only man on the case.

"Honestly, we have little to go on, but I wanted to fill you in on a few details. See if you could offer some assistance."

"Oh, Jesus...I'll try, but good lord...what actually happened...I saw him out my front door just yesterday. He waved to me."

"Well, this Julie girl literally ran him down in a car yesterday. Pinned him against a dumpster...over on Wisconsin.

"What? Was it an accident?"

"Not from where I sit. The girl is in the hospital right now. A total mess. Claims she blacked out. Didn't even know what had happened. But there's, uh, a tidbit or two that kinda has me questioning the whole thing."

This had gotten Mrs. Schneider's attention once again,

and she leaned forward. "What are you talking about?"

"Well, first of all, this Julie girl is a Georgetown student...just like your husband's killer. I mean, *suspected* killer. Wouldn't normally be that big of a deal. I mean, we're only a mile from campus, after all. Nothing more than a coincidence. Right?" Wisdom hesitated. "But...two GU students with no priors...no obvious axe to grind...involved in separate murders within three days of each other? In my twenty years, it's just simply unheard of. And..."

Mrs. Schneider had stopped listening. She was spent. Emotionally done. She had tried to put on a tough front for the Detective—mostly because she hated him—but now, it was too much, and she collapsed back into the couch...eyes closed, both hands pulled up to her face.

Wisdom was silent for a moment...waiting for Mrs. Schneider to come back to the living. Finally, he just blurted out, "Mrs. Schneider."

She shook her head tightly, like one would do to get rid of the dizzies and then leaned forward...her eyes watering up once again. "I'm sorry...I'm sorry. Go on."

"Well, you see, I keep asking myself why would someone kill—sorry to be blunt—but really, why *would* someone want to kill a lowly patrolman? I mean, he normally just hands out parking tickets for god sake. I've had my fair share of scumbag criminals want to take me down over the years, but hell, he hasn't been around long enough to have enemies. Any enemies. Shit, you met him."

Mrs. Schneider eased out the smallest of grins. "Yeah, he is...I mean, was the nice version of you...to say the least."

"True. That's my point. Who would want to kill him? The thing I keep coming back to is that maybe...maybe someone didn't want him snooping around your husband's murder. But hell, we've been on this case for what...two...maybe three days. Hardly enough time for that theory to make sense."

"Did these girls know each other?"

"It's early but by all accounts, no. I'm pretty convinced neither of them even knew you...or your husband. There's certainly no evidence of that…so outside of being coeds from the same college, they seemingly had almost nothing in common."

"You said, almost."

"Well, it's slim, but both were Psychology students."

"Classmates?"

"We are checking on that, but it doesn't look like it. The Bard girl was a Freshman. Brenneman, a Junior. Not likely they would have classes together."

"So, what are you getting at?"

"I'm not sure. Nothing, probably. They didn't know each other. Apparently, didn't even know their victims. The only thing that can tie them to each other is the Psychology thing…which is, like I said, pretty slim. That, and the fact that both girls shared the same tutor."

At this point, Mrs. Schneider felt the veteran detective was more than grasping at straws. "So?"

"Mrs. Schneider, do you or did your husband know of a Georgetown teacher named Professor Poeltz?"

The question barely registered. She was clueless, and she knew it. Wisdom pointlessly probing her without any realistic likelihood of success had worn her out. And so, she answered with an empty "No."

"Hmm."

He didn't know what he was expecting, but he knew what he hoped for…some small bit of information from the grieving widow that could help him piece this sonofabitch together. He stood up and turned toward the front bay window staring blankly towards her neighbor's homes. This was just a waste of his time, and he had hounded her enough. It was time to leave.

Behind him, he heard the ruffled sound of Mrs. Schneider abruptly stand. "Wait. Did you say Poeltz?"

Wisdom turned to meet the widow's now animated face and then cautiously offered up a careful and drawn out "Yes."

"I know a Poeltz. I know a Poeltz, very well."

Chapter Forty-Eight

Dupont Circle, Theodore's

1962

It wasn't long after she left that his father told him the truth about the overbearing brick of a lady who had posed rather awkwardly as his mother for all those years. When he had arrived home after breakfast that strange morning ten years ago to find his stumped son sitting patiently on the front porch, he offered little in the way of a proper explanation. The funny thing was, the boy didn't even look disappointed—just confused. At the time, he tried rolling out the typical thing he assumed most parents told their kid when they got divorced like… "She just wasn't happy."

But the boy countered with questions like… "But who were those men…?"

And so, the two went back and forth like that a couple more times before he realized that whatever bullshit he tried to unload on the lad it was met with a more logical retort. The kid was smart…and observant—both traits the old man was sure he picked up out of absolute boredom. He stalled for several days trying to get a handle on his new situation as best he could but in the end…the only answer that was going to work—for either of them—was the truth. The whole damn truth. No matter how hard it would be to explain, it would be the only thing that would make sense.

And so, after a couple of days, Alfred Poeltz asked the boy to enter his second-floor office. It was a dark room…containing only one small window which stared directly toward the tiresome brick façade of the house next door. Behind a large cluttered desk, sat his father. His gaze fixed on the boy as he entered the room. Atop the desk sat a small green lawyer's lamp—the kind with the dangling on/off pull-string. A floor lamp stood haphazardly beside several wooden file cabinets that were placed like guards by the entrance. These two lights and the restricted daylight coming from the small obligatory window was all that gave life to the room…which was not much life at all.

He had never entered the room before. Even if he wanted to, the only way to do so was with permission…and permission never came. Entering by more surreptitious means was not a consideration either as the old man kept the room perpetually locked. It was quite clearly not his place. At least not until the day when he heard the thick-accented voice of his father bellowed out from upstairs.

"Jonathan, come up to the office please."

Those booming words—words the boy had never heard before—set off a dramatic shift. It had been a relationship that at one time seemed almost adversarial. But the truth was, they both needed something from each other. After fourteen years of confiding to only himself, Alfred had become so withdrawn that even the most plainly cordial behavior was strained. He had his cat, and that had been enough. But now…now that *she* was gone he realized that he did need someone. Someone he could trust. For Jonathan, who was short on friends and even shorter on feeling loved, the idea of an actual relationship with the man he called Father was like an adrenalin shot. Finally, someone to look up to…and like all young boys, someone to mold himself after. Consciously or otherwise.

Over the next hour or so, the old man told Jonathan everything. Almost. Though his version of events was undoubtedly biased, he held little back. As he talked, the boy sat stiffly on a wooden chair that was so small it was only suitable for a child. He said almost nothing as he listened frozen to the details of a secret life that explained everything. The boy had always felt like he was stuck in a maze—confused about where to go and where he had been. Finally, someone to show him the way out. When you're fourteen-years-old, you have a lot of questions. The trouble is, most times you don't have the confidence to ask *anyone* those questions. Let alone, an adult. For Jonathan, it was worse. His questions ran deeper than most, but he never dared to pursue any of them. At least not until the spring day in 1962. For years, he had lived with people he called *Mom* and *Dad*, and yet there was nothing familiar about them. Nothing hereditary, that is. Like any child, there is a natural link that ties you directly to your parents –different for each. Maybe a creative gene you inherited from your mother or a biting sense of humor your father passed down. There was always something binding you together. But for Jonathan there was nothing. And strange this was, he had always known it. Now, he would know why.

He had started off by simply telling the boy that his name was not actually *Alfred Poeltz*. "Jonathan, I am not who you think I am." He paused for a moment—made sure he had the boy's attention, then continued. "My real name is Dr. Sigmund Rauscher…and I am not American. Certainly, not in the traditional way."

When he was abruptly ushered upstairs, the boy didn't know what exactly to expect, but he certainly didn't imagine his father's name was a farce. So, with a quizzical expression, the boy sat in rapt silence as his father told him of the glorious days of old Germany, his only-child upbringing, his medical practice, and finally his rise within the ranks of Hitler's inner circle and ascension to Medical Chief of the Schutzstaffel. He explained the research he was doing for Himmler on mind control, and of course, he told him of World War II.

It had been thirty years since that devastating war but, for Poeltz, it still felt like yesterday. He recounted his capture at the hands of the Americans, the war tribunals, and his subsequent kidnapping, as the old man described it, to America to work in involuntary servitude for the U.S. Government.

He went on to explain his mother was not a mother at all but rather a government agent acting the part. Her job was not to love the boy, for she did not, but rather to monitor the father. His secret work for the government was merely an extension of the work he had been doing for his country during the war. It was dangerous work but vitally important to the U.S. Government, and they needed every edge they could get. Using their old enemy's experts was simply one way to gain an advantage over their new enemy...the Russians.

When he finally finished, the boy cut to the quick. "But why did my mother...uh...why did she leave?"

The old man paused, wondering if he had gone too far already, and then... "She left because her services were no longer needed. She has moved on to some other case, I imagine."

"But why...why now?"

"My boy, for twenty-five years I worked reluctantly...but I worked diligently for this government. However, much of our work failed to meet the stated goals. It was a terrible waste."

"What do you mean, goals?"

"Mind-control, boy. We were seeking to quantify a reliable method to control one's minds. Their actions. Fascinating work."

Just the idea of 'mind-control' would send any fourteen-year-old boy's head spinning. All he could think was that it was like Star Trek where there was always some kind of mind-control thing going on. But that was TV...not real life.

"Much of the research these people *would* find of value...well, I kept *that* to myself. I was *not* interested in helping their cause any more than I needed to. But you see boy, they discovered my clandestine studies and promptly dismissed me from my position." He shook his head, and for the first time pulled his stare away from the boy and looked out that dull little window pausing for just a moment. Then, after a deep exhale and with about as much pride as someone who just got sent to the principal's office. "I was simply no longer needed."

"What does that mean?"

"Fired. Yesterday's *papier*. The old man's German accidentally leaking out before correcting himself. "Rubbish. Yesterday's rubbish." He paused, "It's funny. If they had only looked closer, they would have discovered that I had secured the very answer that they had long sought after."

Jonathan, virtually dismissing all the other drama, burst out of his chair, "Wait…Really? You can really control people's minds? Like Spock?"

An almost imperceptible laugh escaped from the old man. "Spock? I know not of any Spock, but yes, I know how to control minds. But not in the way you are thinking. You see, all these mind control studies had become too controversial. They were planning to shut down the program anyway. With or without my research, the project was dead. They no longer needed me…so they no longer needed her watching me. That is why your mother…that is why she left."

Jonathan paused for a moment. He had been thrown off by the news and dazzled a bit by the whole mind-control thing…but then it finally hit him. He had never felt much of anything for the lady named Charlotte who had manned his life for all those years. But he still considered her his mother if for no other reason than by default. But now, he had no mother. Even at fourteen, he knew enough to know that that was not possible. So, he abruptly blurted out, "Who *is* my mother?"

Alfred said nothing. Instead, he calmly stood and walked over to the small window peering through it like it would provide some sort of divine clarity. But it didn't. With his back still to the boy, he offered up only a very curt, "Your real mother is dead."

Jonathan slumped back down in the small rigid chair, shoulders rounded, eyes now locked firmly on the silhouetted figure by the window as if he was waiting for the old man to let him in on the joke. But it was not a joke.

Over the next several minutes Alfred Poeltz told the boy what little he actually knew—bits of information he had gleaned from Charlotte and just plain old common sense. Prior to his arrival to the States, Gottlieb and his team had desperately run mind-control tests on all sectors of the population. Old, young. Black, white. Male, female. It didn't matter. All comers. Some tests, Alfred had learned, included pregnant women. The only pregnant women that would dare subject their bodies and unborn children to any kind of experiment would either have to be conned into it, or they were simply disregarded streetwalkers desperate for money or food or a place to sleep…if only for a night or two. It wasn't uncommon for any desperate near-do-well to die at the hands of these nefarious tests. With no one to claim them but the streets, their bodies were summarily disposed of. Lost to the wind. Their experience forgotten by no one for there was no one to remember them. However, it *was* rare to hear of a mother, late in her third term, abruptly die only to have her child born prematurely…and survive. This was indeed rare…but memorable. It was the kind of story that had a way of sticking around, too. But even cold-hearted MKUltra had a soul…tiny though it was. And now with a newborn on their hands, they could not simply disregard him. Just couldn't do it. So, they found another use for the infant. While he had no way to know for sure, Alfred had long suspected the toddler that showed up in his life a decade ago had been one of *those children.* The afterthought of some test gone bad.

Jonathan didn't get it. *His real mother had been killed by his father's boss? I don't understand.* But in reality, the boy understood it perfectly or at least as well as a fourteen-year-old new minted orphan could possibly understand.

Alfred didn't respond. Rather, he walked over to his desk, grabbed the backrest of the chair and slid it over next to the stunned child. He looked at the boy ever so briefly, then sat down beside him. Both father and son now sitting side by side staring out that tiny refuge of a window—the only thing providing any natural escape for either of them.

Jonathan sat dumbfounded in that bleak room for several moments as Alfred nervously fumbled with a freshly lit R&J. Finally, the boy asked the only other question that had been left unspoken. "But you *are* my father, aren't you?"

The answer was abrupt and firm. "No."

Alfred took a deep drag on the R&J, letting the smoke float like a stale haze around the two of them, then reached over and placed his left hand lightly on the boy's shoulder. He repeated his answer again...this time more gently. "No. I'm afraid not." He paused. "But I will endeavor to fulfill that role to the best of my ability. You will not be alone. We'll not be alone.

It was awkward...but it was real. And for the moment, it had its desired effect...providing the boy with a sense of comfort that he so likely needed.

And so, from that day on, almost on cue, the two—the aging professor and the orphan—were virtually inseparable...if not by blood then by a common purpose. Each provided the other what they so desperately needed. Loneliness can do that to you, taking whatever you can from whomever to fill that void. The father relishing the opportunity to inspire the boy...like he truly *was* the son he would never have on his own. The son soaking up every bit of it like a thirsty hiker. You couldn't really blame the boy for it, either. His mother stolen from him by some heartless and anonymous creature. Who else was he to turn to? So, no matter how subjective his father's position was, the boy bought in. Maybe it was by default. Or, maybe it was out of revenge...or even redemption. Depends on your vantage point, I guess.

It began a long and unlikely partnership—the old scientist and his young boy-apprentice. When Poeltz wasn't holding court at his newly arranged faculty position at Georgetown, he and the boy worked in lock step…researching and testing compounds. Analyzing doses. As he aged, Jonathan even became an advance-man of sorts for the old doctor. Tracking victims. Staging the *events*. Planting the necessary *tools*. In fact, if you heard of a strange unsolved Beltway death during the late 60's it is possible it could have been traced back to an old psychology professor. But why bother? Any number of gruesome deaths went unsolved during those days.

It took years to get just the right dosage and just the right dupe. And actually, it didn't completely fall into place until Poeltz was abruptly denied tenure by the university and set out to pasture. With no other source of income, Alfred devoted himself to overseeing the now thriving antique business while also developing a tutoring service that served two purposes: extra money…and access to just the right case subjects. Turns out, being a female Psych student at Georgetown in the early 70's should have come with a *user warning* label.

Chapter Forty-Nine

Arlington—The Crystal House

Wednesday, December 20th–6:05 p.m.

He couldn't believe it. The desperate and virtually impulsive reference of an old Psych professor had shockingly brought a spark into his investigation. He threw the query out to the grieving widow like a fishing line flung into a vast and lifeless lake with little more than spittle on the bare metal hook to entice his catch. Surely a waste of time…but Mrs. Schneider bit, and Wisdom reeled in what she offered.

She told him of a young antique dealer named Poeltz who contacted her about her interest in obtaining an original Wooten desk. Her husband had long admired the one his father worked over in his private study. Made in the mid-18th century by a little-known Indiana furniture maker, the secretary-style Wooten became the must-have office piece for the moneyed elite. With its wide assortment of drawers and secret nooks and crannies, the desk served as more of a piece of intrigue due to its elegant complexity and abundance of ornaments. The desk's use was virtually obsolete just as it was born—who needs twenty hidden drawers, anyway?—and thus production was limited. Now, a hundred years later, the Wooten was hard to find, and if you did locate one for sale, it would likely cost as much as a new car.

On a whim, Mrs. Schneider had mentioned her interest in the desk to one of the antique dealers she had shopped with. Due to the high price of the item, word spread rather quickly to other dealers in hopes of securing a very profitable transaction. She had received other calls from dealers, so she wasn't surprised when she also heard from the young gentleman from Theodore's, as well. She had, after all, shopped at his store in the past, though she recalled working with a woman…not a man.

Regardless, when she received his call in the fall, he offered to make a visit to her home…get a better feel for her needs. With the Wooten being in very short supply and way out of her price range, she begged off. But the gentleman was politely persistent, no doubt hoping to see what other pieces he could acquire on her behalf. Plus, he seemed generally benign. So, a visit was arranged.

For the most part, the appointment was forgettable. She remembered his beard—scruffier then she would like—and his name. Actually, just his last name—*Polts*, she thought—but little else stood out. The visit, which had only been two weeks earlier, had quickly been forgotten. At the time, it seemed like a sales formality, and she just went along with the game. He toured the downstairs, inquired where she might place the Wooten, inquired about her other needs and in an entirely friendly manner, asked about her family. The young man—whom she accidentally kept calling *Theodore*—was certainly pleasant but in hindsight and with the clarity that can only come from having a husband murdered, he seemed much more interested in her family then would be customary.

"What does your husband do for a living?"

And…

"Oh, he must travel a lot."

And…

"Do you have much family in the area?"

After a while, with little interest in the Wooten and a house already full of well-appointed antiques, she politely ushered him off. On his way out, he formally offered to remain in touch. "I'll discuss the Wooten with my father. He's the real expert. When your husband comes back in town, we'll come by for a visit. Maybe we'll discover something worthwhile for both of us." It all seemed very innocuous at the time.

As he listened to the telling of the encounter, Wisdom knew *the father* would have to be none other than Alfred Poeltz. Mrs. Schneider begged to know why this *Polts* fellow was so important. Wisdom had no real clue. Certainly wasn't going to speculate with the Widow Schneider about it, either. Best to remain coy.

"It's hard to say. If I'm correct, *the father* the young man mentioned to you...might be a retired Georgetown professor."

"So?"

"You know, it's kind of a Ripley's moment. He should have nothing to do with this case. Nothing at all...and he probably doesn't...but...his name keeps coming up. Strange is all."

But strange wasn't even the meat of it. From the moment he met him—quite innocently—he knew he was entirely too anxious for the occasion. Even for a normal doddering old man. His combative nature was off. In some warped way, Poeltz was part of the case...but in what way? He was tied to both girls through tutoring and now was also tied to the Schneider's, through the antique business. He couldn't make sense of it. It was kind of like being left with one piece of a jigsaw puzzle that clearly won't fit. The old professor simply did not fit. After he initially met the man, he wanted to chalk up his edgy demeanor to nerves or general elderly bitterness, but after his confusing discovery at the Pentagon, he decided to tuck his suspicion away in a box marked, *don't discard*. He had a feeling Poeltz would re-surface, and he did...all from the random inquiry into a quirky old desk.

It was just before rush hour when Joey pulled his Dart

into the crowded lot of the Crystal House, some Waylon leaking from inside. After his visit to the widow, he had dropped by the station to grab the ballistic data from the Bard/Schneider case and the blood work from the Brenneman girl, preferring instead to pour over the reports at home and away from the ever-lurking Sargent Frankel. As he opened the creaking door and stepped into the brisk evening air, he tossed the remnants of his still burning smoke into the bushes. The sun hung low as the shadows of the seasonally early sunset made their depressing case. Joey always hated this time of the year. It just felt heavy.

Joey walked up to the glassed front entrance of The House and breezed past Frank the Doorman. The funny thing is that when you say 'doorman', it usually implies a sense of class. But that just wasn't the case at the Joey's apartment. Nope. A doorman at the Crystal House didn't stack up to ones that served the upper crust residence buildings like The Watergate. Not in the least. Yes, Frank dutifully wore the customary hi-tone costume—the long wool navy overcoat emblazoned with gold ticking and brass buttons topped with a military-style cap—but he wore it reluctantly. Cap askew, overcoat unbuttoned almost as if he couldn't wait to get out of it. That, combined with the general tubbiness of Frank, led to an overall disheveled look. Even his interactions with residents were equally uninspiring and forced.

Today was no different than any other as Joey gave the ever-present Frank virtually no consideration as he moved through the lobby, past the woeful gatekeeper, and towards the elevator. He was anxious to twist open a Schmidty and fire up a Winston while reviewing the latest evidence report. He might even eat something.

As he approached the elevator and reached out to press the call button, the gruff voice of Frank the Doorman broke Joey's thick daze.

"Uh, Mr. Wisdom…your wife came by…said she didn't have her key. I let her in."

Clearly befuddled, "What?"

"Uh yeah…she didn't have her key." Frank the Doorman

paused, wondering if he just screwed up. "That's okay, right?"

A loud ding came from the elevator as the door opened. Joey shook his head. "Geez...some frickin' doorman." He turned to see Ginny, standing right in front of him.

It was a mutual understanding. Joey was too beaten down for Ginny, and Ginny was too wild for Joey. Hell, maybe even too wild for someone a decade younger.

Practically from the get-go, they both knew they were poorly matched. Ginny was a fox –way better than he deserved, even during his best days. How could he pass that up? And Joey? Well, Joey provided stability. That is, stability in the way that only a twenty-six-year-old imagined...steady money. Joey wasn't well off by any means. After all, he seemed to still be paying off his old man's debts. But, a detective's salary was pretty respectable, and it showed up twice a month. Much more regularly then Ginny's job, which didn't exist...unless you count the waitress gig she had for a month last year. Yep, she needed the stability, and he liked the idea of that tight little ass hanging around. It was that simple.

The funny part was that when they fought it was always about money and sex—the very two things they craved from each other. He wouldn't share the money, and she wouldn't share the sex. And if you asked him, he had actually begun to lose interest in the sex thing, anyway. By the end of the day, he was just plain wiped out, and it was *a lot* of work just keeping up with her. Handful of times a year was just fine for Joey. And so, Ginny simply withheld the sex...kind of as a punishment...or more to the point...as a tease. At home, she would strut around in flimsy cotton panties and a loose tank top acting the part of his little tart. On the rare occasion that he would pull his gaze away from his beer and the game and show some interest, she would twirl away and say teasingly... "You couldn't handle it anyway." And she was probably right.

But the thing is…he liked her. Not *love* mind you…but *like*. She was fun…and funny. When they were out, she would cling to him like he was truly important. Looking up to him like he knew the answers to everything. It made him feel…well…it made him feel wanted. Important. He really didn't want to lose that.

That's what was so maddening about the last Saturday night at the Pall Mall party. This was the first time she openly flaunted her sex appeal to other men…in front of him. He couldn't tell if it was just her way of torturing him further or was she simply just ready to move on. Call it quits. He didn't want that.

So, when Frank told him she was here, his heart double-skipped with a jolt that reminded him of the old days…two years ago. The feeling he had was a welcome respite from the grind of the Schneider thing. And when the elevator door slid open to reveal her cute lightly freckled face with cascading strawberry blonde curls framing her squinty little eyes, he just couldn't help himself. "I'm sorry."

Chapter Fifty

Dupont Circle—Sauf Haus

Wednesday, December 20ᵗʰ–6:30 p.m.

Alfred Poeltz left the note where Jonathan would easily see it. It was placed between a small rubber tourist magnet of the White House and the metal façade of the General Motors harvest gold refrigerator. It hung there delicately, lightly wafting at even the smallest movement from a passerby. For Jonathan, it would be hard to miss as he always returned home through the side 1810 kitchen entrance and his movements alone would undoubtedly cause the precariously hung note to flutter. Plus, he loved a beer this time every day. It was going to be hard to miss.

He had spent the last several hours researching hotels within the five-mile radius of Theodore's. Why? He did not know...only that his father requested he look for the most discreet of the bunch. Which meant the most likely candidate probably would come from southeast part of the city–just beyond the Capitol. It was a crime-ridden area with more than its fair share of flophouse hotels. One thing was for certain…you'd have to be up to some pretty shady shit to have someone call the cops on you in this neighborhood.

He saw the note dangling there even before he pulled the long-levered fridge handle. He swiped it off the door front sending the little rubber magnet to the floor. It said simply:

"Meet me at SH at 6—back room."

Strange request. "SH" would be none other than Sauf Haus, but his father rarely went there for anything other than breakfast. Certainly, not for happy hour. Yet here he was, being randomly summoned to a bar on a weeknight by his seventy-two-year-old father. It was like he was on this long-winded secret scavenger hunt…first that quick dash to Nicaragua, then to every dumpy hotel in the Capital, and now finally, to this sparsely attended non-descript watering hole. What next? He didn't know exactly what his father was up to, but he knew from experience the old man's plan was wired tight and purposeful. He learned long ago to never question—just do.

It was a bit after 6:30 and teetering towards winter's early darkness when Jonathan entered Sauf Haus. The heavy spring pulling shut the abused front entry door as quickly as it had opened. The frantic sounds of rush hour behind him, now replaced by the more comforting noise of the corner juke, the clunking of bottles on tables, and the muffled conversations of a handful of twenty-somethings just off work.

In the rear of the bar hanging as a dismal obstacle to the back room was the tattered curtain that separated the drinkers from the thinkers. It was beyond that thin piece of smoke drenched fabric where you could easily find the professor—whether he was holding court with his college students or, like nowa-days, having his daily breakfast with Bruno, the cat.

Jonathan stepped purposely down the middle of the joint passing by the bar patrons with nary a glance by either party. If his father were indeed here, he would be beyond that curtain…waiting…probably frustrated that he was late. Pulling the curtain aside, he saw the unmistakable back of his father—thinning hair, slumped shoulders, tweed jacket, the ever-present Bruno on the floor beside him and a simmering R&J teetering in his right hand. On the wall beyond his father, hung a small RCA television. Warner Wolf of WTOP was doing some kind of piece on the Redskins. His father seemed transfixed.

"Father?"

The old man didn't budge, nor say a word but lightly patted the tabletop summoning the young man to sit down. He then looked briefly at his Croton… "You're late. Where've you been?" But before Jonathan could answer, Alfred cut to the chase. "Did you narrow down the list…get us a good one?"

Jonathan took a seat with his back to the tube as the old man turned his gaze towards him. "I think so…. Be easier for me if I knew exactly what you wanted it for. We expecting visitors?"

"No…it's for you."

"Sorry?"

"I need you to stay there for a while."

"What? When?"

"Tonight…." From his lap, he lifted that familiar worn burgundy leather journal and slowly slid it across the table to Jonathan. "Tonight."

"You giving this to me? Why? What's going on, Father?"

"Three questions in one sentence?" The old man raised his eyebrows tightly. "Indicates confusion and weakness." He was always doing that—pointing out traits of weakness and strength as if by saying them often enough the boy would adopt them unconsciously.

"Jonathan, you know most of what is in the notebook already. I just need it out of my possession and in a safe place."

He looked at him quizzically, wondering when the punch line would hit. "You think the Astor Hotel is a safe place?" His sarcasm hanging in the air.

"Is that the one you selected? It needs to be a place where no one would expect to find you. Where no one would feel compelled to report you."

The name belied itself. The upper crust pedigree that

came with a name like The Astor was in complete contrast to the real deal. It was a decaying four-story brick building over on D Street by Folger Park. Just south of the Capitol, it was on the edge of the worst part of the District...stuck between misery and hope. And though it wasn't a slum house with prostitutes and dealers milling about, it was still just north of sketchy. The few tenants who lived there were scraping by on minimum wage...or green stamps...or both. His arrival would be abnormal, mostly because he was white. But like dust under a rug, he'd likely not even be noticed. At worst, simply ignored. No, those people had enough issues to deal with.

"Yeah, it'll work."

"Yeah?"

"Sorry...Yes, sir."

His father took a puff of his RJ and looked down at Bruno. The tubby cat was sleeping idly at his feet—a comforting and muffled snore occasionally rolling from his nostrils. He stared at his lazy companion, paused...then leaned forward and whispered... "Jonathan, things are coming to a head. I, uh, I have some...uh." Then rather intently, "Well, I have trouble on my doorstep. I do...but, I need to keep *you* sheltered from it." Alfred Poeltz eased back into his chair while pulling another draw off the R&J. "I'm not afraid of trouble. Had it all my life. But, there is too much valuable information in here," now pointing to the journal, "to let it get into the wrong hands."

He knew exactly who his father was referring to. If the authorities got a hold of his work, it would surely make its way to the inner sanctum of the CIA...to his old colleagues. If that happened, his retirement would most assuredly be short and likely coincide with a stiff electrical charge or a thick rope around his neck. No, Alfred Poeltz—the careful planner—was designing his exit...and not the one his enemies would have for him.

"I need you to disappear. If questioned, I will say you are traveling in Europe for the business. It'll make sense but...they'll need to confirm it...and that will take a while. Long enough for you to set the ball in motion.

Jonathan fidgeted with the edge of the battered journal, but otherwise sat quietly and listened. Listened to the man's plan of redemption.

"Proceed to the last pages. You'll see three names mentioned followed by a contact details for each."

Jonathan opened the worn journal, flipped to the end and then scanned the last few pages with his index finger sliding it across…until he came to the list of names:

> *1) Dr. Edward Obendorfer*
> *Address: 12384 Exchange Ct South –Walbrook, MD*
> *Ph. #424-3405*
> *2) Phyllis Evans*
> *Bethesda, MD*
> *3) Joseph Wisdom*
> *Address: 1600 South Joyce, Crystal House Apt #1414,*
> *Arlington VA   Ph. # Unlisted*

Now thoroughly confused, Jonathan looked up at his father—eyes wide, eyebrows raised.

Alfred Poeltz spared no emotion…or tact…but countered the young man's obvious confusion in a purposeful whisper. "Each need to be eliminated. You will be the one to arrange it. Not I…you. It is now your time."

Stunned. Jonathan stared back down at the list of names. He recognized not a one of them. For his own reasons, Jonathan shared his father's bitterness. He too sought some form of redemption, but none of these names meant anything to him. "Who are these people?"

"That first one? My former lab partner. The only one at Dietrick that could connect my work to…the deaths of." He paused as if suddenly worried someone had bugged the joint. "Well, you understand. If he ever makes the connection, it'll be bad for me." He stared intently at Jonathan. "And you."

Jonathan shook his head tightly as if in disbelief. "What about these…what have they done?" now pointing forcefully to the other two names.

Poeltz looked down at the names then shifted his gaze to the TV set before taking a deep, impatient breath. "Ah yes. The cop. Wisdom. He doesn't know what he doesn't know…yet. But he will. He's a suspicious bastard. He will eventually come back to me. He'll have nowhere else to go."

Jonathan got the point and said nothing in return. Instead, he slid his finger back up settling on the name in the middle. He looked at his father with his palms out and head tilted as if to say, "And?"

Alfred ignored the boy's unspoken query and leaned back, reaching down to pet his motionless cat. He said nothing for a moment then reached forward and pulled the notebook back to his possession, flipping to the front where a large rudimentary envelope had been crudely taped to the inside front cover. He reached inside the envelope and pulled out a sheet of paper with what Jonathan could see was a long list of names.

"Father?" With an air of frustration asked the million-dollar question. "Surely, these aren't part of this other list?"

Poeltz let out a muffled laugh, realizing quickly how this must have looked to the young man. "No. No."

He slid the paper over to Jonathan who eyed it for a while before looking back up to his father. "There must be twenty names here…they're all females." But before his father could respond, he looked back down and noticed three names that had been crossed out. He recognized two of them immediately: Brenneman and Bard. The third name, Rubin, was also vaguely familiar.

"I'm not going to let you get your hands dirty…any more then I would soil mine. This is the list from which you will operate. You know the first three…the remainder are also operatives on my behalf. Our behalf. Unwittingly, they will do the work for you. When you have used one…you move onto the next. Phone numbers are listed to the right. Instructions are on the back. Very simple"

Jonathan flipped over the sheet then looked at the four-step instructions before turning back to his father. He was familiar with the process, but for the first time, it would be under his direction. One might assume it a daunting task, but for Jonathan who had operated in these thick weeds for years, it barely moved the needle. Then, as if he was under his own peculiar spell, offered up an easy and compliant, "I understand."

"Check into the Astor tonight. Make yourself inconspicuous. Dress down. Keep the journal hidden safely away and begin arranging how you will carry out the plan. You won't have a lot of time. Sooner is better."

The abruptness of the timing startled him out of his conforming compliance. "Really? I don't even know how to find this one." He pointed to that same name in the middle of the list. "This Phyllis Evans lady. Bethesda? That's it?"

"Yes, that'll take some work. More time can be granted for her. Concentrate on the others."

"Yes, sir."

His father stood up while lightly nudging Bruno awake and then began walking towards the curtained threshold. Just as he reached the tattered drape, Jonathan threw out one more question.

"Who is she anyway?"

"Who?"

"The lady in the middle—Evans."

The old man said nothing for a moment, then patted his leg lightly urging the lumbering Bruno to catch up before pulling aside the dreary curtain...plaintively looking back while pausing ever so briefly. "That's the lady who left you ten years ago. That, my boy, is Charlotte Poeltz."

"My mother?" Even after all those years—*and* knowing the whole truth about who she *really* was—he still couldn't reference her in any other way.

Alfred Poeltz didn't respond, and as quickly as he had dropped the bomb, the old man was gone. It was strange, he had always been emotionless and curt. So, to the untrained eye, there was nothing new tonight. But to Jonathan, there was something in the way that he had looked back that gave Jonathan a chill...the same feeling he got when he saw that *mother* for the last time...the very person he was now being asked to kill.

He grabbed the journal and tucked it under his arm. That strange man whom he had always called *Father*—for he knew of no other name to call him—had just walked out on him.

Likely, for the very last time.

Chapter Fifty-One

Crystal City—The Crow Bar

Wednesday, December 20th–8:30 p.m.

He was thrown off his game. He had simply wanted a peaceful evening at home. If not peaceful, at least quiet. No distractions. Some time to review the Schneider evidence and call it an early night.

But he never quite made it upstairs. The two of them stared at each other…momentarily stunned by the randomness of such a chance encounter. She had a pitifully sweet look on her face…almost sympathetic. He wore the look of fluster. He said he was sorry, and he meant it, but he wasn't even sure what he was apologizing about.

She said she was sorry, too…that she overreacted and should have never done what she did—leaving without telling him. She needed her space, needed to figure out what was best for her. She loved him and didn't want to leave him, but she just didn't know what *he* wanted anymore. He had changed…or maybe she had. Distant. One of them, at least.

She didn't know. It was all in a note she left on the coffee table, she said.

"Like the last note you left?" he said.

She tilted her head sweetly halting his aggravation with a simple, "Joey."

They went on like this for several minutes...back and forth. Sometimes biting, sometimes tender. Finally, she promised she would call him in a few days.

As she walked away, he watched, knowing that she might never come back. But for some reason that he couldn't quite pin down, she had left him with some hope. How it went from her needing him to Joey needing her was beyond him. Maybe it was nothing more than how smoking hot she was. Surely, Joey was better than that.

He waited until she drove off...staring intently the whole time...thinking what he could have said or what he should have said. Finally, he shook his head—telling himself those thoughts were *wasted baggage.*

Without giving it even a second's thought, he made his way. Not upstairs with the elevator, but straight outside passing good ol' Frank along the way, who asked, in an obligated sort of way if the detective "would be back soon?"

Joey never looked back but simply said, "Doubt it. Kind of feels like a Crow Bar night."

There were four things you could always count on when you hit the Crow Bar...cheap beer, cheaper liquor, stale peanuts, and staler people. Oh, and drunks. Lots of them and not the timid kind. So, with the din of the stereo filling the room, he pulled up a stool to the edge of the bar right by the server's station. When Joey came to the Crow Bar he pretty much just wanted to be left alone. Sitting in this spot at least kept the riff-raff away from his right. Can't stop what's coming from the left, though. Some people can't help feeding off the energy of other drunks. That was not Joey's style. As he settled in, the nightly ranting of that new WRC disc jockey shot out from the joint's two-speaker Pioneer stereo system:

> "It's the Grease Man and the Grease is
> starting to get the shakes…tremblin'
> all over. I know you're tremblin' too
> with this biiiitter cold …so let's warm
> you up, up, up with 'My Ding-a-Ling'
> by Chuck Berry. Whoa…Someone's
> gonna get in trouble toniiiiggghhhtt."

As the song kicked in… "…*won't you play with my ding a ling*" …all Joey could wonder was which he hated most…that Motown rock and roll crap or that blowhard DJ. What he'd give for a little Merle Haggard. Hell, he'd even go for some Charlie Pride over this crap.

It was 8 p.m. or so, and the place was littered with a handful of raggedy mechanics from the airport. Each wearing the uniform of the trade…oil-laden blue overalls with their name in a white patch over the left breast. Each was also knee deep in a beer—not their first—and a smoke. This was the kind of place that had the constant ever-loving stench of cigarette smoke soaked into everything from the ceilings to the floors. Hell, even the Redskin posters of Billy Kilmer and Chris Hamburger had a dingy beige color to them. No doubt, The Crow Bar was Joey's shithole bar of choice. Two blocks away from The House set back on the corner of 18th and Hayes, it was an easier get-away and much more his speed than his other fallback. Unlike Gadsby's, this joint was a true blue-collar bar catering to everyone from mailmen to mechanics and every swinging dick in between. A place for the beaten and the brash. Hardly a weekend would go by without a good fist fight over a pool game or more likely, the Skins. Sunday afternoons were not for the faint of heart.

The place was called *The Crow Bar* for a reason, but it took Joey, smart detective that he was, a year before he bothered to figure it out. There was no name on the signage out front. Just a crudely painted figure of what resembled a large black crow. Smack-dab on the front door. Obviously, it's a bar—witness the Schaeffer and Old Style Beer lights hanging in the window—but then you add in that ominous looking crow, and you get Crow...Bar. Genius, sarcasm most definitely intended. But, Joey didn't bother catching the play on words until one afternoon when he heard the owner talking shop with a couple of car repair regulars. Ah...*crowbar*...the mechanics tire tool of choice. Cute.

But tonight, fortunately...it wasn't a football night. No, outside of the few guys catching a pop or two before they begrudgingly scuffled back home through the bitter night's air to their bitter wives, the place was pretty quiet. He tapped the scarred and moisture-stained countertop to get the attention of the bartender who was shamelessly sucking back a cocktail of his own while chatting up a past-her-prime patron.

The man looked up with a glare of irritation, undoubtedly in the process of drinking away the night's profits while laying the groundwork for an easy lay after closing.

Joey held up two fingers and simply said, "two shots of whiskey and an Old Style." Then turned away and pulled the evidence envelope from inside his Towncraft jacket setting it down on the bar top in front of him.

He was going to put Ginny behind him—at least for a few hours—and focus on this damn case. If it took a couple stiff drinks to make it happen...so be it. Wouldn't be the first time.

As the bartender walked over with his drinks, Joey noticed he was wearing a red sweat-stained game day give-away version of a Washington Senators baseball cap. Joey couldn't resist...

"How 'bout them Senators?"

The barkeep abruptly turned and walked away leaving Joey with his drinks and the simple yet effectively abrasive, "Those mutha fuckas." The Senators franchise had abruptly moved to Texas over the winter. Hell, they weren't even called the Senators anymore...they were the Rangers. An appropriate response and no doubt the one Joey was poking around for.

He grabbed one of the shot glasses—probably Jim Beam—tossed it back faster than a hammer to a nail and then chased it with a big swig of beer…squinting his eyes the whole time before quickly smacking the tabletop for release. He pulled the papers out of the envelope and spread them out on the counter. There were the three police reports and four photos of the Jenner incident along with two separate but detailed toxicology reports—one for Bard and one for Brenneman—along with the results of the GPR test on both Bard and the weapon, itself.

The photos told him everything he already knew…and then some. There was one picture that gave Joey the kind of reaction you get after eating a lemon—bitter…or was that the Beam? He had seen hundreds of gruesome deaths firsthand, but they had always been nameless victims with sad silent backstories. But this…this was someone he knew. Someone who was just trying to help him out. He couldn't say he liked the kid—barely knew him—but Jenner *was* likable. To think Joey dodged all sorts of trouble in his twenty years and this kid gets his reward—so to speak—with barely a year under his belt. Stuck between two immovable objects with no place to go but the next plane.

Joey grabbed the photo, tilting it slightly to get the glare off. He shook his head… "What a shit storm" was all he could say.

The bartender took a break from chatting up the skanky hag down the bar and came over to grab the empties…not missing a chance to sneak a peek at the photo Joey had tilted in his direction. "Jeeesus. What the hell happened to him?

Joey turned the photo away and then with a glare that would undoubtedly make his point. "About five tons of metal happened to him. Now, fuck off." The skinny rat of a bartender got the message and walked off as Joey set the pic down again.

To Joey, it was beyond the pale. Right there…in broad daylight…smashed between the front bumper of a Pinto and the iron monolith of a dumpster. You just couldn't make this shit up. Jenner's body bent over perfectly just above the waist…lower body obscured by the front of the car…upper torso laying facedown perfectly flat against the hood. The kid's face was turned straight towards Joey...eyes closed...relaxed. If you didn't know any better, you might think he was asleep. Until, that is, you saw a massive immovable dumpster attached to his lower back like a tumor and the pool of blood balancing on the hood just beneath Jenner's mouth.

He grabbed the other photo—a close-up showing a pistol lightly pinned between the front hood and Jenner's lifeless right hand. The weapon looked old...certainly not American made. The way it was placed in his hand one could surmise that maybe the Brenneman girl thought he was dangerous. Maybe she just freaked out, and it was all just an overreaction, but of course, she was blacked out and remembers nothing. Too bad for her.

He glanced over the crime scene notes. The witness and suspects interviews, the Medical Eval, then the evidence summary. At the top of the list...right below the Pinto description was the mention of that gun trapped in Jenner's hand. It was listed as a *Leather-gripped 9mm German made Luger P-09, World War II era.* According to the notes, attached to the front of the narrow barrel was a small cylinder—described as *two inches in length and slightly larger than the width of the barrel. CZ Suppressor* was noted in the evidence summary followed by the handwritten notation in parentheses *silencer.* While the weapon was no doubt soiled from lying in the moist contaminated bottom of the dumpster, they were able to pick up contaminated residue of gunpowder... *evidence suggests the handgun was fired recently...very likely discharging a plated or jacketed 9mm.* The same bullet found lodged in Mr. Schneider's skull but...no fingerprints.

He flipped over to the Bard file and scanned down to the GPR report...*no detected residue on either of suspect's hands. Both right and left-handed sleeves of grey down winter coat showed minute traces of GPR. Blue woolen gloves indicate heavy and fresh concentrate of GPR.* The dorm room was exceptionally clean when Joey first arrived, but he did make note in his report of the winter garb hi-lighted in the

GPR summary…both items laying on the floor next to the deceased. Those clothes were literally the only thing that seemed out of place, and they provided the scientific proof that this girl…this strangely benign young lady…was guilty as hell. But why?

In one deft move, Joey slid the GPR report aside while downing the second shot of Beam…this time not wincing in the least. Chuck was done, and The Grease was back on stammering about some White House muckety-mucks being dragged into court for some burglary.

"Glad I'm *Homicide*…not *Robbery*," mumbling only to himself. Certainly, wasn't talking to greasy bartender boy.

He pulled out the Tox report to try and make sense of that jumbled mess. These reports were always a bit of a beating for Joey. Too many scientific words—most of which he couldn't even pronounce. Much of the time he would simply be looking for a blood alcohol level that would indicate impairment—most common in crimes of passion or in vehicular manslaughter cases. Positive tests for drugs like cocaine, amphetamines, or barbiturates were usually tied to drug deals or robberies…or suicides. If any of those contaminates showed up in the suspect's blood work, you could count on the accused's attorney using this data to substantiate a defense of temporary insanity. The higher the concentrate…the greater the likelihood that the accused would get a reduced sentence or possibly a stint in a psych ward for a few years. Beats life in the state pen.

The Tox Report was broken down into four columns. The name of the *Drug* that is being tested…the *Range* necessary for impairment…the *Actual Reading* of the contaminant and finally the *Result*, *Negative* or *Positive* for impairment.

But as Joey scanned down the list of drug test results for the Bard girl, next to each line-item the word *negative* was defiantly listed. From the beginning, Joey never took the Bard girl as any type of hippie drug head but seeing her bloodwork clean of all illegal narcotics had put a pretty big hole in his *jilted lover-drown my sorrows* theory. Kind of hard to OD on barbiturates if you didn't have any in your system.

He skipped the Bard summary notes at the bottom and then flipped over to the Brenneman results. In this case, nine of the ten narcotics tests run also indicated *negative*. Only *THC –Marijuana* gave a positive reading. This hardly surprised Joey, the girl claimed she was out of it, and if pressed, she did seem like the type who had rolled a joint or two in her day. Trouble is the report showed an almost negligible reading…a meager *0.05 mg/g* out of a possible range of *0.01—1.35mg.* The girl may have taken a quick hit that morning, but it was far more likely a reading that low was indicative of someone who still had remnants in the bloodstream from days ago…not hours. Hardly enough to explain her blackout.

Below the line item listing of each tested drugs was a category entitled *Miscellaneous* followed by a summary notation section completed by the Lab tech…in this case *Richard Gestner—Pharmacological Chemist- District 8 Criminal Lab.* Up to now, both Tox Reports gave him nothing to work with…but it was here in the usually vacant *Misc.* Section that Joey finally saw something that peeked his interest level.

It simply said:

S01FA02 Scopolamine, 0.01–0.06mg, 0.11mg, Positive.

Before even reading the chemist notes a confused and stuttered "Sco-po-la-mine. What the fuck is that?" escaped from his mouth. Joey certainly didn't know, but good ol' Gestner did. Because included in the summary notes was a rather detailed description of this drug that he'd never heard of and certainly couldn't pronounce.

It read: *Subject tested for contamination of common illegal narcotics in addition to alcohol. Subject tested negative for all categories except TCH which showed a reading at the lowest range of impairment. Only other notable contaminant revealed was scopolamine, which showed a reading at nearly double the tolerable range.*

Followed by a summary of the drug's cause and effect detail: **Scopolamine (S01FA02) is traditionally used for motion sickness and works by blocking some of the effects of* *acetylcholine. It can best be described as a numbing agent for the central nervous system. Side effects can include fever, confusion, lethargy, hallucinations, and constipation. Severe contamination can lead to seizures, dyshidrosis, (inability for the body to cool itself), lack of gastro mobility, and inflammation. Overdose is rare.'*

His heart raced as he flipped back over to the Bard report quickly scanning down to the summary notes he so willingly dismissed earlier. And there it was…the seemingly innocuous reference of scopolamine with an almost identical summary of its cause and effect. Only this time…for the now deceased Bard girl…the blood absorption rate was listed at 0.25…over four times the amount humanly tolerable. Joey Wisdom set the papers down and then leaned back on his stool, now deaf to the droning radio and the muddled chaos in the bar. He bit his lower lip while darting his eyes about in flustered thought. The Bard and Brenneman girls both showing toxic levels of some drug he never heard of called scopolamine. And what about those OD cases from '68? His mind clearly spinning. Then the thought of that dead girl from the Potomac River a few years back came to the forefront re-affirming the now obvious similarities of each of the girls: All Georgetown students, four dead, one in the hospital…and each showed virtually identically strange bodily conditions—fevered-red skin and distended torso and upper extremities.

As he sat there in astonished isolation, the only thing that came from his lips was the same question he benignly asked a few moments ago…

"What the fuck is scopolamine?" Only this time he had no trouble pronouncing it.

Chapter Fifty-Two

Georgetown—32nd Street

Thursday, December 21st–9:45 a.m.

"Goddam reporters," Sarah Schneider yelled from upstairs. "Just don't answer it." She had had about all she could take.

Her mother-in-law, domineering in a classic blue-blood sort of way, ignored her pleas. "I'll handle it." She walked from the back family-room to answer the kitchen phone. Her son's death had made her angry more than anything else. She somehow felt, as all mother-in-law seem to do, that in some strange, illogical way, this was all Sarah's fault. It made no sense really, but she couldn't shake the thought.

Just as she reached the kitchen, Sarah called out "It's going to be a reporter...don't tell them *anything*." No phone call was going to bring back her husband, and no reporter was going to feel the emptiness she felt. Quite the opposite. They were frothing at the bit...full of prodding disrespectful energy.

Who could blame her bitterness anyway? It had been five

days since her husband was murdered, and the longer it took Wisdom to get traction the more the news media slobbered over her own personal disaster. With nothing concrete to go on, they were free to make up their own interpretations—with the appropriate disclaimers, of course. One reporter was insinuating daily in each of his bylines that there may be a connection to the Bard girl's death and that of her husband's...practically thrusting the theory of an inappropriate relationship between the two into prominence. This, a storyline her mother-in-law seemed pre-occupied with, was more than she could handle. The venom in which they attacked the story of her husband's death was tantamount to a daily barrage of emotional assault. She could barely take it anymore. If only Wisdom was working as hard.

The phone rang a fourth time before it was picked up. A firm and formal "Schneider residence," was offered up.

"Uh...yes, Ma'am...this is uh, Detective Wisdom, D.C. Homicide. Is this Sarah Schneider?"

"No...it is not. I am David's mother...if you haven't brought us any developments, then she doesn't want to talk to you."

Wisdom, clearly caught off guard by the stern sentry manning the phone, backtracked a bit. "Yes Ma'am...I apologize for the disruption. I do have a couple items to run by your daughter-in-law. Is she available?"

"I suppose so..." She paused, toying with the idea of just putting the phone down...or, simply telling this detective exactly what she wanted to tell him. And then she did exactly that. "Look, Mr. Wisdom..." She conveniently dismissed the Detective title. "...you better hurry and solve my son's murder and put that scumbag...whoever the hell he is...at the end of a long rope."

This not being Wisdom's first go around with a bereaved family member he offered up what all good cops do in this circumstance...condolences. "Yes, ma'am. I am truly very sorry for your loss. Rest assured, Mrs. Schneider, we are doing the best we can.

"You damn-well better be." She then followed it with a

simple but tauntingly defiant, "And my name is not Schneider." An obvious clunk of the phone hitting the counter as the increasingly louder sound of footsteps made their determined way to the phone. In the background, Wisdom could hear the two women's curt exchange. "Who is it, Cynthia?"

"That damn cop."

Sarah quickly glared at her mother-in-law as she picked the phone off the counter and with its long cord walked it determinedly into the nearby laundry room closing the door behind her. "Yes, Detective…this is Sarah. What is it?"

It had only been a few days, but Wisdom had gotten used to Sarah Schneider's rightfully irritable demeanor. Shockingly, it was a nice respite from the mother-in-law…whatever her name was. "Yes, ma'am…we have been following up on some loose ends, and I wanted to run something by you."

"What is it?"

"Well, it is a bit of a longshot—I doubt it will make a difference but…"

"Detective…" Clearly exasperated. "What is it?"

"Okay, do you keep medicine in the house for motion sickness?"

"What? What do you mean?"

"You see, we received bloodwork back on both Georgetown girls and each tested positive for a drug called scopolamine…it is used for motion sickness."

"So?"

"Well, according to the bloodwork, each girl had heavy…potentially lethal doses in their system—which is odd since their level of toxicity serves no practical purpose. According to my lab guys…it's not even recreational."

"The answer is no."

"Are you sure? You might know it better as Dramamine or…uh…Bonine."

"I said the answer is no." Clearly agitated, she pivoted into an accusatory tone. "Are you suggesting my husband doped these girls. Go to hell, Wisdom."

"No, no…loose ends. Checked their dorm rooms, and they don't have any prescriptions for anything like that. Just trying to nail down its origin. It's early, but our coroner believes it may have contributed to the Bard girl's death."

"You know detective…I could give a shit how that girl died. I just want to know who killed my husband."

Wisdom knew who *probably* killed her husband, but the last person he was going to tell was the widow who was getting a dozen press calls a day. Couldn't be trusted to keep her mouth shut, or for that matter, her mother-in-law's mouth. So, he gave the standard practiced reply. "I understand. We are doing the best we can. I will let you know when we have something more definitive. One more question, though. Curious… Your mother-in-law…?"

Clearly irritated "What about her?"

"She said her name isn't Schneider."

"So?"

"Just unusual, is all—your husband's mother. I called her Schneider. I think I offended her."

"That's easy to do…for both of us."

Wisdom couldn't help but appreciate the less than nuanced dig. He stifled a small snicker and went on. "Oh, did she remarry or something?"

"No. Widowed."

"So why does she have a…"

"…Different last name? My husband changed his last name in college…before we got married. Too much Beltway drama with his real last name."

And for no other reason but his own lame and awkward attempt at comedy, Wisdom asked, "What name is that, Agnew?"

"Really? Very funny. No, not Agnew. You're just a damn cop, you wouldn't know anyway. It's Gottlieb. Is this actually important?"

Wisdom briefly froze before finally asking her to confirm what he thought he just heard—a name he most certainly did recognize. "Gottlieb?"

"Yes, Gottlieb. Look, if there is nothing else, I gotta go."

Wisdom heard an abrupt click followed by a dial tone. He reached into his back pocket opened his notepad, flipping back a few pages to the front where the notes from his Pentagon visit were documented.

There it was...plain as day. *Gottlieb*... Poeltz's former boss. He stood there...dumbfounded. Pointless information at that time...but now...what the hell does this have to do with anything?

"Ridiculous," was all that came from his mouth.

And now, quite by accident...from nothing more than simply curiosity, he finally had something to sink his teeth into. He'd been looking for a good excuse to visit that cantankerous old professor again. Now he had one.

Chapter Fifty-Three

Dupont Circle—Theodore's

Thursday, December 21st–10:30 a.m.

Call it self-imposed exile…or better yet…vacation. Hell, call it whatever you want, but Alfred Poeltz was leaving, and it couldn't have happened any sooner.

After abruptly discarding Jonathan at Sauf Haus the night before, he came home to the same quiet isolation that had tormented him all these years. His wife had not been his wife. His son was not his son. His business was not his business. Hell, even his professorship had been arranged. He'd had almost no direct impact on his own life, and he certainly had no one who truly understood his neutered solitude. Even Jonathan, his accidental accomplice, couldn't completely relate.

The only time he felt he was contributing anything was during his time with Gottlieb and MKUltra, but even that godforsaken program was a rabbit's hole of ineptitude. Every advancement he made—all of which were for causes he did not subscribe to—was met with resistance or derided as useless. Any calculable progress was accomplished on his own...in secrecy...away from Gottlieb. His payback for decades of indentured service was isolation and the ever-watchful forces that made sure his isolation remained intact.

But *redemption* can be a very powerful force, and in that silent solitude, he set about a seemingly interminable plan to not only prove his thirty-year-old theory but also pay back the bastards who would not embrace it. The same bastards who hijacked his life but not his will. And now...the plan was a fait accompli. Sure, he left Jonathan to tie up the loose-ends, but what he had accomplished would be talked about and studied for decades. If only they knew where to start.

As soon as Wisdom checked his notes for *that* name, he called her back. It took just seconds. There it was...plain as day. Just below his cryptic description of Poeltz was the name *Gottlieb* followed by *Boss* and then the quizzical series of traditionally governmental three-letter acronyms, *HSA, CIG, CIA*...followed quickly by a darkly scrawled question mark.

There were too many acronym-labeled agencies in the District. He had a hard time keeping track of who's who and what's what. What was meant to be a convenient way to label the litany of government departments ended up being a blur of letters to Wisdom. He had no idea what the HSA or CIG was...nor should he...but he certainly knew the CIA. It had raised an eyebrow when he visited Sniffen at the Pentagon, but really, it was nothing more than an irrelevant side note. Now? Now it was a critical component to an otherwise very confusing series of violent acts. Frankly, the optics were not good. Having the CIA involved in anything...let alone a murder...just brought a more nefarious element to the case. Even if it *seemed* incidental to the events...there was nothing ancillary about it. The CIA was never anywhere by accident.

And so, he called her right back and got the story as best as she could recount it:

Her husband was born David Stuart Gottlieb. His father had the same name—though he went by Stuart and the son went by David. It was common and indisputable knowledge that the elder had worked as part of the intelligence arm of the government for decades...since World War II, at least that is what David told her.

Though neither he nor his father ever spoke of the work he did, it was assumed and widely rumored within the Beltway scuttlebutt crowd that Stuart Gottlieb oversaw Black Ops for the government—the secret lair of the Intelligence agencies. CIA to be most specific. While no one talked of the work he may (or may not) have orchestrated there were random rumblings about assassinations, coups, moles, brain-washing...you name it, and though it was in hushed tones, it all seemed to circle back to David's father. D.C. craves to put a face on anything...especially its dark under-belly.

All just a part of David's life. The rumors. The whispers. Mostly, he was agnostic to it all...until that day he interviewed for a summer college internship with a big investment firm. It was that day when the reality of his family name came to fore. By the end of his freshman year at Georgetown, David was ranked near the top of his class...practically guaranteeing any summer internship, he desired. It also happened to be about the same time the movie *Manchurian Candidate* came out. It was a movie about the brain-washing of a U.S. military officer as an unwitting assassin for an anti-American communist conspiracy.

While it had been several years since the heady days of McCarthyism, the authoritative impact of that oppressive government stance still lingered. To make matters worse, the nubile presidency of JFK was dealing with the Bay of Pigs disaster. At the time, the country's confidence in their government was at an all-time low. But it wasn't until the movie came out that the potentially damaging impact to David's future came front and center. No high-dollar firm was going to take a risk on the son of a well-placed government spook whose fingerprints were all over all sorts of nefarious government dealings.

It was a shock to David who had nothing but admiration for his father, but it was the father who provided the most logical solution. "Change your name, son. That's the best I can suggest." And so, he did—much to the chagrin of his mother. He also changed schools, "And get the hell out of D.C." he was told, and so, he transferred to Yale. He got on with his life putting all that D.C. government conspiracy nonsense behind him. He kind of enjoyed his new identity—reveled in the idea of being his own man.

"And that's pretty much it. We never really talked about it. Is this actually important?" she asked.

Wisdom shifted gears. "I discovered Poeltz may have worked for David's father?"

For a moment, there was no reply on the line, but then she blurted out with dismay… "You mean that young antique dealer?"

"No, no…the father…the old Georgetown Professor."

You're fucking kidding me?"

"I'm afraid I'm not." At the time, Wisdom paused wondering if he should tell her what was *actually* on his mind…that the old man not only may have worked for the CIA and David's father, but he also was very likely tutoring both the Bard and Brenneman girls—maybe even that girl from the Potomac River. To make matters worse, according to his Pentagon documents, he may still be working for the government. But he didn't tell her. "Another question. I know Mr. Gottlieb passed away a few years ago. What happened to him?"

Clearly flustered by this peculiar news, it took a moment to catch up. Almost stuttering, she offered up a distracted "Oh…uh… well, uh" before getting to the point. "Yeah, uh, back in '69, I think. He was on his daily walk by the canal and collapsed. Heart attack—died almost instantly."

"Heart attack?" His voice held just a touch of skepticism.

"That's what they said." Long ago resigned to accepting the official government press release on the matter. At the time, her husband David raised his eyebrows at the conclusion, but his mother would have none of it. She knew full well the ways of the world her husband lived in, even if David didn't.

Dr. Alfred Poeltz woke that morning with a renewed sense of purpose. Sure, he could've chosen to sit there in that battered old house for the next umpteenth years peddling battered old furniture. Instead, he preferred to choose his own path…for a change. He might truly fade into oblivion. Hell, he'd been in oblivion for decades. But now, he would disappear as an irrelevant cog…on his own terms. Truth was, he had a self-preservation instinct that had always served him well.

So, he began his morning as he always did: a pre-breakfast pond-side cigar. In that crisp morning's dawn, he tucked himself inside layers of his disheveled bathrobe and his son's winter parka and pulled on what he believed would be his last morning smoke…at least in this place. The previous day, he had visited the bank and had opened an account for Jonathan…moving most of his savings into the lad's name…withdrawing the meager remains for himself. He would need money…if for no other reason than to get out of town. To get settled.

He had packed up two travel cases. One full of clothes. Just the basics. Clothes, toiletries. That sort of thing. The other case, a much smaller one, was filled with…well, there was really no other way to say it…filled with remnants of his life. But, where most people might pack fond memoirs in the form of family photos or quirky keepsakes, Alfred chose instead to cling to the bitter memories of the farcical life he was forced to live. Almost a mocking reminder to get as far away from this cold, cold world as he could.

Inside were what seemed to be mostly irrelevant items. A tattered copy of the German classic, *The Sorrows of Young Werther*. A set of rusty old skeleton keys. Some faded newspaper clippings. Each of these represented the silent struggle that he fought: The keys were to the attic where he hid that battered old journal full of his secret science. The book, one he must have read a hundred times, provided a taunting escape to the Germany of old and the life he could never have. The clippings referenced items as old as the war and as recent as the death of Schneider. There were other items, too but none of them brought even the slightest of grins to his face. None, but one. Tucked beneath the tattered book and papers was a faded polaroid of Jonathan as a young boy sitting on a borrowed 10-Speed. Maroon Toughskin jeans, striped crew shirt, and a lopsided grin to go along with a crooked towhead haircut. He was the son he never had. But even the boy's photo brought its own level of angst. His childhood had been stolen, his future undoubtedly stunted, and while it wasn't all Alfred's fault, for some reason, he felt responsible. Where had the boy actually come from? Alfred had never even bothered to ask.

Wisdom didn't care much for the government in general. Hell, it was kind of a byproduct of the times. Most people didn't. But here he was, unfolding clue after clue and the stench of the government—or at least the CIA—was sitting right in front of him...concealed beneath name changes and cover jobs. How deep did all this go? Was it a conspiracy or simply a series of random rogue events?

The government, certainly wasn't going to be of any help anyway. Neither were Gottlieb...or David...or Bard and most likely not Brenneman. No. She was just north of worthless. There was really only one person who could shine light on this mess. The question was, would he? Doubtful, but Wisdom didn't care. He had been hoping for a chance to make a run at the old man anyway...if for no other reason than he enjoyed the competition and tension that came with it. From the get-go, Poeltz had seemed inappropriately combative, setting Wisdom back on his heels.

But now Poeltz was like a piñata hanging from a rickety tree limb...waiting to be hit with a hard cross, spilling out truths like candy to the ground. Wisdom couldn't wait to be the one to take that swing...and pick up the pieces.

Though it was normal procedure, he was so anxious to get over to Dupont Circle that he didn't even register his schedule with the Desk Clerk or Frankel, for that matter. He simply burst out of the District 2 front door, leaving almost everything but his sidearm and his smokes behind. No jacket...no notes. Nothing but his mind and his wit.

He climbed into the Dart, and in seemingly one smooth motion, lit up a Winston, fired up the engine, turned off the ever-present 8-track, and then peeled out towards Mass Avenue. Straight to the professor's. In ten minutes, he would be there. In ten minutes, he'd have the old man right where he wanted him...if he was still there.

Dr. Alfred Poeltz longed for that old German countryside. Perfectly manicured as if by God himself. The hills rolled on and on, colored in the lushness that only deep-green can provide, surrounded by neat patches of forest. There were farms dotted about with precisely tilled fields separated only by lonely solitary strips of roadway. It was a place he frequented many times as a young boy...and more times than he could count in his own longing mind as an adult.

He wanted to return. Return home to those graceful highlands and fields of solitude, but that was no longer possible. After the war, his motherland had been surgically divided in half as the Soviets and Americans battled for the soul of the people and the soul of Europe. One half—The East—was the stepbrother of Stalin. For them, an easy transition from the days of the Third Reich. The other half— The West—was a petri dish for democracy in a land that had never warmed to the idea. It was a volatile place and one not too welcoming to old Nazi-era doctors.

And so, he found the next best place he could think of in a country he was now compelled to call home—the swelling countryside of Montana. Magazine pictures of a land a full country away made him long for his past. He would be far away from the clamor of the Beltway and far away from the probing eyes of...*those people*...the unseen.

He would find a little cottage to let, hopefully tucked in a field of reminiscent green, strategically placed right next to some lonesome little stream. He would try to get some light work. Maybe teach at a high school or maybe even the local college. He would let the breeze blow him whichever way it wanted. He simply wanted to blend in...and then disappear. Anything would be better than this place.

He had grabbed his last greasy made-to-order breakfast at Sauf Haus recalling the conversation he had with Jonathan the night before with just the slightest tinge of guilt. It was a lot to put on him, but in reality, the boy had his own issues to settle. While his father's life had been a charade, the boy's castrated existence had been both a mystery *and* a charade. Maybe those next steps, as distasteful as they were, would provide their own sense of cleansing. Their own redemption.

And so, Alfred Poeltz, having liberated Jonathan while vanquishing his so-called life, would plan to visit the local library in Bozeman and make a habit of glancing through the late-arriving D.C. newspapers, looking for references and evidence to a closed circle—a story that needed to end.

His train departed from Union Station at 2 p.m. It would be a two-day journey, so he booked a sleeper cabin for the duration. He would welcome the privacy if not the wait. Waiting, he was tired of.

It was just after noon when he had gone around locking up the old house and turning down all the lights inside. The cluttered main floor—loaded down with the heaviness of old desks, bureaus, and armoires—was dark on its own accord, but now with only the filtered daylight of a cloudy day seeping its way through those big wood-framed glass front doors, the place produced an even more ominous air.

This place and its sterling reputation in the antique world would be waiting for Jonathan. If he owed Gottlieb and his minions anything, it was gratitude for making sure Theodore's was more than pretense. If Jonathan played his cards right, it could be all his. At best, he could continue to man the store. The unwitting orphan, an innocent side story—nothing more. At worst, he would be in jail. The odds were likely somewhere in the middle.

Alfred Poeltz poured an extra-large bowl of kibble for Bruno and walked over to one of the timeworn Queen Anne chairs—retail, $800—sitting idly near the front entrance. As usual, the cat was at his heels. He bent down, placing the bowl at his feet and then dropped his tired body into the depleted cushion. He would wait here, comforted by the presence of his near-constant companion and the muted sunlight that slipped through those big glass doors. He would wait here until his old Croton hit 1 p.m. then ring up a taxi to deliver him to Union Station—deliver him to the freedom he so rightly earned.

He let out a tired sigh then grabbed just one more R & J from his breast pocket, lighting it up with a series of practiced repetitive puffs, sending the smoke hanging defiantly in the stale air. It may have taken almost thirty-years, but now the end was so near he could literally feel the heavy cloak of oppression falling from his shoulders. It was only a matter of time.

Little did he know.

As it turned out, it really did take ten minutes. Maybe it was the lighter than normal traffic or maybe it was the fact that Wisdom pretty much ran every light on the way there. He turned onto P and much like he did last time, forced the Dart up onto the curb…this time more in defiance of the old man's state of comfort than out of any real need for convenience. He took a quick look up at the store's front. Dark and empty. It was a bit before 1 p.m., but the place had more of an *Out of Business* feel than a *Back After Lunch* vibe.

Wisdom flipped the dash-top police light on—its rolling red flashing light out of synch with the stately ambiance of the neighborhood. Even if Poeltz was not here, he wanted the neighbors to know who *was* here. At the very least, it might keep the old man in check.

He crushed out his smoke in the stub-laden car ashtray and cracked open the door, stepping out into the brisk midday air. Though it had warmed a bit, the sun struggled to make its presence felt through the thick winter clouds. And then, as he made his way up the path he realized for the first time that he had left the coat back at the District house.

Stepping up on the store's front porch, he eased his right hand to his hip—finding comfort in the confirmation that at least he had not left his service revolver behind. It was strange. He didn't trust the guy at all. But, come on, the man was old. Why did he feel the need to be careful? Looking through the glass entryway, he surprisingly laid his eyes on the very person he came for. Oddly stoic, Poeltz sat there, cat by his side, in the relative obscurity of the darkened foyer behind a thin veil of cigar smoke, the midday's murky gloom the only faint source of light.

He paused, squinting tightly to confirm what he saw. The man was so still, it was almost as if the old professor had been waiting for him.

He may be an old man, but the exhilaration he had been feeling as he sat there waiting was like that of a teenager on his first date—plenty of nervous energy. It was awkward, but for the first time in a long time, he felt alive...until, that is, he heard the familiar thump and creak of an old car stopping on his curb. Poeltz knew right away.

That obstinate cop was back. Sitting there in stunned silence—unable to move—he forced out a thick burst of smoke as if it might provide some sort of refuge, worthless though it was.

As the cop made his way up the front steps, Poeltz glanced at his watch. His train left in an hour. This was exceptionally bad timing.

Wisdom slowly walked right up to the front door cupping both hands by his eyes and pressing them firmly against the glass. Maybe he had mistaken what he saw…that of a solitary figure sitting stoically alone in a dark room staring—or was that glaring—right at him…or through him. He couldn't tell.

He knocked once—pointless though it seemed—expecting the professor to wave him in or…even better…get up and at least portend a welcome. But no…there was zero movement. It was as if Poeltz was stuck in some stunted stroke-like state. The only proof of his viability was the still smoldering cigar sitting idly in the old man's hand. It hadn't lit itself, and it surely didn't smoke itself, either.

Four damn days and one hour. All he needed was just one more fucking hour. He stared at the cop through that murky glass and wondered to himself what kind of angle he'd take with the unwanted guest. The cop had a thing about him that he appreciated—irritably patient, if there was such a thing. It was the kind of trait that one could only acquire after years of practice. This was no excitable, distractible rookie. If Alfred didn't have a selfish interest in his own future—like catching that train and getting the hell out of town—then he probably would consider the stubborn pest at his door an admirable challenge.

He glared at the frumpy silhouetted creature peering through the glass…the pest stared back…their eyes in lock-step. For some reason, he enjoyed this pause as if waiting gave Alfred at least one more sliver of control.

Once more, the cop raised a balled-up fist for another almost irrelevant knock. In that split-second, Alfred simultaneously stood up…slowly, of course. After glancing briefly at Bruno—as if for some kind of silent support—he walked to the door, opening it no wider than his own face.

"You know, it's open?"

"You don't look very open, Professor."

"It's Doctor…. The store is closed…the door is open.

What can I do for you?"

Wisdom glanced past Poeltz into the darkened storefront. Sitting just steps behind the old man, lay the leering cat. Wisdom couldn't help but compare the two as if they were delivered from the same womb. Haughty and suspicious. Behind the cat were two small suitcases placed tightly next to each other. He looked back at Poeltz and with one raised eyebrow asked, "Going somewhere?"

"I was…." Then shifting gears. "Officer, you look a touch anxious—something wrong?"

Wisdom stifled an amused, "hmm." "It's Detective…. Dr. Poeltz, I feel like we have had this dance before. May I come in?"

"Indeed." As aggravating as it was, Poeltz appreciated Wisdom cutting to the chase. He pulled the door open, stepped back, and with a slow sweep of his arm, ushered the cop inside.

"Thank you." Wisdom stepped inside and looked about the main room of Theodore's and all its organized clutter. "You know, last time I was here, I didn't even think to ask. If I may…how did you come to be in the antique business?"

"How do you mean?"

"Well, you're a doctor and a professor and if memory serves you used to work for the Defense Department."

"Your point?"

"Just seems an odd transition, is all?

While waiting for an answer that wasn't coming, Wisdom worked his way around the room. "Do you mind?" as he slid his stubby fingertips across the intermittent bureau and table…idle dust pushed aside with each swipe.

Poeltz said nothing, just watched as the cop meandered through the rows of old furniture as if he was getting his bearings, flipping at price tags along the way. "Expensive."

"Well, depends on your perspective." It had only been a few moments, but Poeltz had already grown weary of the pace. What had initially seemed like a determined man, set in motion, now felt like someone simply biding his time. "Detective, what can I do for you. I have a train to catch."

Wisdom glanced again at those two bags…teasingly sitting idle behind the cat. "Yes, I guessed as much. Where to?"

"Visiting friends." Poeltz glanced at his watch—a nervous habit more than anything—then looked back up to Wisdom. "Can we reschedule this for later? I really must be leaving."

And then rather firmly, "I am afraid not." Wisdom looked about the main floor again and almost as an aside… "You said, I think, that I uh…looked anxious. Didn't realize I was so transparent."

"Well, you seemed a touch lively, is all."

"I would say more determined than anything else."

"If you are so anxious…or determined as you said, why don't you please inform me of the meaning of your visit?" His own impatience betraying his confidence… "So we can, you know, get on with it."

Wisdom turned back towards Poeltz and walked toward the man who still stood isolated by the front door. "Professor, we've had some developments on the Bard girl."

Poeltz saw this coming…he had been watching the Althage reports and reading the morning papers religiously, consuming the information as if it were an elixir. It was the lack of details that had him most concerned. If it all worked the way he had planned, they would have quickly surmised murder-suicide and closed the books just as quickly as they did a few years ago with the Rubin girl. Surely, they had bigger fish to fry.

But no. Specifics were lacking, meaning they weren't sure exactly what had happened to Schneider…or if they did know, they weren't saying. The Jenner death only added to the confusion. In hindsight, that was probably a mistake. Now, the detective was back to pick at him like a scab…until he bled. Only this time, he saw Wisdom's intentions as clear as day, the moment he first caught his determined expression, filtered through cigar smoke and that old door's wavy glass.

"Bard? You told me before that the poor girl overdosed."

"Well, she did overdose but not in a typical fashion."

Wisdom looked around the room. He did not want to interrogate the man standing in the front foyer of his cluttered store. It seemed harried. "Is there somewhere we can sit. I have a few things that I'd like to ask you about. Things you might be able to help us with." ...saying *us* as if there was a team on the case...and there wasn't.

Impatiently, Poeltz had stood by the opened front door as if the mere sight of the opening might tempt the cop to leave. It didn't. And so, Poeltz firmly pushed the door back into its framing. He turned back toward Wisdom and with nary a glance started making his way to the back of the store. "I suppose so...follow me to the kitchen."

Wisdom moved through the maze of stately furniture pieces pausing briefly at a glassed encased tabletop display. Inside were a series of what were, Wisdom could only surmise, antique pistols. "Professor, that's quite a collection. You got an armory over here."

Looking back, Poeltz paused at the swinging kitchen door. "Don't worry Detective, they're not in working order. All their firing pins have been removed. Even so, most would not be safe to fire anyway."

Wisdom took one last glance, noticing what looked to be empty spaces where three pistols once sat. Dusty outlines like body chalk at a crime scene...evidence of their recent removal. He walked up behind Poeltz who had now pushed open the swinging door to reveal the familiarity of that poignantly well-lit kitchen. Maybe it was the unfettered windows or the white décor, but it served as an enlightening escape from the cluttered gloom of the storefront. "You know, looks like you're missing a couple pieces. Uh, guns."

"Sold them" and then with a feigned politeness that bordered on transparent, "Come on in. Have a seat."

Poeltz pointed to a chair by the little metal-topped kitchen table. He then took a seat himself opposite Wisdom...something, in an act of defiance, he had bypassed last go around. "Please..." his frustration more than showing. "Can we just...let's have it, Wisdom. What do you have?"

Wisdom had always believed in being abrupt with

suspects…accusing them of a crime in almost a rushed way. He felt, as he had with the Mrs. Schneider, that the response you received—even if they were lies—could be very telling. Wisdom sat down…looked straight into the irritably tired eyes of the old professor. "So Professor, why did you have David Schneider murdered?" It was an almost identical question to the one he asked the Schneider lady, but this time he hoped it produced different results.

To Poeltz, it was an inevitable question, though one he hadn't expected so soon. He couldn't help but be impressed by the bravado. But, he didn't move a muscle, his eyes remaining equally fixed on the unkempt cop as if it were some sort of unspoken battle between the two. And then, with his traditional arrogance that had thus far escaped him, let out a sly smile. "You amuse me, Wisdom. Is that what you think? I'm a retired professor of Psychology that runs an antique store. I'm seventy-two, for the good lord's sake. Do you really believe I would kill that man? Any man?"

If the guy sitting across from him was ten years younger, Wisdom would already have his hand on the revolver. Hell, he'd probably already have him arrested and given him those damned Miranda rights. "Let me just say this…I've seen everything…and for every reason imaginable. Long ago, I learned not to exclude anyone from anything…no matter how ridiculous it would seem."

"You have quite a life. How do you sleep at night?"

Wisdom laughed. "Alcohol."

Poeltz, tittered briefly then slid back in his chair. "Okay, Detective, I'll bite. What for? Why would I kill…", pausing briefly as he shrugged his slumped shoulders while pointing back to himself, "Better still, how would *I* kill that man?"

"I never said you killed him."

"Well then, you have me perplexed."

Shifting gears quickly, "I know…that you know…that David Schneider's father is Stuart Gottlieb. I also know that Gottlieb was your superior at the DOD. Our investigation has discovered that the Bard girl was, in fact, the shooter…the killer…and, as you already admitted, she was also your student."

"What are you driving at, sir. I have many students."

"No doubt." And then with blatant sarcasm, "You mean, like the Brenneman girl?"

"Who? Look, I've had many, many students…" as if the pure number of former students would somehow dilute the possible connection. "And for that matter, hundreds of people worked for that man. So what?" his contempt now clearly showing. "Surely, you haven't pinned your case on old employee records and eighteen-year-olds?"

And once again, out of left field. "Tell me about scopolamine."

Nothing…literally nothing leaked from the old man. Was his stoicism belying his guilt or quite the opposite? Poeltz now felt the noose tightening, and he had to decide if he would simply continue the 'pompous-deny' strategy or instead embrace the brilliant truth of it all. He chose the latter…but with a twist…and at the pace of his choosing.

"Scopolamine…such a big word for such a…uh… simple man. Just asking tells me all I need to know. I am quite sure you know very well what scopolamine is. What you probably have no clue of is how beneficial it can be in my line of work."

"Oh…and what line of work is that? Murder?"

Poeltz appreciated the direct and disdainful world in which Wisdom liked to operate, but he wouldn't capitulate. Instead, he let out a haughty laugh. "Wisdom, I'm seventy-two." Repeating his age for effect. "I don't stun easily. You *are* amusing, though."

Wisdom, as was his practice, let the suspect do as much talking as possible, so he said nothing…just waited until Poeltz continued.

"Education, my good man. Education is my line of work. Scopolamine, when used in the proper dosage breeds susceptibility…which tends to enhance retention. Quite useful when it comes to learning, don't you think?"

"I'll take your word for it, Professor. So, you're saying you use this in your tutoring?"

"Quite right—in combination with the hypnosis therapy," which wasn't true on any level. He had never used it in tutoring. Hypnosis, yes. Scopolamine, no. That came later…when needed…and for other reasons. But Wisdom didn't need to know about that.

"So, it wouldn't surprise you that the Bard girl had scopolamine in her system?"

"No"

"Lethal doses of scopolamine?"

"Well, I can't say that."

"Can't or won't?"

Amused by what was clearly a rhetorically familiar question, Poeltz shifted gears. "Wisdom, I provide scopolamine treatment to my students at their request. What they choose to do with it on their own time is up to them…though, I would hardly suggest ingesting a large dose purely for the amusement of it all."

"Really? Why is that?"

"It doesn't provide any sort of enlightened state like maybe LSD can provide…no buzz or high, like say uh, cocaine or marijuana."

"Well, educate me. What does it do, then?"

"Detective, surely you have lab technicians that can tell you all this?"

"Oh, I do, but…you are sitting right in front of me. Why pass up the opportunity?"

Wisdom drifted to silence and just waited, for several long seconds it seemed, until finally. "Small doses, the kind you get at a pharmacy, are used for motion sickness. Larger doses are…well, they're my specialty. A certain amount will send the brain into a neutral and accepting state…but one that's hardly pleasurable…for it's neither a good nor a bad state."

At the right dose, this was most definitely true. But Poeltz left out one important item…while on the medication your memory would actually be void of any and all things. You would not recall your actions…anything you said or heard…and you would very likely not even utter a single word. When Poeltz said that you would be in a neutral and accepting state...you were, but *mindless* might be a better description. Scopolamine was hardly a tool for education. Far from it.

"As far as an overdose...I couldn't tell you what would happen."

This was most assuredly not true. It was Poeltz's aim that whomever he had ingest the scopolamine would effectively overdose and die. Taking a sufficiently large enough measure that, at the very least, would restrict the subject from recalling anything. But the coup de grâce of the calculated overdose, if all went to plan, would result in the subject succumbing to cardiac arrest. What happened to the Brenneman girl was an anomaly as she had—unfortunately—received proper medical treatment almost immediately after taking out Jenner. In his many case studies, Poeltz had learned that simple but heavy hydration would reverse the effects of the overdose. Brenneman was, as per protocol, put on substantial IV fluids upon her admission into George Washington Hospital. This was not expected.

"So, you administer the scopolamine...and..."

"Oh, hardly, Wisdom...the student will take it themselves on their own accord. I administer nothing."

"Okay, let's not mince words, Poeltz. They take it because you told them it would help them. Like it or not, if they are overdosing on your drug...the drug you're providing them...then that puts you in a pretty crappy position."

Poeltz had stepped right up to the edge of the rat trap and sniffed. He did not like the smell. He had put himself in a position as an accessory to a crime. He knew that much from watching *Mannix*, if not from Wisdom...and he didn't care.

"Wisdom, the drug is not illegal and if some clueless girl takes more than I prescribed and then dies...well then, I am sorry...but that is hardly my responsibility.

"So, anyone can get this at the pharmacy?"

"Don't be so naive Detective. No, you can't simply get a prescription for scopolamine at the dosage necessary for what I am talking about. The FDA is not going to approve the drug for what I use it for...for memory retention? Hardly."

"Well, then how do you obtain the prescription?"

"Detective, I have my ways."

"You have your ways?" with emphasis on *ways*...only Wisdom mimicked the word with the same heavy *vays* pronunciation that Poeltz had used.

The phrase itself was a gift on a platter, and it gave Wisdom the opening to dig further into the old man's past. Maybe it was the accent, the Defense position or his redacted past. Hell, even the fact that he was unmarried. It was all taunting. It may have been circumstantial, but that single phrase gave him the excuse he was looking for... "So very-German of you, Professor."

"What?"

"You're German, are you not?"

"Oh, please...what, because of my accent? That's all it took?

"Well?"

"Well...if that's true, then I suspect you probably aren't much of an admirer of mine."

"So far, not so much...but why would you say that?"

One Jim Palmer fastball deserved another so with contempt literally dripping off every word. "Because you're a Jew, of course."

Wisdom had never given his heredity much thought. Hell, when it came to religion...agnostic came to mind. But he got the point and it allowed him to poke further. "So? Would *Nazi* be an even better description?"

"Wisdom, you can take up my birthplace with the Department of Defense...they have been running my life for the better part of thirty years. But I wouldn't expect much from those people. It's a big black hole over there. I honestly wouldn't wish it on anyone."

"Well, you seem to be doing just fine."

"Sitting across the table from you...having you insult me...and my intelligence? Damn you."

Poeltz got up and walked toward the small escape of a kitchen window...looking out at the jumbled mess of a backyard, it's murky pool surrounded by looming and ominous stone figures. The whole scene was a metaphor of his life and he couldn't miss the irony. One damn hour from freedom. One damn hour. He knew his way out...hell, he knew it the moment he saw the cop on his stoop. He would feebly try a more benign route...it wouldn't work, he knew that. But if it did work, it would be better...for everyone.

"Are we quite through, Detective?"

"Hardly. Are you familiar with Miranda Rights?"

"No, I don't know what that is. And guess what. I don't care."

Wisdom had heard enough. He lifted his hand towards the chest pocket of his overworn and perennially wrinkled blue dress shirt for the folded-up and creased Miranda Rights cheat-sheet that he kept there. Only it wasn't there. Wisdom looked up at the tiny white tin chandelier light that hung so delicately above that little table and realized that the battered and worn crib notes that he so hated likely sat crammed inside that old Towncraft coat...back at the station. With Poeltz's back still facing him, he shook his head lightly and smiled. This would be more fun.

The old man was a cantankerous creature, but maybe he was right...maybe he had good reason to be. Wisdom could only wonder what had befallen this man. How did he come to this place? No doubt he was guilty of something. He could be arresting him for any number of crimes...accessory to murder might be tough, but trafficking and negligent homicide wouldn't be a problem. But there was something about him that left him wanting. More information. More answers. To Wisdom, waiting for it to all come out in trial—if it came out at all—was tantamount to one of those striptease acts over on Wisconsin. It always left you needing more...or worse, empty. No, this story was far from complete and Wisdom wasn't going to wait around to get his answers. He wanted to know now.

And so, he set his empty hand back on that cold metal table and returned to the one thing he truly didn't understand. "You know...Professor, you said that you have your ways of getting the drug... So, I guess I could assume you have some here...some scopolamine."

"Ah, Detective...curious, I see."

Wisdom said nothing.

"So, uh...would you like to see it?"

"If you would be so kind."

Poeltz moved across the small kitchen room, and as he breezed through the swinging door, he partially stifled a barely cryptic laugh. "All right, Detective. If you must... Wait here."

He most assuredly didn't trust the man, and so, as Poeltz made his way through the house, the sound of creaking wood flooring echoing his every step, Wisdom stood up and took a seat at the opposite side of the table...facing the still swaying kitchen door...holster unsnapped...hand firmly on the revolver. Just in case.

And then he wondered, had his curiosity gotten the best of him?

Little did he know...the die was now cast. The full story to be laid right in his lap. Everything he wanted to know...and more. Wisdom didn't realize it, but it was now *he* who had stepped right up next to the trap. The whole truth could now be told...or as Poeltz might say...the brilliant truth.

Chapter Fifty-Four

Dupont Circle—Theodore's

Thursday, December 21ˢᵗ–1:25 p.m.

Wisdom sat patiently wondering what he had gotten himself into. He had been dragging his tired body around this city for decades…his daily ritual comprised mostly of staring smack-dab in the face of death. Anguished and ugly death. When death happens unexpectedly—as is always the case with homicides—there is a torment of sorts to the body or their expression…or both. Most times, both. The Bard girl had that look…so did Schneider and Jenner. But he was numb to it all…or at least that is what he told himself.

Truthfully, he felt guilty. Guilty that he chose to ignore the brutal and sad way these nameless people's lives ended. Maybe blocking out the reality was simply his defense mechanism. But as he waited for Poeltz's return, Wisdom couldn't help but wonder what the old man's excuse was. If he was right about Poeltz, he not only had three people murdered but he seemed rather tactical and detached about it all. Did they deserve it? Not in any normal sense. Maybe the old man was simply tormented himself, and he took out his own anguish over his frustrated life on these false tangents of his oppression. Or maybe he was just plain crazy.

As the thump of steps and their accompanying creak grew louder and the professor's presence grew closer, Wisdom gripped the butt of his revolver tighter. He did not want to alarm the old man into silence, but he also didn't want to find himself facing the wrong end of someone else's gun without being prepared.

Suddenly there was silence in the steps. The door was now being pushed ever so slightly open, almost as if the unseen was intending to sneak up on someone…on Wisdom. He could see it all, though. Almost always saw what was coming next, and for him, it would be very hard to be fooled by such amateur trickery. But as Poeltz eased his tilted frame through the doorway, Wisdom could see that he did not return with one of those archaic pistols but rather a round silver container, small enough to sit in someone's hand.

Poeltz took his new seat opposite Wisdom. "You like that view better?

The detective's hand still rested lightly on the revolver's butt. "You could say that."

"Aww, Wisdom. I'm honored…but you expect too much of me." He paused, looking sheepishly then shifted. "You know…the two of us…we're not so different."

Wisdom rolled his eyes. "I doubt that?"

"We're both just two beleaguered beasts, that's all. Toiling about. Kowtowing to our own duplicitous and oppressive overlords. Day after dreary day."

"So profound, Poeltz. Maybe you, man. Not me. I answer to no one."

"Oh, I'm sure your right…but look at you. Wearing your bitterness like you've been answering to someone else all your life." The old man paused. "I know the feeling. It's like a coat too heavy to remove. Mine has been building up for decades…like a thick callous. Almost impervious. Almost. What about you?"

Clearly impatient. "Okay, Poeltz. Enough." Then pointing to the little container that had been placed on the tabletop. "Is that the scopolamine?"

Poeltz was not done. "Where will you go from here? Another murder case. Another box to check. For what purpose?"

In a way, the old man was right. Tauntingly so, and Wisdom knew it. He fired back...defensively. "You think we're the same? Well..." he leaned forward a bit, "...at least I'm not a minute away from being taken to the station in cuffs."

And then, in almost mocking surprise, "Cuffs. Arrested. What forever for?"

"You know what, just show me the damn scopolamine, Professor."

"Okay, fine. You ask to see the scopolamine?" He slid the slightly tarnished and delicately jeweled container across the table and flipped back its lid to reveal a padded blue velvet lining with six small pills nestled inside. "This is scopolamine."

Wisdom took his hand off his gun and looked closer at the pillbox...a box he quickly noticed was very similar to ones found in both Bard's and Brenneman's room. Though theirs' were empty and could easily pass as a small jewelry box, they were very much like the one now placed before him. But this one was most assuredly not for jewelry. "What are these, pills?"

"Scopolamine, of course."

Wisdom picked up one of the pills and held it in front of both men's eyes. "I get that, Poeltz. But these look plastic."

"Ah, you mean the pill casing? Yes, yes." And now with a subtly giddy nervousness. "Quite new...very ingenious. It's a hardened aspic casing that telescopes open and..."

"Telescopes open?"

"Yes, slides open. Inside you will find the pharmaceutically milled scopolamine. Here, let me show you."

Poeltz took one of the other capsules from the pillbox,

placing each tip between the thumb and forefinger of each hand and, while lowering to just above the tabletop, carefully pulled the two ends apart. Slowly spilling out and settling on the table was a predominantly milky-white powdery substance peppered with tiny specs of dark grey.

"There you have it, Detective. Scopolamine. Satisfied?"

"Not so much." Wisdom peered closer at the innocuous substance and then looked up directly at Poeltz. "Okay, no games…I ask you again…how do you come about obtaining this?"

"Very well…I assume you will simply pester me until I succumb to your harassment…is that how it works? Is that how you do your job?" Not waiting for the answer to his own rhetorical question, Poeltz slid the pillbox to the side and then leaned forward over the small, fragile mound sitting idly between the two men. "Wisdom…" pausing as if he was about to reluctantly give away a secret hiding place. "It comes from the Borrachero tree. Central America."

"The what tree?"

Poeltz smiled. Couldn't help it. "Borrachero, my good man. You know." Knowing full well, Wisdom had no clue what the hell he was talking about. "It has quite a reputation. Mothers warn their children not to sleep under the tree as they may never wake. Utter nonsense, of course."

"How so?"

"There is nothing toxic about the tree itself. It essentially looks like a diminutive palm tree, though the Borrachero has drooping white trumpet flowers that hang from its branches. The flowers, though…when dried-out, milled, and cooked will produce the substance you see here. Scopolamine. It's quite a feeble concoction, though."

"I thought you said the flower was white…what are those black specks?"

"Ah, the stem and the stigma…both strangely almost a blackish-green on the Borrachero…their density won't allow them to blend organically with the powdered petals and stamen. We use the whole flower, of course." And then he spoke in an almost prideful tone. "Look, you see…those black bits are coarser than the rest."

Wisdom briefly looked down at the powdery mixture before him and then looked back up at Poeltz. "You said it was a weak drug. *Feeble*, you said?"

"Such a pleasure to be comprehended. Yes, feeble."

"I don't think Jennifer Bard would agree with you."

It was true that Poeltz was nervous. His breathing now more labored than normal. But that's not why it had suddenly become even more pronounced and so, before one last deep breath, he teased the detective with "It all depends on how much you ingest…"

Wisdom leaned forward to get a closer look. "How much is too mu…"

But before he could even finish, Poeltz leaned forward and let out an enormous exhalation, one that sprayed the powdery substance directly onto his tormentor's face and then yelled out a taunting, "This much."

Stunned, Wisdom frantically shook his head and abruptly stood up, stepping back from the table while reaching for his gun. He let out a furious "What the fuck." He kicked his chair across the kitchen floor, its clanking in sync with his confusion.

But in all the panicky moving about, Wisdom had unwittingly ingested a staggering amount of the scopolamine. Not only through his nose and mouth but it had also settled in his eyes. A most potent repository for medicinal intake as the toxins went almost immediately into the bloodstream.

As Wisdom fumbled with his gun, Poeltz had also stepped back from the table. Now putting both hands straight out towards his victim, he coolly urged his victim to "remain calm…just remain calm," as if he had done this many times in the past.

Before he even had a chance to un-holster his weapon, a thick, muddled veil began to come over Wisdom. If he could tell you—and he couldn't—it was as if he had stepped into a pool of clear, breathable gelatin. His movements so contained that it was as if he was operating at half-speed. He felt as if he could talk but as the medicine completely enveloped him, he could only stammer a few useless words before settling into a living-walking coma.

Poeltz took his own calming and deeply measured breath and looked at the now tamed and helpless Wisdom. He walked over and removed the officer's sidearm, laying it calmly on the kitchen counter. His path now clearly set in stone. The detective had cornered Poeltz, and he was paying for it. He had wanted the whole story. The whole truth. He just had no clue what that actually meant.

And now in an accent so pronounced as if he had never left the motherland... "You want to know my whole story, Wisdom. Achten sie darauf, was sie fordern."

Chapter Fifty-Five

Dupont Circle—Theodore's

Thursday, December 21–1:45 p.m.

What's it like to be cornered? Trapped? To feel like you're caught at the end of a long, dark, shapeless hallway with only one seemingly treacherous path in front, and to your back, the taunting shelter that lay behind an unlocked door? A door that you know will only take you deeper into the now familiar black maze that had enveloped your world nearly three decades ago.

Poeltz understood the kind of man Wisdom was, and it had forced his hand. He'd seen plenty of them in his life—immovable and stubborn objects. They could taste the meat on a bone without even seeing it, and they knew well enough how to get to it. It was a deliberate trait and one he envied, even aspired to. Truth was, before that dogged cop even sat down at that little kitchen table, it was Poeltz who already knew the score, even if Wisdom didn't…and it left him with only one real choice.

And so, the small powdered mound of toxins that Poeltz had deliberately set in front of Wisdom had now opened the forbidding door behind him. It would indeed take him deeper into the very world in which he was trying to escape but, in a warped way, it may also provide the refuge he had long sought.

The Croton read a bit after 1:45. No, he would not be calling that taxi. Not enough time. Nor would he effort to make that long walk past the White House and the Mall to Union Station. Even if he wanted to, it would take thirty minutes. Too long. Much too long. It was as if both time and Wisdom had conspired against him, pressing him into a solution that was both daunting and desperate.

Wisdom stood there on the other side of the table in a sort of paralyzed shock. He didn't move...nor did he seem to even try. His stance was matched by a heavy gaze-like stare. After the initial fit of muddled babble, he had said nothing. Stoic would be a fair description, though even that wouldn't fully describe the muted condition. He would know nothing but what was told to him. This thick grey place wrested complete control from its victim. Poeltz had seen this state dozens of times, and he knew that the poor sap across from him was now subject to all his whims, tortured or otherwise. If only for a mere three hours.

Once he placed that little mound of powder in front of Wisdom, he had no intention of making his train. No, he needed to make things clear, if not to the cop, at least to himself, *and* he needed to take care of the reoccurring problem that was Wisdom. But not here. Not in Theodore's. For all he knew, the place had been bugged long ago, and *they* were probably already on their way over...with their matching grey suits and sedans. No, he needed to leave quickly, and so he gave his newly minted minion his first tentative instructions.

"Detective, follow me. We are going for a walk."

A simple "Okay" was all that was returned.

With loyal Bruno just a step behind his master, the three of them—now awkward partners of sorts—made their way down that hall, through the main foyer of Theodore's and onto the posh streets surrounding Dupont Circle. As they stepped outside, Poeltz felt the change. A gloom had settled in, as the air abruptly turned from brisk to downright cold. A foreboding front, now in route. It surely wasn't going to be the only storm this afternoon. And Wisdom, who was both jacketless and defenseless, was now most assuredly ill-prepared for either.

They headed east on P and made their way to The Circle where they would meet up with Connecticut…a route that would take them straight into the heart of the city. Where exactly they were going, Poeltz didn't know. What he did know, however, was that whenever they got there—wherever *there* was—he and Wisdom would part ways…forever. Hopefully.

Poeltz stopped at the corner, Wisdom pausing dutifully behind him, pulled another R&J from his breast pocket, and fired it up. The warmth of it all gave him a false sense of comfort against the bitter freeze. He looked back at Wisdom to make sure he was still there—and of course he was—then looked skyward as thick blackish-grey clouds rolled in as if on waves. He turned back toward Wisdom. Strangely, his first instinct was an apology of sorts.

"You know, my friend, I feel sorry for you. You have nothing to do with my life. We've never crossed paths nor each other. There is no need for you to even be here…except to do your unfortunate job. Such bad luck, for you."

Wisdom looked at the thick blur in front of him and said nothing…nor moved a muscle. A passerby, of which there were none, might mistakenly think the under-garmented cop was simply politely listening to his elder. The obvious chill in the air apparently of no consequence to him.

Poeltz began walking again, deep in thought, both cat and cop in tow…each always one step behind, until he got to Connecticut where he stopped and abruptly turned back towards Wisdom. "I have never been prone to carelessness, my good man, and I am not about to start today but you…you make it easy…so easy. Look at you."

Wisdom's head obediently bent ground-ward glancing down at his waist and then towards the street-side glass storefront beside the trio. The myth of it all stared back at him. He squinted his eyes briefly at his blurred image. But, not only did he not recognize the figure in front of him, he didn't seem to even bother to try. Both figures equally disinterested in the other. No, Wisdom was clearly gone—now playing the part of the perfect confessor.

Poeltz, now clearly amused, smiled. It was a perverted and controlling grin that reeked of dominance. This newfound confidence had been, up until a mere thirty minutes ago, very much in question. One couldn't say the same for Wisdom. He was now merely a pointless sponge sucking up information that would never be dispensed. Information that would remain stagnant, evolving over time into worthless mold. Poeltz knew this fact all too well.

"You want to know about scopolamine? I will tell you everything you need to know."

So, as the motley trio continued down Connecticut, seemingly with no real destination in mind, Poeltz began reciting his backstory and acumen for the drug like a laboratory dissertation, its data points floating around Wisdom like the bitter chill that foretold the looming storm. It would be Poeltz's missing final journal entry…told to a party of zero.

"Detective, your suspicions are in fact, correct. I am indeed a member of the National Socialist Worker's Party." He looked at Wisdom briefly. Would the cop even raise an eyebrow to this news? Hardly. "Before the war, I was an ordinary family physician. I know…so inconspicuous. But I was happy serving my people. Then the war came and, well… everything changed. And though this is now quite inconsequential, I became, through matriculation and promotion, the Chief

Medical Officer for the Schutzstaffel. Do you even know what that is?"

Wisdom looked at Poeltz, offering up only a slight shrug of the shoulders.

"The SS, my man. The SS. Everything I did for the Schutzstaffel was for Deutschland. Do you understand? For my people. I had many tasks, but none were more invigorating than advancing the effort into mind control." Pausing ever so briefly for Wisdom's sake if not his own. "We studied and tested Sodium Fluoride, Polygala, and Peyote-based Mescaline for mind control…but all possessed marginal reliability.

2:05 p.m.—Connecticut and N: Madhatter Tavern

Poeltz glanced over at the vacant *Madhatter* across Connecticut, its flashing neon 'Open' sign apparently tempting no one, then back to Wisdom. "Marginal at best. So, I gambled. What else was I to do? As the natural state of war's conclusion became a reality, I made a desperate attempt for a breakthrough turning to Scopolamine." And then, as if it were a two-way conversation, he continued. "Yes, that scopolamine. Discovered by a German, naturally. It had been used primarily for managing discomfort associated with childbirth as it neutralizes the pain neurons while possessing the duel psychological benefit of easing anxiety. I had used it many times in my private medical practice. But for mind control, well…it was, by all accounts, a completely unreliable compound. A method of last resorts. But as the clock ticked down on the battlefield, I pressed my studies on a handful of Jewish subjects…the results promising but incomplete. Exact dosage proved to be wanting…too much induced a terrifying hallucinogenic state characterized by a powerful trance with violent effects, temporary insanity, and possibly a tortured death. Hardly a reliable compound. Too small of a dose and the test case would indeed present a brief neutralized demeanor but hardly an impressionable one. As my days slipped away, I was discovered I was trapped. Caught between my inexact science and your government's forces. So, I shut it down. Destroyed it all. The tests…everything. And then simply awaited my bitter fate."

2:12 p.m.—Connecticut and Jefferson: Riggs Bank

As they passed the marbled pillared façade of Riggs, Poeltz stopped and rested his hand on Wisdom's shoulder. "The man you keep asking about…Gottlieb. He showed up that dark day in Nuremberg and never left my life for twenty-five goddamn years. That Gottlieb. The father of your military's experiments of the mind and, just as you had suspected, yes, the father to *that* son. He became the overlord of my intellect, squeezing every bit of usefulness from my very mind. I no longer pursued innovation for my people but rather for your people…the very enemy I had long pursued. Ironic, I know. The mocking aspect of all this to me is that your people believe that it was the Germans that were the sole despicable participant in that callous war. But Wisdom, there were no innocents to be found. You see, the difference between my country and yours is that we were attacked from within. The Jews were wresting control of all our institutions in an almost benign way. The purity of our culture threatening us from within. We sought to rid ourselves of that infestation and pursue a world without the conniving. What is so wrong with that? We used all the tools at our disposal to achieve that goal."

3:05 p.m.—Connecticut & M St: People's Drug Stores

As they stood at the corner waiting to cross, Poeltz looked at a beggar sitting crouched outside the *People's*. A small tin cup in his hand. Then turned towards Wisdom. "Your people are doing the same. What's your excuse?" And then without waiting for a response that would surely be slow to come. "Your Gottlieb manipulated, tortured, and even killed the unwitting…the weak. Your own. And he pursued his agenda with a vitriol that made my endeavors appear almost ancillary. And for what purpose? By my arrival, the war was over. My country left in ruins. Who were you trying to press your will upon? The Soviets? Your own people?"

"With your government, I had been made to do terrible things…many terrible things. I never got any sort of perverted thrill out of it. Honestly, as I look back, I preferred what I was doing before the war…helping people…not tormenting them. But the war changed everything. I could have demurred…made myself less useful…but I didn't. I simply didn't. Instead, I chose to help my country defend itself from all you self-righteous Americans…and the Jews. Those damn Jews, eating us from inside…like some sort of bacteria. And if a few Jews had to die along the way, so be it. I did what I was asked to do…and then I did it again…for your people. Only this time I had no choice. It was either help your government or die a slow death in some frozen Russian camp. At the time, it never occurred to me to choose any other option but Life…but today, looking back, maybe I made a wrong choice. I spent the last twenty-five years trying to recapture my core while selling out my soul to your perverted agenda. To your Gottlieb. All just to be alive…and what kind of life was it?" Rhetorical questions require no response…and there were none coming.

3:08 p.m.—Connecticut and L: Kaage Newsstand

Poeltz walked over to the knee-high stack of Posts fluttering in the wind and pointed to the banner story about the Vietnam War. "None of this is new. Rinse and repeat. War will make demons out of all of us. I have seen so many vile things. I have seen a man claw his own brother's eyes out for a bowl of dog food. Why? Because we convinced him…or his adulterated mind, rather…that this was the only way to survive. The idea of it made me wretch. We violated the very sanctity of one's mind …not because we wanted to…or even needed to…but because we could. Because we thought we had to. It's a perverted addiction. Having that kind of power over someone. The thought of it burned me from the inside and yet I kept doing it…over and over for your government. For all the perverted wars you have yet to wage."

"Maybe I should have been grateful…provided work…money…a place to live. But each day, a constant watchful oppression incessantly lurked around my life…my work…my home. It was suffocating, and it only sought to hasten my angst. My heart raced always…I spoke to virtually no one. Paranoia was a constant companion. The fear of retribution lurking around any corner. I had heard stories of agents who simply disappeared. If I was going to vanish, it was going to be on my terms, and so I developed my plan." He turned and looked towards Wisdom, "The plan that brought *you* to my doorstep."

The three continued their lonely trek moving past convenience stores and office fronts like an isolated battalion…each irrelevant milestone receiving little more than a passing glance.

3:17 p.m.—Connecticut and K: Farragut Square

As they approached K St. which was now nearly void of traffic—no doubt waiting patiently for the daily chaos that rush hour would soon bring—Poeltz paused and peered through the shadowed and vacant park that now lay in front of him. With the pending winter storm discouraging any midday activity, the normally bustling Farragut Square now stood virtually unoccupied. If one peered from the right angle, it could provide an almost unfettered view to the black iron gates that surrounded the White House grounds. "The thing is, long ago we learned how to create monsters...but only I would discover how to create monsters we could control." Poeltz smiled. "Like I am doing to you right now...toting you around the city like some kind of dimwitted disciple. "

As they cut through the park, Poeltz disclosed many of the details of his pivotal discovery to Wisdom. Like...

> Why he used female subjects as opposed to males for his assassin mules: "Their mental capacity was naturally more susceptible...their digestive system processed the toxin more evenly...more rapidly."
>
> Or, how he was able to finally perfect the correct dosage: "Through literally dozens of side trials 1 Milligram (mg)/39.65 Pounds (lbs.), if you must know."
>
> And, how he was able to elude discovery from his superiors: "Covered my tracks with hundreds of duplicate and doctored test reports."
>
> And, where did he obtain the raw scopolamine compound: "Jonathan's business travel to Central America provided a most excellent cover."

"But one problem always remained. Indeed, with scopolamine, I could implement a reliable level of control over my test cases. However, what use was clandestine mind control if you always needed to be there to administer the drug? Furthermore, a dupe would never voluntarily subject themselves to ingesting an unknown drug...or any drug for that matter. If we simply wanted someone killed, the agency had plenty of trained assassins for that. What we didn't have, and what I personally needed, were assassin mules...killers who didn't know they were killers."

"For that, I researched the earlier analysis that I did for Himmler and the Schutzstaffel...where I layered hypnosis beneath a mind-altering drug...in that case, Mescaline. The drug was wrong, but the idea was compelling. Could I simply hypnotize a subject so that when later hearing a pre-arranged trigger word, that person would then voluntarily ingest a Scopolamine tablet? A person under hypnosis will not commit an act that goes counter to their moral core. We have known this for decades."

"They will, however, follow seemingly benign instructions...such as swallowing a tablet...a tablet that would then make them susceptible to any deed...criminal or kind...it did not matter in the least. The scopolamine superseded the hypnosis." A proud smile came across Poeltz's face. "It was brilliant. A person under the influence of scopolamine alone would commit any nefarious deed requested...but only under the specific prompting of the administer. The element of timing and secrecy lost...but combined with the underbelly of hypnosis...any deed could be committed...at any time...at any location. The assassin mule...both completely willing and unwitting. It was as pure as one could get to complete mind control. And so, my students, those pretty and sweet young girls, became my guinea pigs...then my own personal killers."

They reached the edge of Farragut and saw before them the prominence of the White House. Between them lie Lafayette Square, a park once used as a racetrack, a graveyard, a zoo, an encampment for soldiers, and even a slave market. It was now the unofficial residence for the city's homeless. The battered and beaten. And the angry—protestors of any and all things.

Poeltz reached down and lifted Bruno, easing him into the protective cradle of those aged boney arms. The cat purred with a calmness that taunted Wisdom's predicament. "How unfortunate you are, my friend. I am the purveyor of all you seek, and yet you stand there wearing that queer quizzical expression...like some kind of comical costume. For years, I have pondered the very predicament you find yourself in. What must it feel like? Lonely? Can you even see beyond your eyelids?"

With a lull in the traffic, the two men crossed H. Now at the edge of Lafayette, only the cocktail blend of human debris and their protesting cohorts separated the two wanderers from the world's leader. Shouts of *Nixon is a crook* blended seamlessly with the stench of human grime—a scent that can only be earned from months on the street and one that now drifted effortlessly on the edge of the impending storm and the crisp winds that came with it. Poeltz pointed to the spectacle in front of him. "I wonder, Wisdom, are you any different than these poor souls? Are any of us?"

The old doctor, now doubling as a pre-ordained dictator, ushered Wisdom through Lafayette like a worn-out maître d' from a past-its-prime French restaurant leading a solitary customer to a lonely table and an overpriced and unfulfilling meal. Strangely, he could not shake the feeling that started to settle over him. He'd felt it before…with Bard, Brenneman, and Rubin…and all those other nameless dupes. Guilt? Sounds about right

Poeltz walked Wisdom to the only vacant bench in the park and sat down, motioning the dutiful detective to do the same. He did. All around them lay the remnants of the age. The frustrated and forgotten. Withered faces and worn out minds lying atop cardboard mattresses and blankets of today's news. They were here every day…waiting for no one…someone…anyone. Most weren't picky, but some had an anger so deep-seated in betrayal that it begged for specificity. You could kindly bring them an apple, and they'd throw it back screaming as if you were the only person in the fucking world that didn't get it. "Orange...not an apple. Goddammit. You fucker."

Poeltz considered his options. He could direct Wisdom to walk straight into the now escalating traffic on H. That wouldn't end well. He could have him scale that forbidding black ornamental iron fencing that subtly protected the President's perimeter…the itchy trigger finger of a rooftop sniper awaiting the poor cop. Problem solved. He could direct Wisdom, at least for the next hour or so, to do anything he chose. But the power that Poeltz felt time and time before, now seemed completely hollow. No, he would part with Wisdom here. Whatever became of him today would no doubt be better than what became of Bard or Rubin...and the others. And now the old doctor was tired. Very tired. He finally met his match, not in Gottlieb, but in a determined detective who would likely never give until the story was over.

"Silly name, really. *Wisdom.* Apropos, but silly." He paused and then turned his gaze skyward as the first flakes of the bitter winter storm began to filter through the grey above. "You've been so clever to piece it all together. Bard and Schneider...Brenneman and Jenner. Though I seriously doubt that you even considered Rubin and Gottlieb." He took another drag of the still smoldering R&J and blew the smoke skyward as it battled each falling flake while blending effortlessly with the grey above.

He turned and looked toward Wisdom. Wisdom dutifully looking back. Waiting...bated breath. "It's queer. You know so much, but you still have no clue. Connecting Schneider to Gottlieb surprised me." He glanced over at Wisdom. "Nice work, but have you not noticed? Bard is a Jew. So is Brenneman...Rubin. Gottlieb, of course. Even you. All Jews. Have you considered the simple truth? If you leeches just stayed in your own part of the world...none of this would have happened. Those poor girls would be alive. You wouldn't be sitting here next to me. Jenner? Good lord, that wouldn't have been necessary. And me? I would have continued my practice...my simple village...a family, maybe. You see, every man needs something to hold onto. Family, most of all. I had none of that. Love? Hardly. Children? No. Gottlieb took it all from me. But surely you must have wondered about Schneider? Why bother? He's an innocent, isn't he? Is he? Wisdom, apple doesn't fall too far, you understand." He glanced through the park back towards Farragut. His exit. Clouds getting darker, snow picking up. Time was running out. "Wisdom...maybe he was nothing more than the son to a father. Something I never truly knew." Poeltz paused, comforted by the knowledge that everything he said would get lost in Wisdom's mind, now offered up the first reference to the only family he would ever truly have. "Something my Jonathan never knew, either."

And now, for the first time, he uttered his challenger's given name. "Joseph, it is true...I am a bitter man. My redemption...make no mistake...I earned it, dammit. I deserved it. Yes, it was filled with brilliance, but there was so much bitterness. So much..." His voice trailed off unable to finish the thought that hung in the air. He looked skyward once more, the falling snow making his eyes blink repeatedly and then said what he'd been unable to admit all these years. "I hate what I have done, Wisdom. Hate what I'm doing." He abruptly stopped, realizing the pointless reality of it all. Thirty years seeking his redemption and yet, now that it was almost over, he knew it solved almost nothing. His emptiness, unfilled. His happiness, a hoax.

Poeltz dragged the R&J one last time, then leaned forward reaching his hand toward the pavement below and crushed out the smoldering end, tossing the remains on the tattered grass beside him. The snow was picking up as both the homeless and the protestors began to retreat into the background. With Bruno still sleeping idly in his arms, Poeltz stood and looked about the cluttered scene before him and then towards the docile detective. "No, I'll leave you be, Wisdom. Enough damage for today. More than enough. He paused. "Anyway, this is where you belong. Amongst *these* people. At least for a while."

He gave him one last simple instruction. "Stay here, my good man. You may freeze to death...or be ravaged by some equally clueless soul...but my guess is you'll come to just fine. At least I hope so. But by the time you are yourself again, I will be long gone."

Poeltz turned back toward Wisdom and reached forward to shake his competitor's hand. "My true name is Samuel Rauscher." He paused. Saying his blood name out loud—even to a witless tag along—provided the old man with a sense of liberation. "I am from Lehde. Outside Berlin. I am more then you see, Wisdom." He glanced into the greyness above as if lost in thought. "Much more.... I love rolling fields. Brisk rivers—the kind you can stand in. A crisp Riesling." He paused. "Cats, of course." He smiled for no one but himself. "And I love my country." He stared one last time into the detective's dull but compliant eyes. "I bid you goodbye. Auf Widershehan, Herr Wisdom."

He smiled and then turned to walk away for good. Wisdom's gaze followed the old man like a puppy to its master until he could no longer see him. The ever-growing distance and the rapidly falling snow obscuring his view. His fate uncertain, Wisdom then turned to face the now huddled masses before him...each lost in their own world...just as he was. At least for another hour or so.

Chapter Fifty-Six

District of Columbia—Lafayette Square

Thursday, December 21st–5:05 p.m.

He could see him…kind of. A blur, mostly. Hazy. A shadow of something lurching over him. Nothing definitive. Just a presence. Slowly, though, the image began to take form. A human. A man, actually. His face wasn't specific, but there was definitely a face there. Definitely. And arms. They were waving about like a slow-moving windmill. Then there was a mouth. Or at least what looked like a mouth. It was constantly moving. Open, shut, open, shut…, like a malfunctioning robot. There was no sound to speak of, just a slight ringing amongst the hollow. But then…

"Datsmibiishufkr"

At first, it was just a whisper…or maybe a wave of a whisper. The mumbled nothings from nowhere. But just as quickly as it arrived, it began to slowly morph. "Dats mi bnsh u fkr." Still not into anything precise, but something that sounded more like the teacher in the Charlie Brown cartoons.

You knew who it was, and that she was talking, *and* you knew she was mad…pissed off, more than anything…but that was about all. Until finally the reality of it all, at least in this case, began to seep clear.

"Dats my bensh you foker."

"Whah?"

"That's my bench you fucker…you damn son of a fuckin' bitch!"

Wisdom peered through the now thinning veil that had surrounded his world. With what appeared to be teeming snowflakes serving as both a background and foreground, the clear presence of an awkward mess of a man began to reveal itself. A disheveled creature partially concealed in a tattered blanket that was wrapped lightly around his shoulders in the same teetering manner as his body. He was scraggly—long stringy hair, hollowed features, dingy Redskin cap sitting lopsided on his head. Smell was another issue. To his right was a grocery cart…not the big ones you get from Safeway…the small one from the local Peoples. It was filled with stuff. Stuff of no apparent consequence. Wisdom thought he saw a telephone sitting on top. No, there was nothing important about this thing—this man—outside of the fact he was virtually screaming at Wisdom…over and over again. That was it. All he could take.

Wisdom didn't know where he was. Didn't even realize he was on a bench until the madness in front of him made a pretty dramatic point of it. He looked down and saw two…maybe three inches of fresh snow building up around him. Then he looked up:

"What are you saying?"

"You…are…on…my…bench, dammit." The man spoke, making a point of carefully enunciating each word…especially the last one.

Wisdom slowly stood up and instinctively reached for his revolver. Not there. So, without warning and with little more than a fleeting thought, he reached back with his right hand and decked the berating spectacle in front of him.

Wisdom hit him so hard, the homeless man quickly fell

to the ground as if his entire being had been instantly sapped of life.

"You can have the damn bench, you son of a bitch."

He looked down at that jumbled heap in front of him...a faint murmur mixed with a whimper was the only thing that told you there was life at the bottom of that pile. For a brief instant, he was sorry. It was a pretty brief instant.

Wisdom rubbed his hand then looked at his Timex—5:10 p.m.

"What the hell happened to me?" He looked around the park, getting his bearings when suddenly it clicked. "The old man. Where's that fuckin' old man? Son...of...a...bitch." He wrapped his arms tightly in front of him...a shiver leaking uncontrollably from within. No coat, no hat, no gloves. He wished he had gloves. For the first time in three hours, it finally occurred to him.

He was cold.

He was also very pissed.

Wisdom looked frantically around the park in search of a police call box. This wasn't his precinct, but surely there would be one here...in Lafayette of all places. With the chaos and crime that resided here daily...right in front of the White House, mind you...he could hardly think of a more prudent location.

He moved away from that poor jumbled mess lying on the ground to get a better view of the park. The deranged guy had clearly been in over his head. Lesson for the day—one he undoubtedly won't remember—don't scream at a D.C. cop. Especially when he's been blacked out for three hours...lost his weapon...and was freezing his ass off. Odds were against homeless Redskin fan.

Suddenly, he spotted it. Beyond Lafayette and across H by a light pole near the corner of Farragut stood the familiar painted blue police call box. Sitting atop an ornamental black iron pole, the box itself was sealed to the public. Only a police officer had the key—a master key—to enter any box anywhere in the District.

Wisdom reached into his pants pocket with dread. No key and he was pretty screwed. But nestled at the bottom, lay the chain of keys that kept his life in order. Dart keys, apartment key, District House key...and the Call Box key all attached to the worn leather keychain that Ginny had gotten him for his birthday...lovingly stamped with *Joe* across the band. They were out of *Joey*.

He grabbed the keys like a baby to a rattle and sprinted across the park towards the police box. If it wasn't a sprint, it was still as fast as any forty-two-year-old waking up from a walking coma had ever run. Crossing H, he practically fell into the pole, grabbing it for support as his body heaved forward in exhaustion. He slipped the master key into the slot and pulled back the cast iron door. Next to the Patrol Signal Switch was a telephone that circuited right to Central Command. Wisdom grabbed the phone, and after an initial static, the desk manager answered.

He thought for second, "What do I tell this guy?" but quickly realized there was no need trying to explain the mess he was in. He couldn't even explain it to himself...at least not yet...or even quickly. So instead of the details, he cut through the bull.

"This is Detective Wisdom, District 2. Please issue an APB for a Dr. Alfred Poeltz. Approximately seventy years old. Grey thinning hair." He paused for a moment, shook his head lightly to break the cobwebs of uncertainty, and then added. "He may have a cat with him."

"What now?"

"Don't ask—just get it out there."

"Yessir, Detective. Polts?"

"Yes, dammit. P-o-e-l-t-z."

"What's the reasoning?"

"Person of interest in the David Schneider murder?"

"Who?"

"Goddammit, man just do it...and send a couple units over to Union Station and National. He may be looking to skip town."

Wisdom hung up the phone and immediately waved down an oncoming Red Top who abruptly swerved from the middle lane on H to stop perfectly in step with its new passenger.

Wisdom pulled open the back door, and before he even sat down, barked out, "1810 P Street...and hurry the hell up."

The cab sped up Connecticut to the roundabout at Dupont, circling around to the third exit...P Street. What normally would have taken fifteen minutes or so was accomplished in about five...the extra twenty dollars tossed over the seatback a likely stimulant.

"Third house on right...pull in right there behind that green car."

He looked at his watch...5:30...it had been twenty minutes since he woke from that fog...or whatever it was. Very little was coming back to him, but seeing his Dart curbside in front of Theodore's reminded him of one very clear detail. He knew only this: three hours ago, he had been sitting in the kitchen parlor of *this* house questioning the very person he was now frantically in search of only to suddenly find himself sitting in three inches of fresh snow. Bewildered on a bench. Those three hours now lost to infinity. The old man had clearly outsmarted him.

He tossed another ten over the seatback and with the car still coming to a stop, he jumped out, immediately slipping on the wet snow beneath him. A bitter *Mother* was followed by the prerequisite holler from the cabby, "Should I wait?"

It was ignored.

Steadying himself on his feet, he gingerly ran up the path, then gambled and took two quick steps up onto the dry sanctuary of Theodore's covered porch. The only thing that stopped his momentum was those forbidding glassed front doors.

Looking into the storefront, it appeared that on the

surface, nothing had changed. The place was quiet. Dark. Just as before. The only illumination came from beyond that gloomy foyer and its connecting hallway. Like a looming train in a tunnel, that lone light cast an ominous shadow through the ornaments of the dead beasts that adorned the walls of that equally bleak hallway.

But as he leaned his gaze heavier against the glass, Wisdom noticed the two travel cases that earlier had sat idly next to Poeltz's feet patiently waiting for a departure that obviously never happened. But now, one case lay open, its packed contents exposed as if someone was frantically looking for something. And then, beyond the darkness, down the hall and through that opened swinging kitchen door, he saw something. A glancing movement of sorts.

The old man was still here.

Wisdom stepped back and simultaneously reached for both the door handle and his sidearm, but one was locked…the other gone.

Wisdom screamed out, "Poeltz." The shadowed movement from the kitchen abruptly stopped. From behind its concealing walls, emerged a gangly silhouette. It stood there motionless for just a moment then slowly walked down the hallway until it met the edge of light…its image becoming clearer. The old man looked off. His mannerism stiff. Too stiff.

With no weapon, Wisdom was left with nothing more than threats and anger to entice his entrance. "Let me in, Poeltz. Son of a bitch, let me in."

The shadow of Poeltz slowly turned, and with an uncommon rigidness—even for him—the old doctor walked back to the kitchen as if he never heard or saw a thing. It was almost as if Wisdom was nothing more than an invisible and silent presence. But then, Poeltz turned his head slightly and just before he disappeared into the kitchen's deceptive sanctuary, he said everything that Wisdom needed to hear.

"You're too late."

It was muffled and stuttered, but clear enough for Wisdom.

As Poeltz swung closed the kitchen door behind him, the detective took two steps back and kicked the locked framing once…then twice. The old hickory, firm and indifferent to Wisdom's frantic efforts. But suddenly, right by the lock, a crack in the glass appeared. He took his elbow and with one good smack to the fractured surface, a silent spider web of cracks sprinted towards all corners of the door. And before he could even pull his arm back for another go, the whole thing shattered and collapsed with the tinging sound of a thousand nails falling to the floor.

His entrance now clear, Wisdom stepped through the hickory portal and quickly maneuvered around those old Queen Anne's until he got to the edge of that murky hallway—stag antlers still dutifully guarding the way. Behind the light-edged door, the now apparent and distorted sounds of grunts and muddled moans briefly stopped him in his tracks. Like a tangled path to Purgatory, Wisdom eased down the hallway, the sounds of desperation escalating along the way. And then, with a plaintive curiosity that belied the circumstances, he softly called out the man's name one last time.

"Poeltz?"

And with no response but the continued sounds of torment, he slowly eased the door open and then saw before him a twisted version of the man he knew. Now sitting bolt upright, a dull brooding expression on his face, the old man stared vacantly at the floor, his moaning mouth was closed tightly…almost convulsively. His nostrils flared. Cold sweat covered his forehead. His complexion was tortured-red.

Wisdom stepped back in shock. Stunned, he couldn't take his eyes off the tortured spectacle. The man's jugular veins on his throat were swollen as large as fingers. He groaned as his chest rose and sank slowly. His arms hung down stiffly by his side.

"What the fuck?!" Wisdom desperately looked around the room for some clue to the disaster in front of him, and then he saw it…an empty glass on the table and the separated discards of four gelatin capsules. The last remaining scopolamine now officially finished. "Aw man, what the hell did you do?"

Poeltz's eyes suddenly misted over and filled with huge tears, and his lips twitched convulsively for a moment. His carotids were visibly beating, his respiration increased, and his extremities jerked and shuddered of their own accord.

Wisdom looked around the kitchen. "Phone. Where the hell is the damn phone?" Acting as if the stunted professor would be able to comply. And then he saw it…the phone…and his service revolver both lying together next to a small counter-topped TV. He scuffled over to the phone…dialed 0 and now, with a coolness that confirmed his true feelings, calmly requested an ambulance and police backup.

With the stunted doctor now clearly of no threat, Wisdom hung up the phone, slipped the gun back into the holster, and then slowly walked back towards Poeltz, stopping just in front of the old man. He leaned forward and stared closely at the damaged professor for several moments. His eyes were now dry but had become bright red and rolled about wildly in their sockets. All his facial muscles now horribly distorted. A thick white foam began to ooze from between his half-open lips. The pulsing on his forehead and throat was beating too fast to be counted. His breathing was short and extraordinarily fast but did not even seem to lift the chest, which was also now visibly fibrillating. A mass of sticky sweat covered his face and arms which now became shaken by convulsions. His limbs were hideously contorted.

Wisdom just watched. Couldn't take his eyes off Poeltz. He knew he couldn't help the old man…even if he wanted to. And, as if he had all the time in the world, the detective who had seemingly seen everything, simply took in the strange scene before calmly stepping back and over towards that small kitchen window.

He looked out—snow now coming down hard—then back over to Poeltz, "Why did you do it, you son of a bitch. Why?" With no memory of anything Poeltz had told him mere hours ago. "What kind of hell came over you, man?"

He paused and stared at the faltering old man half expecting a response, and then as he walked past Poeltz and out the kitchen. "I know one thing." He looked back one last time. "This is exactly how you should go out."

As Wisdom made his way down the hall towards the foyer and the sounds of a pointless ambulance, he couldn't resist one last, virtually silent stab. "Go to hell. Fuckin' Nazi."

Be there in fifteen minutes.

And now, with shattered glass at his feet, Wisdom waited patiently in the very Queen Anne that Poeltz sat in just three hours before. The old man's murmurs and shrieks now blending with a new sound that came from that antique kitchen wall clock...the echoing charm of a cuckoo's call.

It was 6 o'clock.

By the time paramedics would barge into the kitchen, Alfred Poeltz would be dead—his bloated and inflamed torso the only remaining evidence of his preordained dance with The Devil's Breath.

Just as he had planned.

Chapter Fifty-Seven

Crystal City—The Crow Bar

Sunday, January 12th–8:35 p.m.

They had plowed through the battered old antique store like neophyte surgeons to a virgin cadaver. They looked for anything that would explain the scene before them…that human heap lying prone and bloated on that cold white kitchen floor. But beside some dusty remains of the scopolamine and the undisturbed and seemingly unrelated contents of a suitcase gone unused, they found nothing. Nothing of substance, mind you.

With Wisdom's knowledge tauntingly incomplete and with every victim or manipulated dupe either dead or dim, the trail was now as bitter cold as David Schneider's frozen, bloody corpse. So, after several fruitless days of dead-end interviews, along with some very pointed prodding from nameless superiors, the case was unceremoniously closed. Though Wisdom knew better, the official cause of death was *accidental overdose*. Just like Bard. The puppeteer's twisted redemption now seemingly complete.

The only wanting items of any intrigue that were discovered that wintry afternoon three weeks back, were the seemingly purposeful placement of a faded photograph and a folded-over letter that lay undisturbed atop that tiny kitchen table. The picture was of a young boy standing next to a child's 10-speed, a forced smile explaining his lack of interest. The cryptic note, a confessional of sorts, was addressed simply to a Jonathan. It read:

Jonathan,

I am sorry. I have left you a void. Nothing for which to return. When you discover the truth, you will understand who I really am and most importantly, who you are.

When the time comes, and my story has been forgotten by all, remember the good things I have done. I suppose, the very same things that have done me in. Jonathan, I have gone much further than necessary, and I am simply tired. I chose the long way down, and it has taken a toll. I am finished.

I regret many things. But mostly, the time I spent watching the space that dissolved between us. And yet, I said nothing. Instead, discouraging a connection that we both needed. It is too late now, but, though you are not my blood, you are most assuredly my son. Mein Sohn. Mien Sohn.

Lovingly,
Dein Vater.

In the end, the cops made a mostly indifferent effort to find Jonathan. But after a few days, they gave up...releasing him to the winds. They thought that maybe the 'son' would show for the old man's funeral…but he didn't. No one did. The kid probably skipped town. Left the country. And who really cared, anyway? He was just an unwitting extra to the star and his demented story. Seemingly.

Wisdom set down his drink and turned away from the TV that hung above the bar. With another Billy Kilmer interception and the cries of *You Bum* rising above the din of a frustrated crowd, Joey had simply had enough. *Getting to the Super Bowl was good enough. Wasn't it?* Staying any longer would only prolong the agony and likely get him in the middle of a booze-fueled brawl. *Not worth it.* He would miss the flubbed Yepremian field goal and that ridiculous fumble that gave the crowd some temporary life. But that's all it would be. Temporary.

It was an unseasonably warm night for a January as Wisdom stepped out into the tepid darkness. With muted jeers lingering behind him, he lit up another Winston and began the short walk back to Crystal House. Strangely, he hadn't thought of Poeltz or those girls in days, but he had come to realize that there was still an itch there and it wouldn't go away. The itch was simple. Why? He had seen hundreds of murders, and in Windom's mind, there was always an answer as to *why*. Everyone killed for a reason, didn't they? Surely, the old man wasn't simply just another version of The Zodiac…killing only for the sake of superiority. No, Poeltz seemed to want no attention. No fame. If anything, his designs were meant to be private…and temporary…almost like an assignment. When it was complete…he would be through…and he was most certainly through.

He gazed skyward, taking in the distant stars that began to speckle the dark. If only he could remember something…anything…from that lost afternoon. Maybe he would get it. Maybe it would all make sense. He shook his head lightly, dispensing the distraction…then shrugged his beaten shoulders. "Aw…fuck it."

As he approached The House, another taunt eased its way into his mind. How many more years could he do it? This relentless job. He had always loved the mystery of it all. But the effects…the death, the blood, the sadness…had all taken a toll. He had learned to ignore things that would make others cringe or cry. It was the only way to remain somewhat sane. But it had made him stern. Thick-skinned. Almost without care. He thought of Mrs. Schneider and how he treated her. Rough, to put it mildly. Was Ginny right? Was he that vacant? Was Poeltz right? Banging around the city, year after year, solving the leftovers of someone else's disaster. *Checking boxes,* as the old man said, for overbearing dimwits like Frankel. How many more years? How much longer?

He tossed out his remaining smoke and entered the faux-marbled floor lobby of The House…empty and quiet save for the cavernous and static sounds of the Bellman's transistor radio, tweaking out the play-by-play of a lost game. As usual, he paid little attention to the doorman who, quite unnecessarily, aided Joey's entrance.

"Good evening, sir."

Joey said nothing in response and was already several steps past the sentry when it hit him. "Where's Frank?"

"Aw, he's got the night off. Skin's game."

"Oh, right. Gotcha."

And with only the slightest bit of enthusiasm, so as not to jinx things, the stranger of a doorman offered up the tiniest bit of hope. "Making a comeback, ya know."

"Huh?"

"Yeah, 14-7. Only a minute left, though. Dolphins got the ball."

"Okay." Joey didn't actually care. The afternoon buzz of a sixer matched with an equal number of smokes had begun to fade along with his enthusiasm. And so, he shrugged, turned, and walked towards the elevator.

He was just steps away when the doorman hollered out… "Hey, aren't you Wisdom?"

Joey turned back… "Uh, yeah…Why?"

"You had a visitor."

"Yeah?"

"Yeah, a young lady. She asked if you were in. Needed to give you something." The doorman simultaneously smiled and winked.

"Really?"

"Uh, yeah...I offered to have her leave it here, but she said she wanted to drop it off at your place. 14th floor, right?"

"Yep. She still here?"

"Don't know, man Sorry. Had a couple smoke breaks...she could of skipped out. Don't know."

Joey's heart raced as a wave of endorphins streamed into his system. In the back of his mind, all he could think of was how pathetic he must seem. "Frickin' teenager." But he couldn't help it. The Skins could come back to win the game, and it still wouldn't give him the same bolt he felt now. "Was her name Ginny?"

"Ah...didn't say...or at least I don't think so. Real cute, though"

He hadn't heard a thing from her since before Christmas. Thought it was over. Moved on. Well, kind of. Joey turned and, with an extra kick in his step, rushed back over to the elevator pressing the *Up* button repeatedly. It was funny...one silly thought flooded his mind:

"God. How bad must I smell?"

In reality, he'd been in a funk even before the Poeltz thing. He needed this. He needed her. And so, once inside, he hurriedly pressed the *Close Door* button once...then twice, as if the first try wasn't enough. He looked up at the floor display above the door...2, 3, 4. *Was she even still here?* ...6, 7, 8. *What did she want?* ...11, 12...no 13...bad luck, and then...finally...

"Ding"

What would he say?

The doors had barely pulled apart, and he was already in the hallway. *Slow down, you old fart*, as if Ginny herself had whispered into his ear. Wouldn't be the first time. He laughed...to himself, if no one else.

Joey turned the corner and looked down the hall. Crystal House was always poorly lit, but there, further down that dark pathway, she stood...right in front of his door...like she was waiting for him. A solitary ceiling light hanging just behind her, spread a highlighted halo around the girl...and her sweet tiny figure. He smiled. And then, with a nonchalance that disguised his true feelings. "Hey, there."

She stepped back, and as the light eased its way over her face, she turned toward Joey. Even in his booze-induced teenage enthusiasm, he saw it for what it was worth. The face was no more familiar to him then that damn doorman downstairs. It was blank...but focused...and not Ginny.

"Who the hell are..."

Before he could even finish, she raised her arm, pointing something so familiar at Joey that he could hardly breathe. Was it one of the missing pistols from Poeltz's? Yep. Probably. And before he could even move, the sound of a thirty-year old Lugar echoed the narrow hall, a silencer muting the drama.

Wisdom fell to the ground in a ball, grasping with both hands at his stomach, now drenched in blood. A gut shot, and though there is no such thing as a good stomach wound, Wisdom knew this was more than dire. Upper abdomen. Not good. The pain wasn't so bad...numb more than anything...but he already shit his pants and would bleed out in mere minutes. His breathing now rapid and shallow. So little time.

As the mystery moved down the hall, calmly stepping over Wisdom, he made a futile attempt to grab her. A pant leg. Anything. Maybe all he wanted was to see her face...to see the truth. But he already knew the truth. The only problem was, the truth was buried. Buried deep inside Wisdom's mind.

So much for that.

And so, as the girl entered the elevator that would take her down to the now vacant lobby and into the anonymous night, Wisdom let out a slow, plaintive moan and then simply closed his eyes.

Post Script

Capitol Hill—The Astor Hotel

Monday, January 13ᵗʰ–7:20 a.m.

It had been almost three weeks since he first heard the news of his father's death. It had stunned him, as it would anyone. But ever since that night at Sauf Haus he knew that the old man was planning on leaving. Alfred Poeltz hadn't said anything at the time. Nothing specific, mind you, but the feeling Jonathan had was marrow deep. The trouble was, he had no idea that 'leaving' actually meant for good. As in, dead. Certainly, not in the way the paper described it. Accidental overdose? Hardly. Nothing his father did was by accident.

It was ironic. The familial stand-ins in his life provided comfort—a façade though they were. But all along, he had no *real* mother… and for that matter, no *real* father. But it wasn't until that day when the Channel 9 News broke the story of the death of a once prominent Georgetown University professor that he, for the first time in his life, truly felt alone. For days he barely moved. It was as if he was a small child left on the side of a long and lonely country road. Barren fields in all directions. No one in sight. Abandoned. Empty. There was a numbness in his body that felt like he had been heavily medicated...but without the medication. His face, drawn. His limbs, dense. He didn't cry, either. He had wanted to, but couldn't.

But as the fog lifted and reality set in, his purpose slowly came back into focus. Whether his father had known of—planned, even—his own imminent demise was beside the point. The old professor had left him with very specific instructions, and it was now his duty to carry them out...if not for the father's sake then for his own reasons. God knew he had a few.

So, as if he was on auto-pilot, Jonathan Poeltz set about fulfilling his responsibilities. As instructed, he kept a low profile, rarely leaving The Astor. When he did venture out, it would be after sunset, and it would be for quick jaunts to The City Deli next door or to the beaten-down Piggly Wiggly on 7th and C. Each excursion included the purchase of The Post which, along with the static-filled TV news that he soaked up daily, was the only way to keep up with the developments of his father's case. The papers had mostly been filled with the warming scuttlebutt of Watergate and the Redskin's Super Bowl run but even with all that dominating drama, the four deaths out of Georgetown in a span of five days still took up its fair share of ink. For a few days, there was even talk of a rumored and missing son to the deceased old professor. Maybe the young man could shed some light on things. Certainly, he'd be interested in claiming his father's possessions. At least he'd want that note. But no, he was gone. Nowhere to be found. Probably traveling abroad again for business. Or...maybe he was lying in wait over at some decrepit hotel south of The Capitol.

So, Jonathan hunkered down until the strange and violent saga of Schneider, Bard, Jenner, and the professor had faded from the news. Buried. After a couple of days, the story fell from the front page to the Metro section. Then, with no real developments, it slipped to the back pages. Finally, several days later, the story disappeared entirely from both the news and, for that matter, from people's consciousness. Now easily replaced by the nefarious and more entertaining stories of Nixon and his cronies. Buried, for sure.

With the dust now settled he energized the next stage of the plan, treating his room at the Astor like some sort of fortified bunker. Like a bunker, it was dank—lack of proper heating will do that. It was dark, too—one small table lamp and a flittering ceiling light had that effect. On the wall, he had pinned a large paper map of the D.C. metro area. Red stars were affixed near Bethesda and Baltimore and Crystal City, an address and name labeled to the side of each. Handwritten notes in the nearby margins. It was like his own personal war room...and war map. Dressed in an old heavy grey Georgetown sweat suit, he incessantly moved through the sparse room planning his timing—talking to only himself. When it felt safe, he would sneak out to investigate each location. Detailing entry and escape routes, pinpointing spots for weapon drops—all talents he had learned to use rather effectively in both the Gottlieb and Schneider jobs.

So, on the morning after the Skins loss and with the die most certainly cast, Jonathan anxiously plowed through The Post, passing over one Super Bowl article after another...until he found what he was looking for. At first, there was only an ancillary note stuck deep in the Metro section about an overnight shooting in Arlington. It was as if the news had hit the run too late in the day to garner anything more than a simple acknowledgment. But a day later, the sketchy details of the murder of a D.C. police detective started to flush themselves out.

According to The Post:
"Late Sunday evening, an off-duty District police detective was found murdered in the hallway of his Crystal City apartment in Arlington. According to unnamed sources, there were no witnesses to the grizzly shooting. However, the residence attendant

on-call informed the police that a young female, possibly in her twenties, had paid the officer a visit just prior to the shooting. As yet, her identity is unknown. The homicide detective, identified as Joseph Wisdom, had been with the force for almost two decades. According to neighbors, Detective Wisdom was married but may have recently separated. His allegedly estranged wife, Ginnifer Wisdom, was not at home the evening of the shooting and has yet to be located. According to Sargent David Frankel of the District of Columbia Police, 'Mrs. Wisdom is a person of interest in her husband's murder'. Police have issued an all-points-bulletin in hopes of discovering her whereabouts."

Jonathan reread the article over and over. He was beside himself. The whole thing had actually gone better than planned. Nowhere had he taken into account that the detective was married. He simply didn't know. With Ginnifer Wisdom now innocently forced into the mix, it would bog down the police investigation even further. Add to their confusion. Drag out the process. And unlike with Schneider, there was no obvious trail to follow. Jonathan made sure of that. A distracted city on a balmy night was just the solution. Regardless, the police would first need to find the random young female visitor that was so innocuously referenced in The Post article. Of course, that task would be cluttered with the natural assumption that Wisdom's missing wife might fit that bill perfectly. Poor Ginny—newly minted murder suspect—would undoubtedly take the brunt of the investigation until she could prove her innocence. The good news for Jonathan was that this added distraction would now give him the extra buffer he needed to complete his task.

And with that dogged detective now out of the way, Jonathan removed the red star placed near the Crystal House apartment and turned his gaze towards Baltimore. It would likely take a couple weeks to organize, but the Dr. Obendorfer hit wouldn't be very tough. Aging and living alone in a small non-descript suburb made this undertaking much less complicated. The assassin-mule would arrive late in the evening. The streets undoubtedly quiet. The neighborhood battened down for the night. Dr. Obendorfer would not be a challenge.

Jonathan then looked over the map towards Bethesda, where a star was placed near a village called Kenwood. The word 'Evans' was labeled next to it. He had found that even the rudimentary task of just writing down *Charlotte Poeltz* would still piss him off. So, he stuck with *Evans*...not *Poeltz*. Not *Charlotte*. Definitely not *Mother*. The more distant, the better. Easier that way. Too difficult, otherwise. Just too many empty memories. For fourteen years that duplicitous bitch vacantly played the role of *mother*, then summarily and abruptly left him basically sitting in front of a bowl of cereal. It had more than stuck in his craw. She was a cold and callous person who chose to ignore the natural longing that lay in a child's eyes. In Jonathan's eyes. At the time, he didn't truly understand what he was missing, but ten years later, he surely did. So, on that night when his father disclosed the final details of his plan –and Jonathan finally grasped the depth and reason behind it all—he resolved to save her for last. Quite intentionally. That old lady wouldn't have a clue what hit her. Literally.

An uncontrollable and mildly cryptic grin came over Jonathan as he turned from the map and walked over to the window beside his bed. The glass was full of early morning condensate, but for the first time in a while, his life couldn't have been clearer. He swiped the moisture clean with his hand and stared out into the waking city knowing full well that this would all be over very soon. His burden fulfilled. His own redemption complete. He may not be able to repair his father's legacy, but he will secure—if only for himself—the critical remnants of his father's long-suffering study. The wry old German doctor had spent almost thirty years crafting and perfecting a process that would be used on the very people who had so cavalierly neutered his life. Both of their lives. To use *those people's* own long-sought-after 'weapon' against them was truly fitting. More than fitting. His father would be proud.

So, over the next couple months, if one were paying attention one might notice a rather curious mention in the local paper of a random killing…or two. Maybe even an ancillary college student overdose…or two. To the average person, it would all seem to be just a part of the age. Another day…another senseless D.C. death. If you tried—and why would you—to tie them all together, you couldn't. All seemingly random deaths. But in Jonathan's mind, if not Wisdom's, it all made perfect sense.

As the sun began to peak over those prestigious government buildings—bringing light to the dingy city— Jonathan knew he was not long for this place. Enough tortured time had been spent here. The truth was, it had all worn him down. The revenge. The hatred. No way to live. With his redemption almost complete he knew that soon…very soon…he would be gone. He'd pack up the dust of what little he owned and leave. Just go. But where to? He blankly stared out that misty window. Then, as if answering his own wanting question, "Maybe I'll head out west. To the mountains. Colorado, maybe…or Montana." He paused, lost in thought, imagining the swelling green countryside of a land a country away. "Yeah. Montana. Perfect. Sounds like home." He'd find a cottage tucked beside some small forgotten stream. "Maybe open up an antique store in some little town. Just let the wind blow me wherever, man." All he wanted to do was simply blend in.

Jonathan gazed out the moist Astor window, taking in the dreary city below—men in three-piece suits mixing awkwardly with homeless vagrants. Like oil to water. Then, turning away, he simply whispered, "Anything is better than this place."

Jonathan walked back over to that map, pinned defiantly to the Astor's faded wall. He stared it down. Eyes focused on what remained. Mind transfixed by what could be. He had spent twenty-four years stuck in someone else's world. It had all slowly seeped deep inside him like a virus, and there was nothing he could do about it. The prostitute's orphan and the old Nazi doctor, separated only by blood, each longing for the same dream...both resigned to the same burden. The same fate.

And so, in the end, it turns out the apple really doesn't fall far from the tree. In the end...in the very end...it really was like father, like son.

THE BALTIMORE SUN
Saturday January 19th, 1973

Weekend Metro

<u>By Allen W. Robinson</u>
For The Baltimore Sun

Dr. Edward Obendorfer

Police are searching for clues in the death of a 69-year-old scientist with the National Bioresearch Institute at Fort Dietrick, Maryland.

Baltimore County Police spent Friday going door-to-door looking for information to help them solve the death of Edward Obendorfer. Dr. Obendofer was found fatally shot in his home in Walbrook on May 18th.

A preliminary investigation indicates that Obendorfer was inside the home when he was shot several times late Thursday, May 17th. The first officers arrived at the scene in response to a welfare check late Friday morning when Dr. Obendorfer failed to arrive at work as scheduled. No apparent forced entry was detected and it appeared the house was left undisturbed.

Detectives have been interviewing neighbors and leaving fliers. Authorities say they soon plan to hold a community meeting about the case. No arrests have been made.

Next door neighbor, Leslie Jones has lived in the typically peaceful neighborhood for 16 years. "We heard nothing. Just a normal night." She said she could think of no reason anyone would want to harm Dr. Obendorfer. "He was very private but so nice to everyone. Just a total shock."

Anyone with information that can help police is asked to contact Crime-Stoppers at 411-8477 or call the Baltimore Police Homicide Division at 441-2131.

THE WASHINGTON POST
Friday March 9th, 1973

Local News

Police Seek Help Solving Fatal Hit-And-Run
In Bethesda

<u>By Nicholas Davenport</u>

Police are asking for help in identifying a motorist who struck an elderly pedestrian on an early morning walk yesterday in the Kenwood neighborhood of Bethesda and then drove off.

The incident occurred about 6:15am, March 8th on the 2300 block of Pyle Road near Whittier Woods Par and Walt Whitman High School.

Phyllis Evans, 74, a retired government pensioner, was at the intersection of Maiden Lane and Pyle Road when a driver, who had been travelling east on Maiden, ran into the victim Police said. The driver then took off.

Evans, of the 5900 block of Whittier Boulevard, was found by a passing motorist and was subsequently transported to Holy Cross Hospital in Silver Spring where she was pronounced dead.

The vehicle could have damage to the front bumper, hood and front windshield, according to a news release from the Bethesda Police. Anyone with information about the crash should contact the Police Department's Major Accident Investigation Unit at 745-4521.

Mrs. Phyllis Evans

Borrachero is a *genus* of seven species of flowering plants in the family Solanaceae. Native to Central America, they are woody trees or shrubs, with pendulous white flowers, and have no spines on their fruit. Their large, fragrant flowers—which produce a medical compound known at *scopolamine*—give them the common name of *Angel's Trumpets*. Ironically though, the tree itself is frequently referred to as *Devil's Breath or Drunken Binge* due to the rather notorious reputation it has for the mind-altering effect it can have on people.

All parts of *Borrachero* are known to be toxic to humans.

CPSIA information can be obtained
at www.ICGtesting.com
Printed in the USA
BVHW071701211218
536177BV00009B/629/P

9 781633 633582